DEAD ANYWAY

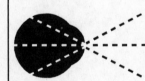

This Large Print Book carries the
Seal of Approval of N.A.V.H.

DEAD ANYWAY

CHRIS KNOPF

THORNDIKE PRESS
A part of Gale, Cengage Learning

Detroit • New York • San Francisco • New Haven, Conn • Waterville, Maine • London

GALE
CENGAGE Learning·

LIBRARY OF CONGRESS CATALOGING-IN-PUBLICATION DATA

Knopf, Chris.
    Dead anyway / by Chris Knopf.
      pages ; cm. -- (Thorndike Press large print reviewers' choice)
    ISBN 978-1-4104-5505-5 (hardcover) -- ISBN 1-4104-5505-X (hardcover)
    1. Life change events--Fiction. 2. Future life--Fiction. 3. Large type books.
    I. Title.
    PS3611.N66D43 2013
    813'.6--dc23   2012041564

Published in 2013 by arrangement with The Permanent Press

Printed in the United States of America
1 2 3 4 5 6 7 17 16 15 14 13

ACKNOWLEDGMENTS

The technical information in this book is the result of talking to valuable sources and a lot of secondary research, mostly done online. My approach was: "If I was going to do all this myself, in the real world, how would I do it?" What I quickly learned is *it's really hard to drop off the grid* in post-9/11 America. But not impossible.

Some readers will see details that they know aren't true, wouldn't work, or are inadequately described. This is not the fault of my sources, but my own misinterpretation, or flawed description. Just know accuracy was my goal and better information is always welcomed.

The following are my indispensable sources:

This story would have taken a very different turn if not for Steve Pedneault, a forensic accountant in Glastonbury, CT, who gave generously of his time and detailed knowledge of dirty financial dealings. My son James, an artist in Pittsburgh, gave me a tour of contemporary art, which I modified to protect the innocent, but used as inspiration for Nitzy Bellefonte's art gallery. Paige Goettel, who has long served as my French translator, pitched in here as well. *Merci.*

Bob Rooney, IT whiz at Mintz & Hoke, who once provided tech support to a team of computer forensic investigators, taught me digital breaking and entering, and all things relating to electronic mischief. Dave Newell, President of Wills Insurance Agency in Bennington, VT, described things he'd never do himself, and when you read the book, you'll know why. I learned more devious ways to render people paralyzed and unconscious from Dr. Peter King, also of Bennington. Do not mess with this guy. My crack legal team of Courtney, Orr & Orr tried their best to keep my hero from completely incriminating himself. Their success you'll have to judge for yourself.

Everything worth knowing about market research, which in many ways formed the basis of this book, I learned from Sean Cronin. The clever money laundering scheme was devised by Merrill Lynch Senior Financial Adviser and guitar collector Bob

Willemin. My local banker, Tom Griesing, showed me how to pull off a few financial shenanigans, including how to stay under the radar when depositing ill-gotten cash.

Janette Baxter, Long Island girl, provided insight into the bar scene on the South Shore of Nassau County (don't know how she knows this). Mathematician David Lampert provided some math terms and concepts which I do not remotely understand, but sound really cool. My good friend Tim Hannon, a ninja of the hospitality trades, gave me a look behind the scenes of a big city hotel. Ed Segal of New York City and Sag Harbor taught me a lot about gold and other precious metals — how to obtain it, assay it and use it for no good.

Note to the FBI: this is all in the service of crime fiction. Emphasis on fiction.

Thanks as well to my intrepid band of readers — Bob Willemin, Sean Cronin, Randy Costello and Mary Jack Wald — for their priceless editorial advice and counsel. And to Marty and Judy Shepard for sticking with me, Anne-Marie Regish and Stephanie Clason for administrative assistance, and as always, Mary Farrell whom I've promised I'll stay on the grid, my newly acquired disappearing skills notwithstanding.

CHAPTER 1

I remember Florencia dressing that morning. I was still in bed, propped up on the pillows, ostensibly reading a book. Moments earlier we were as intimate as two people could be, utterly entangled in mind, body and soul.

Though even then, as I watched her brush out her hair and slither into her pantyhose, I knew she was a separate person, already engaged in the coming day, where she would live apart from me, as her full self, focused and absorbed in her work. I would have plenty to absorb me as well, but never drifting far from that bedroom, and that instant in time. Physically, I'd be one floor below, in the den, at the oaken desk Florencia had given me for Christmas. My mind, at the behest of my clients, would be traversing the earth in search of hidden information — that part of my mind that wasn't lingering with recollections of the morning, the smells and feel of skin-on-skin, the transcendent lightness of unrestrained adoration.

She faced me as she slipped on her pumps, somewhat awkwardly from a standing position, made more so by the pencil skirt that gripped her knees. She smiled through a wave of black hair that fell across her face, amused by her own clumsy impatience. I smiled back and resisted the urge to reach out to her, to grab her wrist and drag her back into bed where I could reverse the process, rewind the clock and delay the inevitable day. I had my chance when she leaned in to give me a perfunctory kiss, and a stroke on the cheek, but I let her leave unaware of my impulse, unfettered by my reckless longing.

Half an hour later I was dressed and sitting at my computer, on my second cup of coffee and regular bowl of granola, strawberries and brown sugar. I was working at my job, the one I'd invented for myself, which I usually called freelance research. Sometimes, in moments of self-adulation, I'd describe myself as a Samurai of the Information Age. A fact hunter. If there was something you really wanted to know, and the usual avenues to acquiring that knowledge had failed you, you could hire me to acquire it for you, or break the news that what you wanted to know was unknowable.

I loved this work. Most of the well-paying projects amounted to classic market research — quantitative and qualitative studies involving surveys, focus groups, phone calls and face-to-face interviews. I wasn't particularly specialized, the subject matter could be anything from toothpaste to social attitude trending, though I'd built a modest reputation for getting answers that eluded other people.

I'd noticed an inverse relationship between the size of the firm doing the work and the quality of the results. So maybe that was the key: my company had a staff of one. Me. And a corporate culture that put a premium on persistence and a willingness to leave the comfort of the computer screen and track answers back to their source.

This meant a fair amount of fieldwork, another favorite of mine. Not only did it get me out of the house, it compensated for my total indifference to formal exercise. Otherwise the extra forty pounds of body weight I lugged around would have been more like sixty. Or worse.

The non-marketing work was usually the more rewarding, if only for the diversity of assignments. For example, that day I was laying the groundwork for a missing persons case. A law firm, one of my regular clients, was trying to close the books on a class action suit they'd won years before. Their accountants had advised them to clear out an escrow account that held the remnants of the settlement, earmarked for a plaintiff they'd yet to locate. My job was to find him or his heirs, tell them they were going to come into a bundle of money, or give up and chronicle the thoroughness of the undertaking, providing justification for turning the remaining proceeds over to the state.

I always began by duplicating the efforts of earlier researchers, which involved a computer search and phone calls to the last known place of residence. Aside from confirming their records, I knew this would shake out a few facts they'd overlooked, or hadn't looked for hard enough. These fresh leads would be the ones I'd chase down first.

I looked forward to the next stage, which amounted to getting in a car, or an airplane, and going to where my subject was seen. Then I got to knock on doors, visit bars and clubs, or churches and hospitals, putting together the links of a chain that usually ended at the home of my quarry. Since few of the people I looked for were intentionally hiding (though I once tracked down a fugitive from a nasty divorce case), good news generally followed.

My client had private investigators who could have done this part of the job just as well, or better, but they were happy to let me provide a turnkey package, and I was happy for the diversion.

This was not the most lucrative part of my practice. Which is why it was nice to be married to an understanding woman who owned an insurance agency. I pulled my weight, contributing equally to our savings and the expenses at our home in Stamford, Connecticut, but it was clear where the latent wealth of the family resided. With twenty-eight employees and established relationships with sturdy carriers, her company churned out enough revenue to assure a reasonably affluent life for as long as we wanted, which as far as I could tell would be a long time.

That's because Florencia also loved her work. She'd say the only people who thought insurance was boring were people who weren't in the insurance business. She claimed those in the know understood they dealt in life and death, safety and disaster. Hopes, dreams, triumph and disappointment were their stock in trade.

She believed the reason people in her line of work seem reserved isn't because they lacked feeling. Rather, they were so exposed to daily triumphs and tragedies that they had to protect themselves, or risk collapsing under the weight of the emotional freight.

I'd done a fair amount of research for insurance companies, so I could see her point. Even though I could never match her passion for underwriting, claims adjustment, loss ratios and actuarial tables.

Few could.

That day, I worked until three-thirty, when despite a sandwich and serial snacking, hunger began to interfere with my concentration, as it always did. The choice was to either munch on more empty calories — like a toasted bagel, or handful of potato chips — or capitulate completely and have a midafternoon lunch, usually the more wholesome decision in the end.

So I dug a wad of Florencia's homemade chicken salad out of a big plastic container, and stuffed it between a toasted, buttered bagel with lettuce and tomato. A concession to both nutrition and indulgence. When I got back to my desk I was sated, but not happily so. The meal resisted digestion, so

14

that two hours later it felt like a ball of unreconstructed protein and triglycerides sitting like a brick in my stomach.

This forced me out of my chair for a walk to the post office, which was about a mile from our house. A walk long enough to create the illusion that I was metabolizing all those useless calories.

I had an uneasy relationship with my body and its most prominent feature — my bulging midriff. For health reasons, I wished for a sleeker profile. But vanity was never a motivation. I knew I wasn't an attractive person. Rippling abs wouldn't have changed that. They wouldn't have grown hair on my balding scalp or turned my fleshy features into Brad Pitt. That Florencia, an undeniably beautiful woman, had overlooked these shortcomings was the root of my greatest surprise and delight. And gratitude.

I was, however, an energetic forty-two-year-old man. Especially when focused on the task at hand, the current quest. I could live on minimal sleep, and even bypass meals. I could stride with purpose (running was always out of the question) for hours if need be. In short, in the right circumstances, I was one of the most vigorous schlumps you'd ever meet.

It was in this mode that I walked briskly

in the clear, spring weather to the post office, where I kept a P.O. box. Much of my research involved correspondence not possible over the Internet, so the oft-derided snail mail system was for me a vital resource, one called upon almost daily. Not giving up my exact location was a soft security measure.

I wasn't by nature very sentimental. If my neighborhood post office was useless to me, I'd never have walked into the place again, with no regrets. Which would have been a shame, because I liked it there. It was an antique operation, thus far eluding modernization. The postal workers were all much older than me. There was stained oak woodwork and uniformed people sitting behind arched windows. The floors were marble and the stamp machines solid brass. The posters and official notices stuck to bulletin boards were the only evidence you hadn't flashed back in time. That and the aggressive impatience of the clientele winding their way down a gauntlet of red velvet rope.

When I got to the window I presented my P.O. number and driver's license. The woman disappeared for a few minutes, then returned with a stack of mail and overstuffed nine by twelve envelopes.

Included in the mail was a check from one of my favorite clients, climatologists for whom I'd been running regression analyses. They had contracts from academia, government and industry, the perfect trifecta, resulting entirely from their ruthless objectivity. Their job was to predict the weather. Not tomorrow's rainy day, but what the mean temperature and sea level might be five years from now. These guys didn't just cleave to the data, they were the data. Pure play empiricists. I didn't pray at the same altar as they did, but I knew the liturgy.

That's why they needed me. The regression equations they'd designed couldn't be controlled by mathematical formulas alone. They needed a little finesse — a tweak or two here and there to stabilize the results and keep the models in reasonable balance. And then, an explanation of what it all meant that anyone, scientist or CFO alike, could understand. They never told me I was meeting their objectives — I never heard a single spoken word from any of them — but they continued to send bundles of DVD's filled with variables and parameters, always paid their bills in less than ten days and never asked me to redo the work.

When I first got the gig, they gave me an application that essentially turned my PC into a smart terminal connected through the web to their massively parallel processing arrays. That was another reason I liked the assignment — the chance to mess around with staggering computational power from the comfort of my home office.

On the way back to the house, I countered some of the wholesome effects of the walk by getting a double scoop chocolate ice cream cone. I was on a first name basis with the head scooper of the place, illustrating yet another of my self-gratifying routines.

Though not without a penalty. I leavened the worst of my fleshy face with a huge Elliot Gould moustache started in college and never shaved off. This was the only feature that ever sparked admiration from the opposite sex, in particular Florencia, which explained why I never shaved it off.

Most foods were easy to work around, but ice cream cones, not so easy.

When I got home, I was surprised and pleased to see Florencia's car in the driveway. Along with an SUV, dark maroon with a trailer hitch, roof rack and decal on the left rear side window granting parking privileges at a local university.

I called to her when I went into the house. She called back from the living room. The sun was still high in the sky, but that part of the house was amply shaded by a pair of sugar maples, so when I walked into the living room I didn't see her right away. In her black pencil skirt and blue blouse, she almost disappeared against the dark leather couch. She sat stiffly upright, knees held tightly together and hands shoved under her thighs. She stared at me, not answering when I greeted her.

"Sit down," said a voice from behind me.

I spun around and saw a man sitting in a small side chair. He wore an almost comically oversized trench coat, with a belt and raglan shoulders, a black baseball cap and sunglasses.

His legs were crossed and he held in gloved hands a gun with a long silencer.

My mind sizzled with alarm and my heart shot into my throat, making it hard to speak.

"Who are you?" I managed to choke out.

"Sit down," he said again, and stood up, waving me toward the couch. I did as he asked and Florencia grabbed my hand in hers, which was cold and wet.

My heart was spinning hard in my chest and I took deep slow breaths to try to bring it under control.

The man took the stuffed chair across from us and put the gun back in his lap. He

19

looked about ten years older than me, somewhere in his early fifties, based on the grey hair sticking out of his baseball cap and the condition of his skin. His nose was long and thin, his lips red. Like me, he had jowls, though his hung more loosely from an ill-defined chin. I didn't know the color of his eyes. They were hidden behind the sunglasses.

"Nice house," said the man, looking around. "You do your own decorating?"

I didn't see Florencia nod, so fixed was I on the man's gun, but she must have, because the man nodded back.

"I admire that," he said. "My wife is always after me to hire a decorator, when I keep telling her, you're very artistic. What need do you have for such expensive ridiculousness? I think it's all the TV shows, with these fags coming in and turning some shithole into, what, a room at the Waldorf? All bullshit, of course, but it gets the women all worked up."

"What do you want?" I asked.

"Nothing. I'm all set. Had my last cup of coffee of the day before meeting up with your lovely wife."

"I mean, what do you want. Why are you here?" I said.

He looked down at his gun, as if surprised

to see it in his hand.

"Oh, you mean, like, why am I sitting in your living room with this gun? Why indeed."

"He told me you'd be killed if I didn't come with him to the house," said Florencia. "I only know him as an appointment. A life prospect."

"A life prospect," said the man. "There's your irony for you."

Florencia's hand tightened on mine. I wondered if I could move fast enough to grab the gun before he could shoot me. Not only if I was fast enough, but if I had the strength to overcome him. The baggy overcoat hid his physique, which could have been far more formidable than mine.

As if to settle the question, he picked the gun off his lap and pointed it at my chest.

"I'm here to perform a simple transaction. You're both professional people. You know transactions are best made efficiently with a minimum of back and forth."

He reached into an inside pocket of his overcoat and pulled out an envelope.

"Actually, in this case, I simply give you this piece of paper." He handed the envelope and a pen to Florencia, who picked the items gingerly out of his hand with her long, elegant fingers. "You read it and fill in the

21

blanks. Or I shoot you. I already know one of the answers, so if you like risking your life on one in five odds, go for it."

"What is it?" I asked.

He shook his head.

"That's only for your wife to know," he said. He looked at Florencia. "You tell him and I shoot him in the balls." He lowered the gun to underscore the point.

The flap of the envelope was unsealed. Florencia pulled out and unfolded a sheet of paper and started reading. I wanted to look down, but I'd already been warned. I didn't know enough to test the boundaries.

After a sharp intake of breath, Florencia asked, "And if I don't?"

"The usual," he said, then reached the gun across the divide between us and flicked the muzzle across her right breast. "Maybe after you and me have some fun and games. You like fun, don't you gorgeous?"

I wondered again about the probability of reaching him from a sitting position, wrestling away the gun, and holding him powerless until the police arrived. I must have telepathically communicated this, because the man reacted by shooting a hole in my left thigh.

"Jesus Christ, Forgiver of Sins," he said to Florencia, "do I have to wait all day for you to fill out that motherfucking thing?"

A second after hearing him say this I was consumed by monstrous pain. I yelled and cried, and wept with fear and agony. I clutched at the wound and watched blood rush out between my fingers. Florencia's hand clutched alongside mine, until the man tapped her in the face with the muzzle of the gun and told her to sit back in the sofa.

"Do it or I put a few more holes in the dumb fuck," said the man.

"He's not dumb. He's brilliant," said Florencia. "You just don't know that, you stupid bastard." Her hand holding the pen raced across the paper, which I tried to read with no success.

Florencia handed it back along with the envelope. The man folded the sheet along the creases and put it back in the envelope, which he stuck in his inside coat pocket. I saw all this through a liquid veil, my eyes gushing tears, my brain barely able to comprehend what was happening.

The man sat back in the chair, making himself comfortable.

"We need to call him an ambulance," said Florencia, in a calm, measured voice. "I did what you asked me to do."

"You did," said the man. "I gotta give you that."

Then he shot her in the forehead.

I felt the spray of blood and brains splash across my face. I yelled, I think, though I don't remember for sure.

"No hard feelings," said the man. "That 'stupid bastard' thing aside."

Then he shot me in the head, too.

CHAPTER 2

Being indifferent to life gives you a fresh perspective. I didn't mind that I faded in and out of reality. In fact, I welcomed the lush euphoria of semi-consciousness, where I could note the staggering destruction that had been done to me without feeling its effects. My sister later explained that this was the morphine talking, which she administered cautiously, negotiating that devil's deal — irrational bliss versus possible addiction, detachment versus horrible pain and crushing grief.

Consciousness, however incomplete, came to me after I was moved to her house, so there was no recollection of the hospital, the operations or the coma I fell in and out of for months, both natural and artificially-induced to prevent the swelling in my brain from killing me before the neurosurgeons had a chance to repair the damage. As best they could.

I remember someone telling me, soon after I became aware again of my own existence, that I was lucky to be alive. That was the most debatable statement of the century.

It wasn't my sister Evelyn who said it, though she could have. She was a doctor, and also Florencia's best friend. Her first statement to me, sadly repeated a few times until it stuck in my memory, was that Florencia had been killed instantly. I would have been killed, too, but for a lucky (that word again) turn the bullet took when it struck the right side of my skull, mostly bypassing the frontal lobe, then cutting a shallow tunnel through the parietal and exiting the back of my head.

The two holes in my head were very tidy, indicating a small bore round, like a .22, with a heavy charge. There were any number of other combinations of bullets, powder and weaponry that would have had a much more catastrophic effect. Which meant I was only near death for part of a year and not completely dead like I should have been.

We'd been found by a neighbor, whose cat I was feeding while she and her husband were on vacation. She saw our cars in the driveway, and when we didn't answer the doorbell, she walked around to the patio at the back of the house. She looked through a pair of French doors and could see the tops of our heads over the sofa, and when we didn't answer her knocking, she called the cops, who got there before I'd completely bled out. Another bit of dubious luck.

I learned this in fragments as my consciousness, hearing and limited motor skills slowly returned.

Apparently my eyes opened before I could process what I saw, triggering an hysterical response from the nurse on duty. In no time the room was filled with anxious, inquiring faces, gentle prods and sheets of paper with hand-lettered messages. None of it made any sense, and finally weary of it all, I closed my eyes again and puzzled over the groans of disappointment.

Sometime after that a version of my sight returned, enough to make eye contact and respond to signals. I know now that this was an important step, but at the time I was merely annoyed at all the ridiculous celebration.

The last thing to come back was my voice. And the first words I croaked out were, "Did they catch the guy?"

"Another country heard from," said Evelyn, sitting at my bedside. "They don't tell me much, but I'd know if they had."

"Any idea why?" I asked.

She shook her head. "I was going to ask you the same thing."

"I need to talk to the police," I said. "I can identify the killer."

"I told them, and everyone else, that you were in a persistent vegetative state, and would likely stay there forever. That's the story that ran in the newspapers. The only people who know it isn't true are Dr. Selmer, the neurologist, and Joan Bendleson, the visiting nurse who was here when you opened your eyes."

"Why the deception?" I asked.

"You said it yourself. You can identify the killer."

I tried to ask her more questions, but had trouble getting the words out. She patted my arm, and held her mildly sympathetic expression, using all her meager bedside skills to mask her deeper feelings. She told me the aphasia was obviously clearing, but I shouldn't tax my voice box. She said to let it rest for another day, and we'd try to catch up again. She had to go back to the hospital, but Joan would keep an eye on me, and then she left.

Two weeks later, my voice was still impaired, but my mind, nearly free of painkillers, approached the functional, or at least that's what I thought at the time. As a researcher, I'd been trained to resist jumping to conclusions with insufficient data. Though I'd also learned that certain determinations could be made based on a small set of data points, assuming they were consistent and powerful. Powerful data is what I had, and some important decisions to make.

The first was to be or not to be. I'd never had a suicidal thought in my life, though now the life I'd had, the one I loved, was effectively over. So choosing to finish off the mangled remains was an entirely rational option. Especially when I tried to imagine a return to normalcy. I played a series of scenarios across my mind, but they were equally repellent. Nothing would ever be normal again.

A vast and fathomless sadness engulfed my mind. An impossible agony of grief. I understood for the first time how black black could be. I felt my heart descend into a snarling well of irredeemable anguish. It was there that I relinquished claim to the hopeful, loopy possessor of inevitable good fortune who once defined my world view, and contemplated what was left.

Then I snarled back and embraced the beast.

When feeling lost its grip on my heart, logic and reason took over. The first logical conclusion was that I couldn't live in this world, even if I wanted to. Not as long as I shared it with the man in the trench coat. The man who likely had the answer to the only question worth asking in this barren reality into which I'd emerged.

Why?

Until that was answered, all other deliberations would have to be postponed. With that decided, I started to block out the necessary methodology, running if/then scenarios. Aside from two hours of uneasy sleep, I worked on this until Evelyn showed up again the next day. So I was well prepared to exercise my recovering speech.

"I want to be dead," I said to her when she walked in the room.

"I know, Arthur," she said, sitting on the side of the bed and gripping my arm. "I understand."

"No, you don't. I want to be declared dead. Not actually be dead. All you need to do is sign the death certificate," I said. "I'll take it from there."

"Take it where? You can't walk."

"I can't walk very well. Not yet. You keep telling me my leg will come most of the way back."

I'd made my first wobbly journey to and from the bathroom the day before, with lots of help from Evelyn and the nurse. My left side was much weaker than my right, compounded by the wound in my thigh, and my future mobility was yet to be determined, but I felt instinctively sure of adequate recovery. My vision was also clearing, slowly, though everything looked a little off, as if I'd awoken into a parallel, but slightly reorganized universe.

My gut was gone. The deflated skin hung around my waist, but I was forty pounds less of a man than I had been before.

"I still don't understand what you're getting at," said Evelyn.

"I want a psych evaluation," I said.

"You think your mental functions are impaired?"

"That's what I want to find out. I want to know which ones are and which aren't. For example, I don't sound like myself. Is that because my voice has changed or my hearing's been damaged, or my brain is interpreting what it hears differently?"

"Okay," she said. "I can arrange that. And about your voice, you have a slight slur, which I think will correct itself over time. The bullet clipped the somatosensory cortex, so you could have a slight reordering of your sensory perceptions in general, which could explain the voice change."

"My eyes aren't working as well," I said. "Things look different."

"That's probably permanent. But you'll get used to the change, unless there's a more profound spatial distortion than we've had a chance to determine."

I'd been trying to look at her while we talked, but the warp in my peripheral vision became too much to bear. I looked up at the ceiling.

"I need to know all that. And a complete accounting of my financial resources."

"You're fine there," she said. "Damien Brandt, Florencia's comptroller, is managing the day-to-day at the agency. He's reporting to Bruce Finger, a friend of mine who just retired after twenty years as corporate counsel for a big carrier. Bruce tells me potential buyers are already lining up, but he won't even discuss it if I'm not interested. Am I?"

"Sure, but not now. Though a valuation would be helpful. Beyond that, when you get a chance, give me a breakdown of all my assets, in particular anything liquid. I'd do it myself, but I can't read."

"You're running out ahead of me, Arthur. Come on back and tell me what's actually going on."

She'd been saying things like that to me since we were children. Evelyn was eight years older than me, and clearly more intelligent. But she tended to think in a more linear, methodical way. She liked to go deep into a handful of subjects, like her specialty, cardiology, whereas I was an omnivore, racing like a water bug across the surface of whatever topic caught my eye.

"I need to permanently disappear."

"We'll be getting you that psych evaluation ASAP," she said.

"Your part in this is essential," I said, "and I apologize from the depths of my heart for what I'm going to put you through. As soon as I leave, you need to declare me dead. I'm thinking hematoma, but you're the cardiologist, I'm sure you'll pick the right C.O.D. The harder part will be coming up with a corpse, which will need to go straight to the crematorium before the cops have a chance to order an autopsy, mandatory in a homicide case. When the corpse is ash, you get news of my sudden death out to the media, then tell the cops. They'll be pissed. I suggest you act dumb. The good doctor, brilliant in cardiology, but naïve in matters of the law. I'll need my original birth certificate and both current and out-of-date passports. I'll tell you where they are in the house, which you'll need to sell when I'm officially dead, along with the cars. You'll need to collect on the life insurance, which is another legal threat, so I suggest you put the payout in a secure escrow account. I need some time to figure that one out. Since Florencia had no family left, you're the sole heir and will inherit all the money. I'll need you to advance me a stake until the estate clears probate."

She took all this in with a look that also went back to our childhood. One of annoyed disbelief.

"This isn't funny," she said. "It's a terrible thing that's happened to you, but of course you can't do this thing you're saying you're going to do."

"Do you see me laughing?" I said, more coldly than I should have. I caught myself, and gently laid it out for her in the linear way she could best absorb. "Number one, since they didn't catch the guy in the first forty-eight hours, the odds of catching him have decreased to zero. Two, he's a professional killer, in my untrained opinion. They almost never get caught. I'm sure he knows

34

I survived and will assume I can identify him. Three, though he likely believes I'm a vegetable, it's only a matter of time before he comes back and finishes the job, just to be on the safe side. He's just waiting for more convenient circumstances. The only way to get some breathing space is to be officially and conspicuously dead. This follows your logic, by the way. It's why you told everyone I was in a coma, probably forever."

"What you're talking about is illegal. You could end up in jail."

"Not if I don't get caught. And if I do, who cares."

"I do," she said.

"I know. You love me. I love you, too. And I'm deeply grateful for everything you've done for me. But I've got to get out of here, because every day I'm here intensifies the danger to both of us."

Evelyn did love me. She virtually raised me, since our parents managed to conceive me when they were in their midforties, exhausted and prematurely aged by the harshness of their blue collar, uneducated lives. Earnest and good-hearted, they never knew what to do with either one of their precocious children, especially since we were precocious in nearly opposite ways.

Evelyn was an indulgent semi-parent, though I rarely gave her cause to discipline me. I was a pudgy and dreamy kid, so she frequently had to protect me from nerd-bashers and benighted authority figures, like gym teachers, den mothers and check-out clerks. This was her greatest test.

"What about the investigation?" she asked. "Without your testimony, the cops have nothing."

"Tell them I've just come out of the coma, and I'll talk to them. But ask if we can keep the coma story going, for safety's sake. How long before I can move around on my own?" I asked.

"Not less than four weeks."

"Let's make it two. And keep the visitors coming. We want lots of traffic in and out of the driveway."

"You're scaring me."

"Sorry. Can I borrow your cell phone?"

She reflexively patted around her jeans pocket, then stopped.

"What for? Who're you going to call?"

"Gerry Charles. He's in Amsterdam. I'll make it quick. I've got his number in my wallet. If you could get it for me, that'd be great."

I told her she could stay while I made the call, but she took the high road and left me alone. Gerry answered, which I was very happy about. I didn't want to leave a message.

"Hey, Gerry, it's Arthur Cathcart," I said when he answered. "I haven't been by your place in a bit — been laid up — but the last time everything was in order."

"Thanks for the update," said Gerry. "But you don't sound like yourself. You okay?"

"I've been better, but I'll be okay," I said. "The other reason I'm calling is your guitar collection. Are you still interested in selling?"

"You bet. Which one do you want?"

Gerry Charles designed and built studio furniture in a shop carved out of an old clock factory. He'd flown to Europe a few weeks before I was shot, leaving me the keys to his shop so I could check up on things while he was away. He'd stopped the mail, but there was always random stuff showing up on the loading dock and in the mailbox hung on the outside wall. The shop also had a small living space — complete with single bed, toilet and kitchenette — which he used when in the throes of creation. And a garage, open to the shop, big enough to fit a Chevy Astro van in which he hauled lumber in and furniture out.

Gerry was also a graphic artist, so in addition to clamps, block planes and power tools, the shop had a powerful Mac attached to a scanner and four-color printer. On top of that, Gerry was a former professional guitar player with a world-class collection of vintage guitars, accumulated over forty years of steady, strategic acquisition.

"All of them."

"Really," he said.

"You once told me you'd sell the lot for a quarter million dollars. You could get more if you did it one guitar at a time, but you were daunted by the logistics."

"You're right about that, Art."

"Okay, today's your lucky day."

"Prices have dropped a lot since we talked," he said. "I'm not sure you could improve on the bulk price."

"I'm willing to take that chance," I said.

"Cool. But how come?"

I gave him a brief rundown on what had happened to me. He could have found out on his own, so there was no advantage in keeping it from him. It also gave me a reason for making the offer: I told him I needed something to keep me busy during recovery.

"Holy crap, man, that's fucking horrible. I'm sorry, I really am."

We worked out the mechanics of the

transaction. Using her power of attorney, Evelyn would wire the money to his account in Amsterdam. When he confirmed the funds had arrived, he'd alert the high-security storage facility where he kept the guitars and give me the combination to get inside the vault. He would also mail a coded description of the collection to Evelyn's address, so I could retrieve the instruments on a guitar-by-guitar basis.

After the deal was struck, he told me a little about his time in the Netherlands, where he was on a year-long grant teaching the art of furniture making. He said it was the first time he'd made money from his lunatic profession without blowing sawdust out his nose every night. He and his wife were having such a great time, he had no intention of returning for at least a year; so if I wanted to mess around in his shop when I felt better, he told me to feel free.

"It's super therapy, Arthur. I'm telling you."

I thanked him, and got off the phone. Then I yelled for Evelyn.

"Can I use your computer?" I asked her.

"You were a lot easier to handle when you were in a coma," she said, walking into the room.

I started to go through the awkward and

painful process of getting out of bed. She watched me without raising a hand to help. She was a doctor. She knew what sort of help I really needed.

"While you're racing to my office, I'll boot up the computer," she said, and left the room.

When I finally got there, with the help of a walker, I sat in front of the screen and called up our online investment and retirement accounts. I sold everything, then directed the proceeds, almost $300,000, into a joint checking account to which I added Evelyn's name.

Two days later Evelyn wired $250,000 to Gerry Charles, and the next day he sent me all the enabling information, completing the transaction.

I now had a ready source of entirely non-traceable cash, available to be meted out whenever needed.

Done deal.

CHAPTER 3

Detective Mike Maddox was a lot younger than I thought a plainclothesman would be. I was surprised to learn he was a college graduate with two years of law school, finishing his third at night. A short, neatly groomed African-American in a conservative suit that complemented his small frame, he looked more like one of Florencia's claims managers than a Stamford police department detective.

He introduced himself, shook my hand and sat in the visitor's chair. He held a pad and small digital recorder. He clicked on the recorder and held it up in the air.

"You mind?" he asked. "So I don't miss anything."

"I don't mind," I said.

"First off, I'm very sorry for your loss. I know this is difficult and I apologize in advance for any emotional stress this conversation will cause. Though I'm sure you want

41

a positive resolution of this case as much as I do."

"Maybe more so," I said.

"Of course. So tell me what happened. Anything you can remember."

So I did, just as he asked. I'd been running through the main event in my head since regaining consciousness, straining to remember every detail. Not that I trusted the recollection. I knew from countless research interviews that memory was an unreliable thing. The mind had a variety of storage and retrieval mechanisms, all imperfect in different ways, even when you haven't had a bullet pass through your brain.

"So you don't know what was on that piece of paper the suspect gave your wife."

"No. But I think it was some type of form — five questions he had her answer. He said he knew one of the answers, that she only had a one-in-five chance of guessing which one. A simple proof that she wasn't fudging things."

"Anything going on with your wife leading up to this? Had she been herself, acting normally?"

"Yes. I would have known if she was bothered by something important. I know everyone thinks they know their spouses that intimately, but this is what I believe."

"So no theories, no possible motives?" said Maddox.

"No. What about you?" I asked. "What's the official theory? Does this guy sound familiar?"

Maddox kept the same pleasant, helpful look on his face, but he paused before answering.

"The description of the individual does not ring any bells, at least with me, but this was an expert hit, I'm certain of that. The hat and sunglasses, the type of weapon, the totally clean crime scene — rounds and spent shells recovered — all the telltales are there. Don't expect anything to come of the SUV. For sure stolen and long gone. I believe your wife knew something, or had something, or saw or did something, to bring this on. Doesn't mean it was intentional, or that she'd done anything wrong in the eyes of the law, but obviously in the eyes of people outside the law."

"And you don't know what that something was?" I asked.

He shook his head.

"Since you've been unconscious, your wife's company has been in the custody of your sister. Miss Cathcart and her attorney have been very cooperative. We've grilled every one of her employees and anyone outside the agency who might have an insight into the case and come up with zilch. We've had forensic accountants from the State Police go over audits of the last three years, and the same thing. Nothing out of the ordinary. Your wife ran a very clean and professional business."

"Not surprised," I said.

"Your business, on the other hand, we know very little about, because Miss Cathcart refused access to your files. She was holding out hope that you'd be in a position to grant us that authority yourself, and lo and behold, here you are."

"Be my guest," I said, without hesitation. "I have no paper records. It's all in my computer. Just give me a chance to copy the hard drive for safety's sake, and you can have it. And you can search my house, my office, anything you want."

"I can make that copy for you," he said.

"You can watch Evelyn make it, following my instructions, which you can approve."

He nodded. "Fair enough. We already searched your house," he said. "We found some external hard drives, but since the warrant didn't cover the computer, we had to leave them where they were."

"Those are archives. You can have them, but I'll need copies."

We negotiated the next steps. He was happy to sustain the coma ruse as well as he could, but noted it wouldn't last forever.

"For example, you need to work with our sketch artist. A little hard to explain that the suspect was described by a person in a coma. Certain people have to know to keep the investigation going, and the more people know, the harder it is to secure. Especially with a high profile case like this. Eventually, whether you like it or not, you'll have to rejoin the living," he said.

"That's what I intend to do, detective."

Easier said than done. The next two weeks were a cavalcade of frustrations. Cursed with full, morphine-free awareness, I was alternately whipsawed by existential rage and despair and the physical stress of my sadly impaired self. As hoped, my mobility returned relatively quickly, though the left side of my face, the one controlled by the damaged right side of my brain, had a slight, but likely permanent droop, as you often see in stroke victims. My left side also dragged behind the other half. The hole in my leg healed better than anyone thought it would, though the bullet wound would likely hamper movement forever. In other words, I had a limp.

The clarity of my vision, on the other hand, came close to what I had before. Evelyn arranged for an optometrist to come to the house and fit me with glasses, which neatly compensated for the minor deficiencies — though I found the weight hanging off my face hard to get used to, even though half the world seemed to manage it with little complaint.

Beginning with walks to the bathroom three times a day, I built up strength in my gunshot leg until I could go two miles at a time on the treadmill Evelyn kept in the basement. I had it set on the slowest speed, and would never move much faster than that, but steady was achievable.

As promised, the sketch artist showed up and spent a few hours with me going through the well-known process. I expected a friendly person with a charcoal drawing pad. What I got was a crabby grey-haired guy with a laptop loaded with sketch art software.

Seeing the man in the trench coat emerge from the screen was an exceptionally unsettling moment. Worse because I really had no idea if it was what the guy actually looked like. There's a reason eyewitness testimony is often disallowed, even when the witness isn't brain damaged. I shared this thought with the artist, asking whether he ever checked on the accuracy of his images after the fact. He said they were usually close enough.

"Meaning the witness had a great memory, or the cops just arrested some poor schlub that looked like the sketch," he said. "And no, I don't care either way."

Maddox emailed a copy of the sketch to my office computer, which Evelyn had secured and brought to my bedroom.

After that, I hosted a few of Evelyn's buddies from the hospital who assessed my physical and mental state, clinically and otherwise. A psychiatrist, the neurologist Dr. Selmer, and a musculoskeletal specialist all weighed in. The result was inconclusive, mostly due to the relatively early stage of recovery, though everyone but the shrink thought I had a reasonable chance at regaining much of my original self. The psychiatrist told me and my sister that my cognitive acuity was remarkably intact, but my social affect, empathy and equanimity factors were nearly immeasurable. She attributed this, breezily I thought, to having been recently shot in the head and witnessing the brutal murder of my beloved wife. I told Evelyn I hoped we hadn't overpaid for that diagnosis.

My right hand was stiff, but still steady as a rock, though my famous grin, now rarely deployed, looked like a sneer. Worse, my sensory acuity was seriously jumbled. Selmer said it had something to do with damage to the parietal lobe, causing a pathology called optic ataxia, where your arms and legs essentially lose track of things your eyes have identified and fixed in the physical world. So I fell a lot and often misjudged the location of common objects like toilets, ottomans, serving dishes and household pets.

This was disappointing, but not as startling as the dyscalculia. I'd had no reason to use any sort of math in the process of recovery, so it was surprising to be unable to add five and five. I laughed, assuming it was a fluke of the moment, and tried other combinations, all completely impenetrable. I told the doctor I'd pulled an 800 on my math SAT's and wrestled with esoteric calculations for a living. He said the part of my brain that did all that had apparently been mashed into glop by the bullet passing through.

The musculoskeletal guy said I'd never run the New York City Marathon, but I'd achieve a reasonable gait over time, until arthritis hit, which could be severely disabling, depending on genetic factors. I liked him the best because he was harshly direct and to the point, which I noticed despite my apparently diminished social affect.

Meanwhile, my personal appearance had been totally transformed. The severe weight loss had altered my morphology, and with my new glasses, shaved head (a custom maintained after the operations), lost moustache, and the downward curve of my dreary, depressed expression, I didn't look anything like the me that was.

This would have been disturbing, if not so strategically helpful.

Strategic is too big a word. It was much more of an outline of a direction with only the initial stages laid out in order. This wasn't my preferred approach. I'm a person who likes to have every inch of a journey determined before I take the first step. But I was weak from injury and the struggle with my altered circumstances. And, worst of all, there was that blanket of grief enveloping my mind, like an evil drug, clouding my judgment and threatening my sanity.

I'd never practiced TM, or Zen meditation, or any other mental discipline that might have trained me to control my emotional state. Instead, I merely immersed myself in the task. I became literally single-minded. Focused and impossible to distract, consumed by an unwavering obsession.

This is what I knew how to do.

It wasn't perfect, but moving into Gerry's shop apartment would get me away from Evelyn and provide an ideal staging area for the next phase. All I needed was to learn to walk farther than down the hall or two miles on the treadmill.

So I kept practicing, pushing my endurance to the limit, which grew greater every day.

I wasn't ready, but almost, which I decided was close enough. My first trip outside was in the dark. It was early in the evening, but the sky was moonless and overcast. I wore a long overcoat and my L.L. Bean washed canvas trekking hat to cover the bald head, surgical scars and bullet holes — now little pink craters, the most conspicuous of which was on the left side of my forehead near where my hairline used to be. I used my rehab-issue cane, an aluminum number with a fat rubber tip and form-fitting grip, that had become a natural extension of my being.

I walked about a block and caught a bus into town, where I got off and walked another block to an Internet café run by a young anarchist whose only restriction was pornography.

"Can't have people just using the place to get a stiffy," is how he explained it to me. He also claimed to have ways around being traced through IP and MAC addresses, though I knew that to be essentially impossible. For my purposes, however, his relative untrackability was good enough.

I paid cash for two hours of computer time, which I spent scanning obituaries. I set these basic parameters: males within four years of my age; born in Connecticut; died in a distant state; minimum survivors; ethnically compatible with my new appearance; uneventful lives.

The same criteria used by identity thieves, which I hoped to successfully emulate.

One of the more interesting assignments I'd had was to test an identity theft protection product marketed by one of my insurance clients. I'd been asked to assess the product's various features and benefits, so in the process I learned a lot about the tactics of the people it was meant to protect you from.

In my budgeted two hours at the anarchist's café, I logged the names and useful statistics of two dozen recently departed, and their closest relatives. I wrote this information in a little softbound notebook and stuffed it in my pocket.

Then I went home and went to bed, utterly exhausted by the effort. This was one of the things people who are recovering from massive injuries know better than anyone. It isn't just the healing, it's the destruction of your former vitality that's the most difficult to accept. But you have no choice. Your body is calling the shots.

The next night I went to another store in Stamford, one that sold pre-paid cell phones. Their record-keeping protocols were on a par with the anarchist's café, amounting to taking your cash and handing you a phone. Very popular with the illegal drug industry.

I took the phone and a pen and paper, illuminated by a tiny flashlight, and sat in a park to make phone calls. Calling people and extracting information from them is one of my life skills, honed over thousands of phone interviews on every subject imaginable, some even more emotionally difficult than the recent death of a loved one. Yet with the right questions, asked in the right order, with the right tone and pitch, most people will tell you anything you want to know.

As always, the first few were a little bumpy,

but by the fifth I had my rhythm, in both the form and content of my approach. I told them there would be no penalty if they agreed to allow me, as a representative of the Social Security Administration, to file the necessary paperwork. All I needed was confirmation of the SS number, along with the number of years they'd lived at their most recent address, to assure I had the right person. They could expect a check reflecting the deceased person's current contribution to the fund, and a written report within three months.

Most wisely hung up, but in two days of fishing I'd collected seven good names with SS numbers and expressions of gratitude for the written report, if not the check.

I felt strong enough a week later to pack a duffle bag with sturdy everyday clothes and a supply of toiletries. I put $20,000 in big and small bills in a leather pouch secured inside the waistband of my pants.

When Evelyn got home that evening, I gave her my final instructions.

"Please put the proceeds from the house and cars into something extremely safe and liquid, like half cash, half treasuries. Put the life insurance payments in something that'll earn a little interest. Like six month CD's.

I'll let you know when I've figured out how to make transfers."

"So I'm just supposed to sit and wait."

"You'll be plenty busy. You can donate all our personal belongings to charity," I said, giving her the name of an organization that would bring a truck and haul it all away.

"Are you planning to work?" she asked, then raised her hands. "I'm sorry. No questions, I remember."

On top of all the other crazy impositions I put upon her was the agreement that I keep my plans to myself. It wasn't a matter of trust; I didn't want to make her more of an accessory than I already had.

"As soon as things are settled, we'll establish an email connection. I just need time to work out the details. I might have to communicate by letter, so please open all your mail, since you won't know what form it might take. After you read the letter, bring it home and burn it, then spread the ashes on the lawn."

"Are you sure you're ready for this? Whatever it is you're doing?"

"Since I'm doing it, I guess I'm ready."

The duffle bag had a shoulder strap, which I used to haul it down to the garage. I got in the back of Evelyn's Jeep Cherokee. I lay in the foot well of the backseat and she put a blanket over me. She drove me to where I could leave the Jeep unobserved and walk a short distance to catch a cab.

"By tomorrow morning, you'll be dead," she said. "Tell me what it's like on the other side."

"Have you figured out the corpse part?" I asked.

"If I can't ask questions, neither can you."

I admired much about Evelyn, but especially her profound lack of sentimentality. Before she left me behind a grocery store next to a dumpster and a stack of collapsed cardboard boxes, all she did was squeeze my hand and say, "I'm hoping someday to give back that insurance money," she said. "If you do anything to make the payout legit, I'll kill you."

Even with the cane, my leg hurt from the weight of the duffle, as did my neck, head and back. But at least I could move under my own power. I made it to the cabstand, and an hour later a jumpy young East Indian took me to a spot less than a quarter mile from Gerry's shop. I fixed my mind on my destination and set out.

The factory was in an industrial area which had given up the industry of clock manufacturing almost fifty years before.

Several low brick buildings covered about twenty acres, and maybe half had been turned into studio space for artists and craftspeople like Gerry. His place was around the back of one of the smaller buildings where he was the only occupant, and reachable by a narrow, windowless alley.

When I got there, I was nearly felled by pain and fatigue, but kept up the effort until I secured the studio, with all the lights on, and convinced myself that everything was as I had last left it. Only then did I lie on the bed, where I instantly fell asleep.

I slept in my clothes until the next morning. My mind was up to full RPM's before my body showed the slightest interest in moving. I ran through my plan, step-by-step, arranging the sequence, identifying hazards, assessing risks, working my way back to the next thing I had to do.

Which was to make a cup of coffee and stare at the names in my notebook. One I particularly liked, Alex Rimes. Alex left Connecticut when he was five years old and spent the rest of his truncated life in Alaska. On that basis, the clear winner.

After unplugging the Ethernet cable connecting Gerry's Mac to the wall, just to be 100% sure I was blind to the web, I refamiliarized myself with the computer. I'd set up a similar system for Florencia. The most important program for my purposes was Photoshop. Gerry had the latest, professional grade version, but I had little trouble working out the functionality. Mastering complex systems was another of my gifts, or just a variation on the core gift — the stubborn ability to figure shit out.

I took my birth certificate out of an envelope held in the inside pocket of my jacket. It was a rectangular sheet of soft, yellowy paper with deep creases, having been folded and stored for years in the family bible. Evelyn had retrieved it from my house, and after close examination, I sent her off on another mission to buy, with cash, a customizable embosser. It took her a week, but she finally found one in a hobby shop: "Hey kids, make your own *official* seal!"

She also bought a selection of paper that closely matched the feel and consistency of the original. She outdid herself on this one, discovering a fifty-year-old paper sample case in a collectibles shop.

I scanned my birth certificate into the system at the highest resolution the system would allow. Ten minutes later it was up on my screen. From there it was two days of eye-straining and tedious painting by mouse, as I methodically turned Arthur Hemple Cathcart into Alex Bryson Rimes, son of Timothy and Sarah Louise Rimes.

The printing process was more difficult than I thought it would be, mostly because the old stock easily jammed the printer, which was geared for modern office paper. Luckily, I had plenty to experiment with, so in the end I had a half-dozen copies I could use to move on to the next stage.

I took one of the ersatz birth certificates, and using black dust harvested from the motor of one of Gerry's power tools, and some regular sawdust from a piece of red cedar cut on the band saw, mimicked the natural decay caused by a document being pressed together for years in an old bible. I cut the sample paper to the correct size, then softened and roughed up the edges.

With all these features in place, I used my toy embosser to duplicate the official seal. It was maybe a sixteenth of an inch smaller in diameter, but otherwise, an exact replica.

Then I moved to the final stage — folding and refolding the document as my mother had folded the original forty-two years before. Then I repeated the process until the seams were ready to part. I laid my creation next to the original under a bright task light.

Perfection in any pursuit is unattainable, but to my careful eye, I could see virtually no difference between the two. I closed my eyes and felt the two documents, confirming the feel was also identical.

It had taken three days to achieve, but I finally had the fulcrum on which the entire plan would rest.

I waited until night to venture out again. I needed food and a chance to catch up on the news. I stocked up on canned goods and frozen entrees at the grocery store, as much as I could comfortably carry in a kid's knapsack bought out of a sale bin, and found the hoped-for news in a deli, after the clerk generously offered to look in the back for recent issues of the local paper.

I didn't dwell on my obituary, but noted the key facts, which held to what Evelyn and I agreed upon.

Soon I was back home again, where I took a much needed shower, ate enough to kill my hunger, and passed out again, still dog-tired, but vaguely satisfied with my progress.

CHAPTER 4

The rest of the week was filled with another round of forgery. This involved one of my expired passports, covering the years 1987 to 1997. There were two pages I had to process through Photoshop to alter names and addresses. The stickiest issue was the passport number, which was unalterable, since it was hole-punched into the first four pages of the passport, including the cover. The other obvious problem was the number itself — which belonged to Arthur Cathcart, not Alex Rimes. Thus the utility of this forgery was restricted to situations where they'd either ignore the number, or be unlikely to go to the trouble of checking its validity.

That put a big burden on the final forgery, Alex's Social Security card. Fortunately, I'd held on to my very first one, issued in 1983, before the days of Photoshop, Homeland Security and international databases. It was a quaint little slip of paper that fit in your wallet, a manifestly stupid thing to do, but that's what they did in those days.

This time it only took me a day and night to recreate a new card with Alex's number. It was a much simpler job, and I was getting more proficient with the computer.

The next day I took the train to Hartford, then a cab to the Department of Motor Vehicles in Wethersfield. There were DMV locations closer to Stamford, but I didn't want to risk someone recognizing Gerry's address at the old clock factory complex.

I'd left the cane behind to avoid messy questions about my ability to drive, so it wasn't a painless trip, though pain wasn't an unfamiliar companion, cane or not.

The train ride gave me a chance to collect myself and frame how I thought the experience might go. It was impossible to fully anticipate every contingency. I was confident that my forgeries looked legitimate. Based on documents from an earlier, pre-9/11 era, they were relatively simple to manipulate. I respected the people working the windows at the DMV, oft-vilified though they were. They were crushed under a mountain of paperwork which they had to process under merciless time frames. You couldn't expect them to be forensic scien-

61

tists. The most worrisome danger lay in security procedures I knew nothing about. Alerts triggered by automatic data scans.

This led to a decision to stick with the birth certificate and the Social Security card, which a simple check would tie together, and leave out the passport. According to DMV instructions, this was enough to get a replacement license. The passport number may or may not be easy to check, so I couldn't risk it, even though in other ways it would handily lock in the deception.

And then there was the possibility that Alex's relatives in Alaska, or some savvy friend, would have already spotted the scam and alerted the Social Security Administration. That was a pure risk, and there was nothing I could do about it but speculate on how I'd survive prosecution and jail time.

Hiding from the criminal world meant hiding from the legal world as well, since the former required violating the rules of the latter. Caught by the criminal world, I'd just be killed, and that would be that. Caught by the legal world, I'd be exposed, and then eventually killed in prison, or have my freedom so sorely compromised that death would be welcome.

My greatest advantage was that none of my potential pursuers thought I was available for pursuit. With luck, they all thought I was dead. As for law enforcement, this would suddenly change if I slipped up on any one thing, especially if it happened online. But that was an exposure I'd have to face. I could have tried to stay completely off the grid, but that would have rendered me helpless to do anything other than simply survive.

I had greater ambitions.

As no one knew to stalk me, I was relatively safe. I would take every possible precaution, put up every screen I could and leave as faint a trail as possible. Though in the post-9/11 world, no one could roam the network fully secure from a determined tracker, who would be invisible to the tracked. And even the faintest trail lasts forever. Every keystroke, whether made for good or evil, was recorded somewhere, becoming your eternal legacy.

I let thoughts like these run free for several hours, then put them all back in the box from whence they'd sprung. I'm dead anyway, I decided, one way or another. Dead men don't have the luxury of speculating about things they cannot control.

The lines at the DMV were predictably long, but things were running smoothly, so it only took about a half hour for my number to be called to the designated window.

"Hi," I said, my whole being pitched for friendliness and an eager desire to please. "I'm in a bit of a pickle."

The woman gave me a slight smile and said she'd do her best to unpickle me.

"I just moved back to Connecticut from Alaska. I looked on your web site for what I need to get a Connecticut driver's license, but when I started gathering up ID, I couldn't find my Alaska license. So now I'm wondering if I have to replace that one first, or can I just get a replacement here."

"You need at least one primary and one secondary form of identification," she said, sliding a small pamphlet across the counter.

"I know," I said, without looking at the pamphlet. "I saw that on your web site. So I brought what I had."

I unfolded the birth certificate, and presented it to her along with the Social Security card.

She had a confident look about her as she carefully gathered up the tattered documents and walked back into the maze of desks behind the counter. After asking a managerial type a few questions, she sat in front of a computer screen. I casually looked around the general area, and counted three security people.

After nearly ten minutes, she came back to the window.

"I checked with Alaska DMV," she said. My heart, as yet maintaining a steady pulse, took off like a greyhound.

"And?"

"Your license is valid, with no encumbrances. They sent me an affidavit, so I can just put it with these and your application and we can get this done today."

"Boy, that was nice of you to do," I said, with a slight trill in my voice, which she might have interpreted as deep gratitude, which it was, only not for reasons she might have thought.

She didn't answer, already busy prepping me for the next stage in the process, which was to pay the fee and get my photo taken.

"Good luck, Alex," she said ten minutes later, as I walked past her window holding a little manila envelope containing my forged documents and an official Connecticut driver's license. "Must be nice to be back home."

I almost said, "Like I'd died and gone to heaven," but just thanked her and left.

The world is a much bigger and easier place to live in when you have a driver's license.

It's the difference between being part of society and being a specter, invisible to all official and unofficial proceedings, civil and commercial. In a period of two days I had three bank accounts and three debit/ATM cards, a replacement birth certificate, officially obtained from the office of Norwalk Vital Statistics, and a car.

This last acquisition followed my first trip to Gerry's vintage guitar warehouse. It was in Danbury, Connecticut, which first meant a bus, then a cab ride to a giant corrugated metal building sitting in the middle of an industrial park just north of town. I paid the Ethiopian cabby to wait for me while I went to the office, where I had to use my real ID as Arthur Cathcart to negotiate the security checkpoints. I hoped the woman at the desk wouldn't check me out against a database of legitimate living identities, noting the irony.

The guitars were in shelves stacked ten feet high lining the walls of a large open area. Using Gerry's code sheet, I dug out three guitars that most closely fit my criteria, based on some research I'd done on vintage guitar values at the anarchist's café. I piled them on a cart which I pushed with agonized slowness back to the office, where the cabby helped me load everything in the cab.

I paid the cabby a hundred dollars to take me all the way to the clock factory and help me haul the musical loot into Gerry's studio. By then, I was deranged by weariness, my hands shaking so hard I could barely get the bills out of the binder clip I was using to hold my cash. The cabbie stood and waited patiently, with no apparent complaint. This built his tip into a heroic amount.

He took the money and gave me his card.

"You need something else in the transportation regard, you call me, sir. I come from wherever."

I spent the next few hours lying on Gerry's cot trying to regain my strength. When I thought I could speak without sounding like my mouth was full of cloth, I used my disposable phone to call another disposable I'd sent to Evelyn the week before.

"Oh, thank God," she said.

"For what?"

"You called. I was afraid I'd never hear from you again."

"No such luck. How did the funeral go?" I asked.

"Everyone honored my request that we skip the funeral. I gave out a list of charities for donations in your name. I think your passing was well publicized. And you're right, the cops were furious, though they bought the dumb doc excuse."

"I saw the obit in the *Stamford Advocate*."

"And it made the evening news. How're you feeling?" she asked.

"It's getting better all the time," I said.

"Nice to hear, but it would be nicer if you told me something that made me less worried."

I thought about that.

"When I went off to college, you told me I could do anything I wanted. You didn't mean that in a 'this is America where anybody can follow their dream' sort of way. You meant I was so omnivorous in my interests and abilities that I could achieve any single thing I wanted to achieve. Remember?"

"I was just trying to get you to focus," she said.

"Well, I'm focused now."

"Thank you," she said, after a moment of thoughtful silence.

"You're welcome."

The next day I went to Wally's Wall of Music in Bridgeport and sold him a mint 1960 Gibson ES-335, with a sunburst finish and a double bound maple body, mahogany neck, bound rosewood fret board, dot inlays, twenty-two frets, two PAF humbuckers, original electronics, stop tailpiece and original Kluson tuners and hardware, for $32,567.

This was about two grand less than what I could have gotten for it, but part of the deal was being paid with a bank check, which I took to one of my new banks and deposited all but $7,000, which I added to the $15,000 I still had in my cash pouch, and went car hunting.

Plowing through a stack of want ad flyers, I quickly spotted a late model Subaru Outback on sale for $21,000 by a guy in Darien, Connecticut. I liked the Outback for its sturdy utility and ubiquitousness, so I called the guy on my disposable phone and arranged to meet him two hours later. I test drove the car, then said I could do ninety percent of his asking price if he'd take cash. Two hours later, the car was registered and parked in Gerry's garage, supplanting his white van, which I parked out in the alley.

I felt a little bad about that, but his van was a familiar sight around the clock factory, and it would only be there for a few days.

The next day, I deposited $2,635 dollars in one of my accounts — an entirely innocuous amount, well below various thresholds for federal reporting. Over the next few days I made other deposits at all three of my banks, being sure to widely vary the amounts. This was after several agonizing hours working out a deposit schedule that would keep a steady flow of cash into the accounts while staying well under the regulatory radar. Something I once could have done in the time it took to write down the figures.

By now, my physical condition had improved to the point where I could get through the whole day without stopping to rest and catch my breath. My right leg, still sore, had become limber enough that it almost had a normal swing, though I liked having the cane in case of sudden collapse. I hadn't completely reconciled myself to the new shape of the world, but I could usually navigate my way around without running into things, or feeling nauseated by the manifold irregularities.

My math skills had developed to the point where I could add, subtract, divide and multiply at the level of a modern third grader. Not bad for a guy who used to unwind by swimming around the equations supporting Einstein's Theory of General Relativity.

I stayed at Gerry's shop long enough to

build up more strength and receive a shipment of some crucial equipment bought online at the anarchist's café: a beefy laptop rigged for wireless and cell phone access, a scanner, printer, router and two external hard drives with a terabyte of storage space apiece.

When I had the laptop up and running and the wireless connections configured, I took it with me in the Outback and prowled around Stamford for public wireless access. After I tested a half-dozen connections, found while parked outside hotels, restaurants and cafés, I was confident that I'd configured everything for optimum receptivity.

Parked in front of an accommodating Starbucks, I opened an account with a major email provider under one of my dead guy's names, with the screen name "MrPbody." I hoped Evelyn would recognize the professorial dog Mr. Peabody from *Rocky and Bullwinkle* — the name she called me through most of my childhood — when it unexpectedly showed up in her mailbox.

From there, I started to surf, tapping "Organized crime, Connecticut" into Google. I didn't expect "Portraits of CT-based Hit Men" to pop up on the first page, but I knew very little about crime, organized or otherwise, and had to start somewhere.

One of the dangers researchers face is the natural tendency to treat as received truth the manifold misconceptions, biases and opinions formed by Hollywood movies. I had trained myself to wipe away all prior assumptions on any subject about which I had minimal empirical knowledge. I used to pretend I was the Man from Mars, a recently arrived alien sent down to study strange Earthling ways.

Now I had a better role to play — the Man Who Just Awoke from a Hundred Years in a Coma and Had a Lot of Catching Up to Do.

The first three Google pages were rich with information, which took almost an hour to read or download for future study, then it petered out. I kept clicking through the pages, however, having learned that some of the most rewarding material was often twenty, thirty, or even a hundred pages in. The Google search algorithm was a marvel of speed and efficiency, but it wasn't omniscient. Often the best stuff was tucked deep inside the search, where the less obsessive never took the trouble to look.

And this was no exception. On page sixty-three was the retirement notice in the University of Michigan alumni magazine of an FBI Special Agent named Shelly Gross, who'd spent the last ten years of his career setting up task forces around the country focused on organized crime, most recently in Connecticut, where he decided to settle down in Rocky Hill, a fact corroborated by an obituary on his wife in the *Rocky Hill Post*.

The singular success of the Connecticut project was noted in several sources. There was no mention of Shelly, but quite a bit on the nature of the various rackets the task force targeted, and the methods by which they seriously compromised criminal enterprise.

I jumped from there into a people search, which quickly yielded results for the only Shelly Gross living in Connecticut. I also tried to locate three crime bosses that my initial research had shown to be deeply entangled in the state's rackets over a long period of time, but not surprisingly, the public search sites yielded very little. There were more legal, professional search programs for tracking people down, but I'd never felt compelled to use them, on the theory that the cost would never justify the improved penetration.

I now abandoned that qualm, which quickly led me to a short list of three over-achieving punks: Ronny DeSuzio, Ekrem Boyanov, and my favorite, Sebbie "The Eyeball" Frondutti. He was an entrepreneurial underboss who'd set up a satellite operation in Connecticut for one of New York's prominent crime families. He had a taste for nightlife, having rolled up through acquisition and intimidation a string of restaurants, strip joints, night clubs and other entertainment venues across the state and into Massachusetts and Rhode Island.

This provided Sebbie with diversified revenue streams, legal and illegal — including unregulated gambling, prostitution, drug sales and cigarette smuggling — enmeshed in such a way that confounded regional law enforcement. Until Shelly rode into town. Backed by Federal resources and leverage, he'd soon built up a rock-solid case against Sebbie, leading to a racketeering indictment.

Sebbie was an hour away from being arrested when he dropped out of sight. There was a lot of conjecture by the media that the disappearing act had followed a tip-off from someone inside the investigation. The team was led by Shelly Gross, but included undercover cops with the State Police. Predictably, the Feds implied the leak came from the staties, and vice versa. That they were able to try and convict everyone involved in Sebbie's little empire other than Sebbie himself never cleared the air of rancor that hung around the prosecution.

Before moving on, I took note of the name of a reporter, Henry Eichenbach, who wrote a long exposé on Sebbie for the *Connecticut Post*. I searched for him on the *Post*'s web site, but he wasn't listed among the editorial staff, so I went back to Google and found his blog. This was expected, since any newspaper reporter with a pulse sets up a blog in anticipation of the mad dash to online media. I read through the site, noting he was working on a book about the Fed's secret Connecticut organized crime task force. The date of that posting was almost three years old. I checked Amazon unsuccessfully for a book.

I was grateful to see that Henry had a contact email address in addition to the regular comment mechanism.

MrPbody wrote him this message:

"Looking for the Eyeball?"

From there, I downloaded what looked to be the remaining worthwhile information, and pulled away from the Starbucks, nervous that more than two hours online might draw notice. I went back to Gerry's studio and spent the rest of the day packing up, wiping down anything that might reveal a fingerprint, vacuuming anything that might capture a fiber, and scrubbing anything where bodily fluid or epithelials might have been left behind. I wasn't a forensic scientist, but I was a world-class obsessive, so if I couldn't be expert, I could at least be thorough.

CHAPTER 5

I felt reasonably secure at Gerry's studio, and would have contentedly stayed there forever, but practicality drove me to move on before others at the clock factory registered my presence.

I'd already picked out the next stop, a tiny, furnished, single-story house in Wilton, a town just northeast of Stamford, Connecticut, with a nice view of an abandoned crushed stone and gravel distribution center, and thus one of Wilton's less desirable properties. I found the place over the Internet, avoiding the owners and limiting personal exposure to a woman at a real estate office. She gave me the key after I showed her my driver's license, signed the lease and paid three months' rent in advance, plus the security deposit.

Invisible from the road, and well removed from other houses, it featured the ultimate in privacy at a very affordable price. Still, I waited for nightfall to move in with my duffle bag and computer gear. The place had a kitchen with an eat-in area, a living room, two bedrooms and a single bath with a metal-lined shower. A drop-leaf pine table in the kitchen opened into a decent workspace, so this became my base of operations.

After setting up the gear, I made out a provisioning list — hardware, software and consumables — before picking out a bedroom, where I slept in my clothes on the bare mattress, registering the need for sheets and towels.

The next day I went to the Wilton post office and secured a P.O. box, then I went back to the house and opened up an email account. I'd come to the decision that cruising a string of wireless hot spots, some intentionally unsecured, some not, was too time-consuming and inefficient. Sitting on a traceable IP address was an exposure, but couldn't be helped.

I continued to harvest information on the New England underworld and outside influencers in New York and elsewhere. I copied the pertinent data into a ten-gig flash drive that screwed into a pen, and then deleted the file on my computer to the extent that was possible, shy of throwing the thing in a furnace.

My last act for the day was checking email, where I found this in MrPbody's box, from "EichenWrite."

"Yes."

I wrote back with a description of a bench in a park in Norwalk that looked out on Long Island Sound. I gave him three time and date options, with the words, "pick one."

He came back almost immediately with his pick, and a request for more information. I wrote, "See you then."

Then I went and did something I really didn't know how to do — buy a wig. I found the shop by searching for wigs designed for chemotherapy patients, on a hunch that the product line would strive for utility over glamour. I wasn't disappointed by the selection, in principle, just the complications involved in getting the most natural look. I couldn't sign up for all the fittings, the back and forth, so I bought a dozen wigs in a variety of cuts and colors, much to the disapproval of the wig seller.

Back at the house, I tried on a sort of Michael Landon mop that demanded little in transitioning at the fringes. I put my L.L. Bean hat over it and a pair of bulky sunglasses over my regular lenses. A little too ridiculous. Without the hat wasn't much better. So I tried it with a baseball cap, with the hair slightly swept back and streaking out the back, which seemed to do the trick.

My appointment with Henry Eichenbach was set for the next morning at ten o'clock, so I spent the rest of the day and evening installing new gear, stocking the house with various necessities and organizing as efficient a domestic operation as possible. Having worked out of my home for years while my wife tended to her time-consuming office job, household management had fallen to me. Florencia was a neat person, but would never have risen to the level of tidy precision that I brought to the task.

She used to mock me that she was Julia Roberts in *Sleeping with the Enemy,* but she liked things clean and orderly, and efficiently configured, without having to make it so herself. In all our divisions of labor we were absurdly compatible, achingly so, I thought as I lay in bed that night, despite all my efforts not to think about such things.

I'd chosen the park bench at the beach in Norwalk because it would be impossible to photograph my face straight on, unless the photographer was out on a boat. The Thimble Islands were out there, lumps on the horizon, but too far away for anything but a spy satellite surveillance camera.

The bench was open to the west, but on the east was a windowless brick building housing a set of rest rooms.

I sat in the Outback before the appointed time — blending in with the cars and trucks whose drivers parked there to watch the water while they caught a smoke, ate lunch or had a cup of coffee — and watched for Henry's approach.

He was on time, which was notable. He didn't look around for a backup, also notable. I'm not an expert on surveillance, of course, but I have some experience with how people think and behave. It's almost impossible to not steal a glance in the direction of a person you think is watching you. Henry's glances were far more generalized, looking for the guy who was supposed to meet him on the park bench.

I was disappointed by his appearance. Full head of curly, but neatly cropped grey hair, heavy black-rimmed glasses, and a creepy grey Colonel Sanders goatee cut so it formed a point directly under his chin. His face and body were round, with most of the mass settled into his jowls and butt. None of which had any bearing on his skills or integrity as a journalist, so I shook off my first impression and strolled over to the park bench.

I was wearing a light coat with a big collar pulled up around my neck, with the lower half of my face covered in a scarf, and the hat, wig and sunglasses obscuring the rest. It wasn't the most imaginative disguise, but good enough for the purpose.

"Give me the recorder or let me frisk you," I said, sitting down next to him. I pitched my voice low and hoarse, like Clint Eastwood, whom I'd mimicked often to Florencia's delight.

"I don't have a recorder," he said, after a pause, "and I'm sure as shit not going to let you feel me up."

"Okay," I said, and got up to leave.

"Wait," he said.

I stopped. He reached into his jacket and pulled out a small digital recorder. I told him to shut it off, rewind and erase our brief conversation. I watched him go through the actions, then sat back down.

"Paranoid, are we?" he asked.

"Cautious," I said.

"Are you one of Sebbie's boys?"

"I can't tell you."

"Then what can you?"

"You're here because you don't know where he is. And you want to know," I said, looking up and down the beach and out over the water.

"I do," said Henry. "I miss the old sociopath. Hasn't been nearly as much fun without him."

"Are you freelance or staff?" I asked.

Henry pulled a small notebook out of his jacket.

"Mind if I take notes?" he asked, somewhat sarcastically.

"Nope."

"Good," he said, clicking a ballpoint pen, "let's start with your name."

"That's up to you."

"Huh?"

"You can call me anything you want," I said.

He was quiet for a moment.

"You're in witness protection. Interesting," he said. "We must've met, but I can't place you, I admit it. Nicely done. You don't have to confirm anything. I know the drill."

"How's the book coming?" I asked.

"Slowly. Who told you about that?"

"It's on your web site. You should check it once in a while. Anyway, it's understandable. You've been on a big story over a period of years. You're eager to track down a key player. Getting by as a freelance journalist isn't easy, now that they've broomed you out of the *Post.* Why wouldn't you be writing a book?"

"Hey, not broomed. I was empowered to seek fresh opportunities."

Henry wasn't a young man. The grey hair, paunch, baby boomer affectations, sun damage on his pale skin figured him to be about sixty, maybe a little more or less. His eyes were widely spaced, and close to bulging. But brimming with a stirred-up mix of defiance and self-deprecation.

I knew the type. I'd always cultivated relationships with reporters at newspapers and trade magazines, print and online. They were my favorite starting points when venturing into a new realm of inquiry, and my favorite sources at the wrap-up phase.

I liked their inquisitiveness, since it was a lot like mine. And their intelligence and eagerness to cross rhetorical swords. I didn't like their arrogance and first amendment-entitled insufferability, but nobody's perfect.

"I have a proposition," I said. "I doubt you're going to like it. But I'm proposing it anyway."

"O-kay," said Henry, stretching out each syllable, unsure.

"I don't know where Sebbie is. But if you give me a few key pieces of information, I'll find him."

Henry had been sitting sideways on the bench. Now he swiveled around and faced the Sound. He slapped the tops of his thighs and huffed a few times.

"You're right. I don't like that at all. What kind of a putz do you think I am? Who're you working for? Sebbie's not my favorite person, character-wise, but I'm not helping you kill him."

"I'm not going to kill him. I just want to talk to him. And I'm not working for anyone but myself. Like you."

"I suppose you can't prove any of that."

"No. If you decide to help me, it'll be blind trust," I said. "You won't know immediately if that trust was justified. But if things go as hoped, your agenda will be advanced in ways that might prove the salvation of your book project." I turned and faced him. "If you help me," I said, "your knowledge of the world will expand exponentially. If you decide not to, I'll just go to the next name on my list and he or she will have that privilege."

I stood up and started to walk away. He called to me to come back, but I kept walking. A careful study of the behavior of anti-hero archetypes, which I'd made when I was about twelve years old, taught me that indifference to the supplications of the recently put-down amplified their desire to restore the relationship.

"Okay, okay," Henry yelled. "Come on back. We can talk."

I took a few more paces, but at a slower pace, then turned slowly, reluctantly, as I'd seen Steve McQueen do. I walked back to the bench, and after taking a moment for my injured brain to locate exactly where it was, I sat down.

"What is your deal, man? I don't get it," he said.

"My deal is my deal. Your deal is your book. Where we converge is a wish to talk to Sebbie. All you have to do is tell me the name of his closest confidant. Based on your articles, I'm guessing it's Wayne Frankenfelder, owner of the Miss Kitty Lounge. Sebbie seems to think of him as a surrogate son. Or so you implied in your reporting."

"Who cares who his friends are?"

"Human connections are irresistible. Whether you're a journalist or a street thug, you risk everything to keep the ones you value intact. Especially a highly social guy like Sebbie who loved hanging around his restaurants and clubs. This underpins my theory that he never left Connecticut."

"Man, this is bizarre."

I looked at him, noticing again that his

irises, bright blue, were surrounded by the whites of his eyes. It added a dash of craziness to his overall aspect. He huffed again and sat back in the bench.

"Killing Sebbie isn't really the issue, if you want the truth," he said. "I just don't want to be treated like a schmuck."

"Understandable."

"Frankenfelder's important, but less so than Madame Francine de le Croix, the accomplished palm reader and chop shop operator," said Henry. "Word is, Sebbie wouldn't take a piss without checking with Francine first. I've tried to get to her, and Frankenfelder, but they know who I am. I agree with your logic. I don't think he'd want to cut himself off completely from his local support system. That's not part of his ego profile. He'd need a way to connect. Outside of a daughter who used to live with him and might still, those two are his closest people. Tells you what sort of crud we're dealing with here."

"I thought you missed him," I said.

"You're right. I miss the encouraging chats with my publisher. The book's dead in the water unless I can corroborate a bunch of stuff only Sebbie can do."

"Okay," I said, standing up and walking away. "Thanks."

"That's it?"

"That's it."

I went back to the parking lot, walked past the Subaru and across the street to another bench at a sheltered bus stop. From there I could see Henry get into his own car, a ratty, sway-backed Ford Taurus, and drive away. I waited another half hour, then started the Outback with a remote control I'd installed the day before, waited a few minutes, then walked over, got in and drove home.

Francine the palm reader. A professional prognosticator. I'd done some work in futurism myself. Surely we could build something on that common ground.

CHAPTER 6

"I wish you'd check in more often," said Evelyn when I called her on the disposable. "All this worry is interfering with my concentration."

"Sorry. You're right. These spatial distortions seem to affect my sense of time as well. Be no surprise to Einstein."

"How are you doing otherwise?" she asked.

"As a person?"

"No. As a giraffe."

"I can move about fairly well, even with the limp," I said. "I'm okay, then I'm not. I sleep. I eat. My emotional range is circumscribed. I don't seem to experience fear. Anger is always there, though I feel no urge to express it. Grief as well. I feel it profoundly, yet it seems to be operating in an isolation chamber, with no influence on day-to-day operations. Strange, really."

She had the good manners not to ask what

those day-to-day operations were.

"We need another psych eval," she said.

"I'm sure we do. But I can't manage it right now. Too much going on."

"Okay, that's fine. But I need to talk to you about the agency. You told me you'd like to know what it's worth. Bruce has a potential buyer. The comptroller Damien Brandt's father, Elliot. He's a billionaire investor out of Westport. Bruce has known him for a long time and likes him. The father wants to keep the staff intact and just carry on as they've been doing since Florencia died."

"Why's that?"

"If a competing agency took over, they'd swallow up the operation and pare down the staff to realize economies, which would likely involve Damien. They'd also want an earn-out provision, which could erode the sale price over time. Brandt is willing to pay full boat up front and be done with it."

"Buying his kid's job."

"Essentially. There are worse ways to support your kids. He'd also buy the building, and more importantly, keep the name. I thought you'd like that part."

"You think sentiment should be part of the equation?" I said.

"A minor part, but yes."

I couldn't help but agree. With Florencia gone, the agency meant nothing to me, but what was wrong with preserving a scrap of her legacy?

"Okay, sure. What do we do?" I asked.

"Give Brandt's people the right to due diligence. Open the books and come up with a valuation. Bruce will keep an eye on things. He bought about a zillion dollars' worth of companies for his old firm. This is not a problem for him. With all the crap that's happened to us, can't we just take a second and enjoy this one good thing?"

She was right.

"Let's," I said. "It can't be that hard."

We talked for a while more, Evelyn pushing me on how I was taking care of myself, me evading and countering with questions about the police investigation.

"It's nowhere," she said. "Maddox has his theories: It was a professional hit. Florencia had unknowingly exposed herself. Or maybe it was one of your missing person projects. I think the kid is trying, but the odds are long."

"But we're not giving up," I said.

"No, Arthur, we're not giving up."

It's not in my nature to enjoy dress-up. As a kid, I loathed Halloween. My only costume was a jacket and tie and a mask my father wore when he was a kid. This served the purpose from the first wearing at age ten straight through to college, after which I avoided Halloween parties altogether.

This distaste extended to my daily wardrobe, which never varied beyond khakis, or jeans, T-shirts or Oxford cloth button-down collar shirts.

So it was no joy for me to concoct a costume for my visit to Francine de la Croix. Even the logic of it was a hard sell to myself, but my better mind prevailed. This was the first genuine penetration into enemy territory. Risking identification, however unlikely, made no sense if it could be avoided by a simple precaution.

I'd already used up the sunglasses, wig, hat and raised collar on Henry Eichenbach. I stood at the bathroom sink at my rented house looking at my face and thought, now what.

The scar on my forehead was more than a pinky slick of nearly transparent skin, it was an indentation, a slight hollow that you don't normally see on a person's forehead. I could cover the deformity with a hat, as long as it stayed put. But that would do nothing to disguise my features, which still looked like a version of me, gaunt and haunted though I'd become. My heart fell as I accepted the inevitable. I needed a disguise.

I started by studying theatrical makeup on the web. Not surprisingly, there were multiple sites offering every possible means for transforming your face, including prosthetic noses, chins and cheekbones. I girded myself and ordered anything that looked possible for an untrained makeup artist. The items would be delivered the following day.

In the meantime, I tracked down Francine's location, a storefront in Stamford, which I cased from a donut shop directly across the street. The crudely hand-painted sign above the blacked-out window read "Francine's Prognostications — Fortunes Told, For the Curious and Bold." The door to the place was also once black, now more a muddy dark grey. There was a huge brass buzzer in the middle of the door that was the only bright spot on the facade, though not from continual use. During the week I spent casing the place and giving myself the shakes from too much coffee, only half a dozen of the curious and bold sought out Francine's services.

I did note the arrival at ten each morning of a white Cadillac DeVille, an early vintage with gold trim and a plush vinyl roof. It left again at about seven in the evening. This I took to be Francine's car. The windows were tinted, so all I could make out was a huge ball of blond hair, but no features.

The next day my packages from the makeup suppliers arrived. The most important thing I'd learned from years of research was that almost nothing you thought in advance turns out to be the case. This is hugely significant if you think about it. It means that most people who aren't researchers go through life thinking things that aren't true, and never discover their folly.

In the case of the makeup project, this principle proved itself in spades. It turned out I wasn't the first to be intimidated by the process, so the manufacturers worked hard to make everything as easy as possible. The prosthetics were so lifelike, it made me think they'd plasticized actual tissue. The bonding material that joined rubber to flesh was also easily applied and wholly natural as long as you took your time and meticulously followed the directions.

Temporarily overcome by the possibilities, I almost turned myself into an African-American, but prudence led to a white lad with a nice California tan, a shock of weathered blond hair sticking out of a Jeff cap, and a sharp, aquiline nose. It took about four hours to build to my satisfaction, but it was an endeavor worth achieving in its own right, and thus, a good use of time.

One of the most surprising things I found was the lack of discomfort. I assumed heavy makeup was nearly unbearable, but all that plastic was light on my face, barely noticeable.

Who knew.

Francine took a long time to open the door after I pushed the big brass doorbell. It was late afternoon, and the hard, dim light did little to brighten her features, though enough to confirm she was neither young, nor attractive, despite the efforts of her hairdresser and plastic surgeon to prove otherwise.

"I prefer appointments," she said, squinting up at me.

"Okay. When can I come back?"

"You don't have a phone?" she asked. Her accent was born in one of New York City's five boroughs, but she'd been away too long to tell which. I guessed Brooklyn, with little confidence.

"Actually, no."

I patted the outside of my jacket as if one might magically appear.

Francine sighed heavily.

"I suppose I could do it now."

"That'd be cool," I said.

She turned and walked back into the gloom of her salon. I followed, shutting the door behind me. Inside was the caricature of a mystic's lair, as if created by a set designer whose only reference was theatrical cliché. Skulls lit from within, shrouds covered with runic symbols hanging from the walls, a hookah on a painted art-nouveau side table, and in the middle of the room, under an ornate ceiling lamp, a round table with a crystal ball. The act fell down a bit with Francine's outfit, a pink workout suit stretched to the limit over her bulging figure, and high-top white sneakers, worn badly to the outside by her tiny, pronated feet. Her only concessions to the role were a necklace made of several beaded strands and long fingernails, better to stroke the frosted globe.

"Sit, sit," she said, dropping down herself into the opposite chair. "Fifty bucks for the first fifteen minutes," she said, looking at the ball as if her rates were floating around inside. "And another fifty if you want the whole half hour. That's a lot of fortune-telling. Most places you're lucky to get ten minutes. Though determining luck is one of the things we specialize in here."

I peeled a hundred dollar bill off a thin roll of cash stored in my shirt pocket.

"I'll go the whole hun'erd," I said. "No point scrimping on your life's prospects."

I couldn't know how much it mattered to her whether she took fifty, or a hundred, or a thousand dollars out of the transaction, but the upgrade seemed to prompt greater interest. She hiked the straining waistband of her workout sweats up over the deep crease below her belly and wormed her butt more comfortably into her chair. She cupped the phony-looking crystal ball in both hands and closed her eyes.

We sat silently for a nearly unbearable ten minutes. Then she took my hands, which she worked between thumb and index finger.

Finally she said, "It's been a very painful recovery, but you've made impressive progress. You have a strong will. What was it, car accident?"

The unexpected accuracy of the reading was nearly rendered cartoonish by her accent, though not enough to dampen the jolt.

"Hit and run," I said. "How'd you know?"

She smirked.

"What do you think, we're a bunch of amateurs here?"

This was the second time she referred to her operation in the plural. I wondered if it was a royal "we" or someone else was watching nearby.

"No ma'am. So what do you see in the future?"

"For me, a new water heater, if that puddle in the basement is any sign. But that's not what you mean. For you, not so sure. You're not very nervous, so I wonder why you want to get your fortune read. Most people are usually quivering over their fates. Do you have a pulse?"

She felt down along my wrist, stopping to press two fingers between ligaments and veins.

"Very strong and steady," she said. "But too slow. What happened to your head?"

I involuntarily reached up with my other hand and touched where I thought my hat concealed the little crater in my skull. All I felt was the hat fabric.

"Not outside," said Francine, "inside. Never felt such a quiet landscape. Not barren, but still."

I almost pulled my hand away, but caught myself. Francine must have felt it anyway. She looked up at me.

"Don't worry, I can't actually read minds. Not exactly. Especially a mind like yours.

It's like a bank vault. You aren't planning on robbing a bank, are you?"

"What if I was? Could you tell me how to launder the money?"

She scowled.

"I can tell you how to launder your shirts, buddy, and that's about it."

"I know that isn't true," I said.

"Now who's trying to read minds?"

She gripped my wrist a little firmer and closed her eyes. Her fingers felt warm and slightly slick, as if from inadequately absorbed hand cream. When she opened her eyes, she stared right into mine.

"I'm not safe with you," she said, calmly. "Where did you come from?"

"California."

"Not that kind of place. A place of the heart. What you came from was cold, dark and a little insane. But you're sane enough now, aren't you?"

"Perfectly."

"No. Not perfectly. You just think you are." She let go of my wrist and I pulled back my hand. "You aren't here for your fortune. You want something else from me."

"I want a conversation," I said. "Though not with you."

She tapped out a little rhythm on the table

99

with her fingers, a series of impatient triplets.

"That'll cost you a lot more than a hundred dollars," she said.

"Though not as much as it'll cost you if you don't agree."

She withdrew further back into her chair, folding her arms and squeezing herself.

"I must be getting senile, not seeing this coming," she said.

I put my hand back on the table, palm up.

"Take it again," I said.

She leaned forward and took it, pressing her thumb into my wrist.

"Do I mean what I say?" I asked.

After a slight delay, she nodded.

"You do."

"I want to talk to Mr. Frondutti. Here is a phone number. I want him to call me at exactly six P.M. tonight. If he doesn't, I can predict your future with exact precision."

She twitched and let go of my hand as if it had turned into a burning coal.

"I don't tell the man what to do," she said.

"Then it would be his loss."

"His? What about me? What're you going to do, blow up my house? Do you have any idea who you're dealing with? Do you think you could do worse to me than he could?"

"Yes," I said, without hesitation.

100

She put her hand up to her mouth and opened her eyes as wide as they would go. Then she nodded, the message understood.

I got up without another word and left, making a sharp right outside the door and another into an alley that connected with the parking lot of a big drugstore. I started the Subaru with the remote control. Gave it less than a minute, then drove around to the donut shop across from Francine's.

If Francine was in regular contact with Sebbie, it couldn't be through conventional means for fear of mail searches, wiretaps and other electronic eavesdropping. It had to be some other way. And given the short timetable, it had to be in a hurry.

Not a bad theory, I thought as I watched Francine rush out the front door of her salon and jump into the DeVille. Just like that.

As with most cinematic stunts, following a car undetected through crowded urban streets in broad daylight is hardly a simple task. Especially if the follower is only a single car. The serious pros do it with multiple cars that tag team each other, come and go, race ahead and even tailgate as the need presents itself. There was little hope that a lone Subaru Outback could mimic any of those maneuvers, but it's all I had.

Francine complicated the effort by being a haphazard driver with only a casual regard for traffic etiquette. The Cadillac frequently approached yellow lights by slowing down, then accelerating just in time to jump the red. I had the choice of racing through behind her, risking a ticket and her notice, or calmly letting her go.

I usually did the latter, and regarded my success in catching up again as the purest form of luck.

She finally eluded me, I thought for good, but I turned a corner and was pleased to see the Cadillac shoe-horning its way into a parking space along the curb. I drove past and found one of my own, with time left on the meter. I crossed the street and walked back in time to see Francine smacking her own meter with the palm of her hand as she deposited coins. I slunk back against a store window and tried to keep a bead on her without looking directly her way.

Moving quickly, she ducked into a pharmacy. I waited across the street, longing to see what she was doing. She came out soon after, carrying a magazine. I was too far away to read the masthead, but the cover photograph suggested *Time* or *Newsweek*. I let her get ahead of me, and then moved at her pace, which was more uncomfortably brisk than I could easily manage.

She stopped at an outdoor news vendor. The man at the counter looked at her with a smile of recognition. They spoke for a moment, then she moved away without making a purchase. The man bent down to do something below the counter, then stood up again.

Perfect, I thought. One of the oldest tricks in the book. And why not? Sebbie's an old trick himself. I looked around and spotted a café with an imperfect, but acceptable view of the newsstand. I went in, bought a coffee and an orange and waited.

An hour later, a short, dapper man wearing a narrow-brimmed hat and sunglasses approached the newsstand. The man behind the counter took that moment to restock some of the merchandise. When the dapper man stopped, lo and behold, he chose to buy one of the restocked items. A newsmagazine.

As he strolled away, at a far more humane pace than Francine's, I left the café and followed along. At the next intersection, I crossed the street and fell in behind, leaving as generous a distance between us as I dared.

The pursuit of Francine, followed by an hour of inactivity, had wreaked havoc on my weakened left side, which was now entirely engulfed in pain. But since I wasn't going to stop following the dapper man, I did the only thing I could. I ignored it.

After covering about three blocks, the dapper man stopped at a door sandwiched between two storefronts. I saw him tap at something, then open the door. He was well inside by the time I reached where he'd stood, confirming that it was the entrance to an apartment, presumably on the second floor, accessible with the proper code punched into a keypad.

I walked on to the end of the block, then crossed the street again and walked back. There were three storefronts with an adequate view of the dapper man's door. A laundry, a gift shop and a shoe store. I looked up, then went into the gift shop. A pale, young woman, wearing black lipstick and what looked like a leather corset was sitting on a stool behind the glass counter. I asked her if there were offices or apartments on the second floor. She wasn't sure, but came up with the owner's contact information after a prolonged search of the desk at the back of the store. I told her the least I could do after all that was buy something, but she said no worries, it was all just a bunch of junk anyway.

I made it to my car with seconds to spare on the meter, and drove back to my house in Wilton, where I collapsed onto the bed after setting the alarm for five-thirty P.M. Then I passed out, numbed into oblivion by unfathomable exhaustion.

CHAPTER 7

The alarm went off as planned, but I was still too tired to move. So I lay there and tried to calculate the probability that Sebbie would give me a call at six P.M. as requested. I couldn't get the numbers to work, but my gut told me he would. My gut was right.

I turned on a digital recorder to capture the message and hit the green button.

"Are you trying to commit suicide?" said a man with a borough accent far more pronounced than Francine's. Clearly the Bronx.

"I need information from you," I said in my Clint Eastwood voice.

"That's unlikely to happen. I don't give myself information if I don't have to."

"You have to, or suffer terrible consequences."

The phone was quiet.

Then he said, "Threats don't impress me much. I been around way too long for that."

106

"Then you won't mind if you're not around anymore."

"There's nothing you can do to me," he said, his voice at a higher pitch, the stress starting to show.

"Not until I'm ready," I said. "Frankenfelder goes first, though I'll take my time with him before I move on to Francine."

Then I pushed the end button.

In the time it took me to write down the number he was calling from, he called back.

"What do you want?" he asked, his voice still angry, but with a different tone.

"I need to eliminate a person," I said. "I need a list of people who could do the job."

"You're not from around here," he said; it was more a challenge than a question.

"I'm not. That's why I'm talking to you. I need five candidates. Their names and contact information. Where I got them stays with me. I move on and you and your friends get to keep living."

"Not a chance. Fuck the friends and fuck you," he said, and hung up.

I used the information given me by the girl in the store to contact the building's rental agent. There were three offices available, and to my relief, the entrance to the second floor was via a parking lot behind the building. The transaction was managed entirely over the Internet. I gave them one of my dead guy's name and Social Security number and booked the unit above the shoe store next to the gift shop. I signed up for a month's rent in advance and the equivalent amount as a security deposit.

I sent the agent two money orders for $850 each and they sent me the key, which arrived the next day to my P.O. box via express mail. I spent the first part of the day getting the lock changed, and the rest shopping for more electronic gear: an HD digital video camera with a long lens, tripod, and a recording device that could download to one of my external hard drives. I got a nice discount by paying cash for everything.

I schlepped the equipment up to the office, which was a stage set for a weary, anonymous hole in the wall, with a desk, a chair, a file cabinet and coatrack. I measured the lower window sash, then pulled down the shade. Then I went out and bought a sheet of one-way mirror cut to size and some mounting hardware. The supplier wrapped it in bubble wrap and put it in a box with a handle, which I used to carry it up to the office. While waiting for nightfall, I set up the camera on its tripod and ran the wiring. An hour later it was dark.

I turned out the overhead light and stood the one-way mirror on the windowsill, and then raised the shade, pressing the glass to the sash as soon as it was clear. Then I used a cordless drill to screw in the tabs around the edges to hold it in place.

I moved the camera into place and turned it on, the controls appearing in LED red. It was past dusk, but I could easily record through the mirror. I filmed the surrounding buildings to establish context, then racked the lens until I had a crystal clear view of the entrance door.

Having no other purpose for being there, I pressed the record button and left.

The next day I downloaded my conversation with Sebbie onto DVDs and mailed them to Wayne Frankenfelder and Francine. Then I went to another gadget store and bought a GPS. It was palm-sized and of startling sophistication. I mounted it to the inside of the Outback's windshield and punched in the address for Shelly Gross.

An hour later I was just outside Hartford, driving by his bland and faceless house in a dull subdivision in the middle-class bedroom community of Rocky Hill. There was an early model, maroon Chevy Blazer in the driveway. As I drove by I held a digital

SLR camera up to the passenger window and fired off a dozen photos in rapid succession.

Then I drove back home by way of Danbury, where I withdrew another guitar, which I sold for cash to a guy in Westport who'd advertised on Craig's List for that precise model. He wanted to consummate the deal in his bank's parking lot, but I directed him to the waterside park in Norwalk, well away from security cameras. I put the case on a picnic table and let him open it, look over the guitar, fiddle with the knobs and machine heads, and test out the pickups through a little battery-powered amp I brought along for the purpose.

Before resting it in the trunk of his 5 Series BMW, he handed me an envelope. I counted the $24,000 and we parted satisfied.

That night I returned to the office with my laptop. I let the camera continue recording on its digital circuitry and downloaded the day's file from the external hard drive. Using an application designed specifically for editing lengthy videos, I scanned rapidly through the night hours. When day broke, I slowed the pace, allowing the software to easily pick out changes in pattern.

The first one came fast. The door opened and a young woman stepped out. Though shooting a storey above street level, I still captured a vivid image of her face. I pulled a few frames into another program and selected the best angle.

She was likely mid-twenties, short and stout with wavy black hair, parted down the middle and pulled back at the forehead with barrettes. Her nose was big and a little crooked, and her heavy-lidded eyes were set wide on her face. She wore a plain raincoat and carried a briefcase.

I assumed she was his daughter.

I noted the time code on the recording, and continued to scan. Sebbie came out an hour later, in more or less the same getup as the day before. He came back two hours later. No magazine.

I slowed the camera speed to a crawl as he punched the code into the keypad. The clarity of the HD and the manipulation of the software made it almost too easy. Five numbers: five, four, nine, one, zero.

That was the last thing that happened that day. Ergo, the woman was still out there. After a quick review of the camera's most recent recording, I resumed filming, the action playing on my laptop, configured as a monitor.

I'm sure there are more tedious things than watching a closed door for hours, but none that I've experienced. Finally, at about nine o'clock, she came home, carrying several shopping bags along with her briefcase.

Relieved, I drove home and went to bed early so I could get up early the next day to stake out the Frondutti apartment. I brought along my big camera with the zoom lens.

I discovered an ideal surveillance location inside a covered bus stop. I had to look through a dirty piece of Plexiglas, but I had a straight shot of the door. I bought a newspaper and pretended to read, glancing every few seconds over the top through my sunglasses.

At about the same time as the day before, the door opened and the daughter emerged with her briefcase. I folded the newspaper and stuck it under my arm and fell in behind her, as I'd done with her father only a few days before.

The weather had warmed enough to inspire one of the restaurants along the street to set tables out on the sidewalk to snare the morning coffee trade. The daughter stopped and ignored the "wait to be seated" sign and sat down at one of the tables. I don't know what the waiter told her, but he took her order. I strolled (can you stroll with a limp?) across the street and affected the look of someone interested in photographing something high above the heads of the café customers. I snapped away with casual abandon, seemingly at random, until I had a half-dozen clear photos of the young, dark-haired woman sipping her beverage and munching on a pastry.

I stayed away from the street after that, stopping in once a day to download the day's recordings and charting Sebbie and the woman's habits, which were flawlessly consistent. The only variable seemed to be her arrival in the evening, though it was never before six o'clock.

I gave it a week. Then one morning I woke up at four-thirty A.M. and spent the last dark hours disguising my face with my theatrical makeup kit. I put a sweater on over a fleece vest, which I further built out by stuffing socks in the pockets. It wasn't an entirely convincing look of a fat man, but neither did it look like me. Not anymore.

I put on surgical gloves, over which I added another pair in leather. It really wasn't the right season for them, but I could keep my hands in my pockets.

113

I didn't bother monitoring from the office, but rather hung around parts of the street until I saw her leave. Then an hour later, Sebbie left for whatever he did for two hours every morning. I waited another half hour, then walked with as little limp as I could manage up to the entrance door and punched in the code.

The door snapped open and I walked inside. In front of me was a flight of stairs, at the top of which was another door. I ascended the stairs and tried the doorknob, which opened into a living room stuffed with furniture, and walls laden with paintings and photographs that left virtually no free wall space. I walked briskly through the apartment until I found the bedrooms at the end of a narrow hall.

The beds in each were neatly made and everything smelled fresh and lemony from a liberal use of furniture oil. Sebbie's room was easy to pick out. I took the 8 1/2 by 11-inch color print of his daughter out of an envelope stuffed in my rear waistband. On the reverse side I'd written with my left hand the number of another disposable phone.

I rested it on his pillow and left, staring at the door as I walked down the stairs, willing it to stay closed, depending on the habituated Fronduttis.

Back on the street, I walked to where I'd parked the Outback, then drove it around to the parking lot behind the office. Once inside, I retrieved the external hard drive, but left the rest of the setup. I scoured the area for any possible residue of my presence, then left again for the last time.

It wasn't until I was safely back in my house in Wilton that I noticed my pulse was elevated, my mouth dry, and my hands slightly trembling. I lay down on my bed and listened to my heart pound in my ears, which I tried to calm with slow, easy breaths.

It wasn't the first time I'd put myself into a dangerous situation. While never rising to the theatrical heights of a TV detective, the fieldwork I did for my legal clients had occasionally brought me close to people capable of more than an angry word. But then I knew what I was going through in real time. I knew I was nervous, anxious, or even terrified, at the time of the experience. This was a strangely delayed reaction, as if all the normal physiological responses had been held in abeyance until the caper was complete.

If so, it was likely the result of my head injuries. And would be a decided advantage. Assuming I could get the postponed reactions under control before I had a heart attack.

As I regained control over my nervous system, I decided on a course of action. If Sebbie was actually the sociopath Henry Eichenbach thought he was, and could stonewall through the torture and death of his closest friends, or disregard the danger to his daughter, then I would have to let him go and move on to another promising hoodlum. Whatever the bullet had done to my social affect, empathy and equanimity, I wasn't ready for any of the things I'd threatened.

Two hours later, I got the call.

"You scum-sucking motherfucker," said Sebbie.

I hung up and he called me right back.

"Civility, Mr. Frondutti, or no deal," I said.

"You call what you did civil? Threatening my wife?" I stayed quietly on the line, absorbing the revelation that the daughter turned out to be his wife. "How does this go away?" he said, breaking a long silence.

"Do you have a computer?"

"No. My wife does."

"Do you know how to use it?" I asked.

"Yea. Evil things."

"I need the contact information for the

five people I requested. No one outside the tristate area. I'm going to provide you with a code. Get ready to write it down."

He cursed some more, but then said he was ready. I assigned each number in the alphabet with a number, and substituted typewriter key symbols, like @, with things like ϖ. It was a very simple code, but I couldn't give Sebbie too complicated a chore, even if I'd been up to providing one.

After he wrote it all down, I said, "Don't use your wife's computer. Use one at the library. Go to a site called wallbox.com." I gave him a login and password. "It's an online drop box. Leave the information I'm asking for in the code I gave you. I expect it there no later than four hours from now. After this call, you'll never hear from me again, unless I don't get the information. In which case, the consequences will follow in due course."

I checked wallbox two hours later and the message was there. I copied it into a Word document, which I printed out, then deleted the message and closed down the wallbox account, which I'd opened with an assumed name, since that's all they required.

Then, using the basic search and replace function in Word, I converted the numbers and symbols to phone numbers, email addresses and names:

Omar Rankin
Pally Buttons
The Jack Hammer
Fred Tootsie
Austin Ott, the Third

It was the first time since I sat with the police sketch artist that I felt palpably close to the man in the trench coat, though it was hardly a given he was on the list. But either way, it was forward motion in the right direction.

I studied the names, all surely *noms de guerre,* hoping for some unconscious perception to signal the most likely target.

The painful stress reactions of the recent past were now forgotten, and in their place was a new set of sensations. My hands were steady and my vision clear. I was calm at the center of my being, and in place of a racing heart was a crystalline ball of silver ice. You might be Omar, you might be Fred. Whatever your name is, I will find you.

Of this, I am now certain.

CHAPTER 8

It was cruel that the better I felt physically and the more present in the world, the more I missed Florencia. No, I didn't miss her, I desperately longed for her, to such a degree that I often thought the longing too great to bear, that the pain of her absence would ultimately topple my sanity.

This wasn't helped by the fact that I'd seen her killed, that the hopeless finality of death was not for me an abstract concept. I knew it to be the last, irredeemable, fundamental truth.

She wasn't coming back.

While I had no precedent for such sadness, I'd always coped with troubles by occupying my mind, by staying busy, throwing myself into my work. It was the only palliative I knew, the only mechanism that could get me out of bed in the morning to get on with the day's demands.

■ ■ ■ ■

I drove back over to the office across from
Sebbie's apartment. I checked the digital
files, which showed a return to routine for
Sebbie and the woman who'd turned out to
be his wife. I downloaded the fresh information, then cleared the hard drive on the
recording device, which would provide
another forty-eight hours of footage. When
I got back to my house, I put together a
little package containing a copy of the key
to the office, a DVD with select video and
still shots of Sebbie, his neighborhood, the
young woman, and an edited audio recording of our phone conversation (which I ran
through a device that distorted my voice). I
put it all in a FedEx box for delivery to
Henry Eichenbach. I included a note, "You
have one week to get whatever you can.
Then your exclusive is over. Thanks for the
help."

Then I made up a duplicate package, ad-
dressed to Shelly Gross in Rocky Hill, and
tossed it in the Outback for future mailing.

The job of a detective, or bounty hunter, in
tracking down missing people has, in a way,
become absurdly simple. For a nominal

subscription cost, there are perfectly legal, universally accessible databases that cross reference details like name, phone number and email address to cough up a physical address. And often even richer information, like age, time at that residence, occupation, years of schooling, etc. Sometimes, there's even a photo.

This is how I was able to eliminate Omar Rankin, a distinguished-looking African-American, in about five minutes.

Though a negative result, the speed with which it was achieved bolstered my confidence, helping to blunt the pain of my complete failure with The Jack Hammer. First off, both the phone number and email address Sebbie had given me were inactive. If I'd been the FBI, or even a regular police detective, I could still get the name and physical address attached to those accounts, but I wasn't. Worse, there were surprisingly few Jack Hammers living in the northeast USA, betraying a surprising reluctance on the part of people named Hammer to inflict a lifetime joke on their children.

I did dig up a Sledge Hammer, but he was a professional wrestler living in Atlantic City, when he wasn't on the road, which was most of the time.

I put my list of three Jack Hammers aside

and went looking for Austin Ott. All Sebbie had provided on Austin was an email address. I found no correlation using the people search engine, though there were several Austin Otts.

I moved on to Fred Tootsie, for whom all I had was a phone number, with a 516 area code, which covered Nassau County, Long Island. I ran it through the search engine and hit a correlation: Frederico DiDemenico, 23 Hartsfield Drive, Apt 3D, Jericho, NY. Age fifty-three. Occupation unknown. Affiliations unknown. I gave him a call.

"What," he said, answering the phone.

"Hello, Fred. I was given your number by a friend in the business. He said I should call you about a project."

"Who's this?"

"Mr. Jones."

"Sure. And this is Mr. Smith."

"I heard it was Mr. Tootsie," I said.

The line was quiet for a moment.

"Who's the friend?" he asked.

"Can't say. You understand."

"Not sure I do. What's this project?"

I strained to find something familiar in his voice, but soon realized that would be impossible. I remembered much of what the man in the trench coat said, but even without a damaged brain, things like the tone and timbre of a human voice are difficult to recollect.

"Rather talk about that in person," I said. "It's sensitive."

"You want a lot."

"Do you normally conduct business over the phone?" I asked.

I said this lightly, trying to make it sound more like a gentle inquiry than a taunt or criticism. He took it as intended.

"I hear you," he said.

"I propose a meet," I said. "I'll toss you some options."

"When?"

"Soon."

"Okay," he said, and hung up.

I moved to the last name on the list, Pally Buttons, and again hit a brick wall. The phone number Sebbie gave me was out of service, and based on the area code, it was likely a disposable like mine. Virtually untraceable even for law enforcement. This was going to be a much harder slog, so I put him in the to-do column and concentrated on Fred.

I wrote down a few dates and locations on the South Shore of Long Island in easy driving distance of Jericho, printed it out and stuck it in an envelope. Then I drove to a

123

FedEx retail outlet and sent it to Fred in one of their envelopes, which would be difficult to open without destroying. It was also trackable, so I could monitor its journey online, for what that was worth. As always, if there was a serious effort by the authorities to monitor Fred's mail, I wouldn't know until it was too late.

I instructed Fred to put his response in the form of a message to a new wallbox.com account I'd opened for the purpose. I included a step-by-step guide to completing the task, not knowing Fred's computer literacy, suspecting the minimum.

I spent the next few days searching the other names on Google and the other subscription search engines. The paucity of information wasn't surprising. It was only when a professional assassin was caught that his story could be told in some detail, though never fully, was my guess.

Omar and Fred Tootsie were the only ones with public records, scant as they were. Fred had shown up in court records, charged in an assault case involving a brawl in Jones Beach between "Rival Italian gangs with rumored ties to organized crime." Fred had been interviewed by the police in a nearby hospital, so at least for him, the brawl hadn't gone that well. The transcript reported the only information he provided investigators was that he was a Caucasian male and a member in good standing of the Jericho Knights of Columbus. Which actually wasn't true.

Compared to the others on the list, Omar Rankin was positively flamboyant. Not only were all his personal stats plastered all over the Internet, he could also be found in news photos cutting a ribbon for a new basketball court in Harlem, protesting with local residents and clergy over lack of funding for a needle exchange program, officiating at a dance contest during a block party and generally establishing his credentials as a protean and relentless community activist in his Upper Upper West Side neighborhood.

Hiding in plain sight? I couldn't tell, but I catalogued the information just in case.

Then one morning a little ping on the computer told me I had a message on wallbox.com. I went there and jotted down Fred's selected time and place. Then I cancelled the account and started preparations.

Fred had chosen a tatty little bar along Freeport's Nautical Mile frequented by a clientele drawn from the older and consequently scruffier neighborhoods to the north. I'd been there a few years before, so maybe the ambience had improved, though their web site seemed to testify that it hadn't.

I'd been practicing my makeup skills, trying for the maximum change in appearance with the least effort. For that day's outing I simply changed my nose and put a baseball cap over a wig, and a pair of glasses with clip-ons. Simple, convincing and comfortable.

I drove to Long Island by way of the Throgs Neck Bridge, and headed south, arriving in Freeport two hours ahead of our meeting time. The place was called Donny Brooks, attesting to both its Irish roots and featured activities. I parked a half block away in a parking lot behind an ancient five and dime.

I wished I'd learned more tradecraft back when I was tracking down people for my law firm clients. In my defense, there really wasn't much of a need, since in ninety-five percent of the cases I was trying to give away money, not exactly a fearsome mission. But I had no idea how to spot genuine undercover operatives. All I could do was secure a booth with a good angle on the interior and hope for the best.

It was midafternoon and the few patrons

holding down barstools looked like regulars, a judgment reinforced by the aimless chatter with the bartender. The only other booth contained a ragged older woman who was having lunch with the waitress. If this was the state of the surveillance arts, the criminal world hadn't a chance.

I ordered a sandwich and an iced tea, which I nursed unmolested for the next two hours, during which a few more guys came in, better candidates for undercover agents, but how was I to know? And since there was nothing I could do if they were, I decided to stop thinking about it and started to read the *Time* magazine I'd brought along to signal my identity to Fred Tootsie.

He showed up fifteen minutes early, holding his telltale, a copy of *Sports Illustrated* rolled into a tube. I saw his face before I spotted the magazine, so I already knew it wasn't the man in the trench coat. The neurologist who examined me felt reasonably sure my visual memory was intact, and I'd tried to keep the man's face fixed in my mind by constant study of the sketch artist's rendering. If that had been a false rendering, it would be another factor over which I had no control, so that was another thought I could only cast to the wind.

Fred looked like a retired salesman. His

face was round and fleshy, unhelped by a bedraggled head of grey hair, mostly on its way out, and a pair of thick glasses in plastic frames. He wore a windbreaker over a striped golf shirt, bulging at the waist, and a pair of polyester pants. He dropped down across from me in the booth and slapped the magazine on the table.

"How long you been here?" he asked.

"Two hours."

"You're a patient fucker."

"Just cautious," I said.

"Was it worth it?"

"I don't know."

"Only so much caution you can have," he said. "After a while, you just gotta say fuck it."

"That's what I'm learning."

He studied me.

"Take off your hat," he said.

"How come?"

"Just cautious." I did. "Now your shirt."

I did that, too, and he motioned for me to hand them over. He shook out the shirt and felt around the seams, then gave it back, along with the hat, also thoroughly examined. No one in the bar seemed to notice.

"What's your racket?" he asked.

"Search and discovery."

"Whatever the hell that means."

128

"I'm looking for someone," I said. "I'm told you may be in a position to help."

He picked up an edge of his magazine and shuffled the pages with his thumb.

"And if I do, what comes next?"

"I just need a legitimate name and address. I'll take it from there."

His dark eyes behind the glasses continued to examine me, his face reflecting little of what he thought.

"I don't work for free," he said.

"I don't expect you to. Write down what you'd want."

I took a piece of paper out of my magazine and slid it with a pen across the table. He picked up the pen and looked down at the paper as if something was already written there. Then he jotted down a number. A thousand dollars.

I took back the paper and folded it away in my shirt pocket. Then I took out another paper on which the names Pally Buttons, The Jack Hammer and Austin Ott were typed out. He leaned over the table and looked at the paper for a second, then sat back again.

"Who's the fuck who gave you that?" he asked. "Is that how you got to me?"

I took out my last sheet of paper, the police artist's portrait of the man in the trench coat. Fred picked it up and studied it with apparent concentration, looking over at the three names, then back at the picture. Then he put it back on the table.

"Come up with the grand and we might have something to talk about," he said.

"I have it with me," I said.

"Really," said Fred. "So you must be carrying more than that. I think I just left some money on the table."

"I'm good for another five hundred if I like what you say."

He showed his first smile, a cold thing that didn't involve his eyes.

"You'll like what I say when I have the fifteen hundred in my pocket."

"I'm happy to do that," I said, "though that shouldn't tempt you to provide false information."

His smile lost its tenuous hold on his face.

"Not a thing for a cautious guy to say."

I leaned closer to him so I could lower my voice.

"I promise to trust what you say, but if it turns out you've lied, there will be consequences." As I spoke, I looked from side to side, as if watching for eavesdroppers.

Then I sat back and let him absorb it all. I thought rather well, considering.

"That's pretty big talk," he said.

I took an envelope stuffed with money and stuck it in the *Time* magazine, which I slid across the table. Fred kept his eyes on me and his hands off the magazine.

"You could bet your life," I said, "or you could take the fifteen hundred bucks and never look back."

My knowledge of the psychology of professional killers was limited at best, though I knew something about professionals in general, which was half the battle. Pragmatism tends to rule, upsides and downsides clinically weighed and decisions usually, though not always, driven by rational self-interest. I trusted Fred to decide there was nothing to lose, and everything to gain in playing this one exactly as I wanted it played.

"Okay," he said, using my pen to circle The Jack Hammer. "That ain't him. I seen him. I never seen the other two, so it could be one of them."

"Can you tell me where they live?" I asked.

He thought about that.

"Last I heard, Pally was back doing security at Clear Waters in Connecticut."

"What's his real name?"

Fred shook his head.

"I want to say Chipmunk, but that can't be it. Chalupnik. That's it. I don't know what nationality that is. Bulgarian or some shit."

"First name?"

"Pally? Other than that, no fuckin' idea."

"What about Ott?"

He looked even more strained to recall.

"Definitely New England. The biggest of the independents. Even the wise guys are afraid of him. Originally outta Boston, though I don't think he's there anymore. He's kicked a couple jobs to me over the years. Subcontracts. Doesn't get his hands dirty. Polite guy. Very calm. Everything went down according to plan, so no beef from me."

"So no guesses," I said.

He pondered some more.

"Both jobs were up in Connecticut. So maybe he's there. But you said guesses, and that's all I got."

"Do you have a way to get in touch with him?" I asked.

He scoffed.

"No way. He gets in touch with you."

He sat back in the booth, put both hands in his lap and studiously ignored the *Time* magazine filled with money. I slid it closer.

"Thanks for that," I said.

"I ain't guaranteeing I got it all right."

"We're okay," I said.

"Unless I lied."

"Unless you lied."

"Or I coulda just made a mistake. And you'd think I'm lyin'." He lifted the tip of some sort of firearm up above the surface of the table, then put it back down again. "Which is why I'm gonna put a slug into your belly right now and be done with it," he said, glancing down to where he had both hands under the table.

"Noise," I said. "And eyewitnesses all over the place."

"Worth the risk. They're all a bunch of rummies. And this piece is quieter than a wet fart."

I was a little disappointed that I hadn't foreseen this possibility, given the nature of my booth companion, though I felt no self-recrimination. I was in a daily contest between precision and expedience, trying to attend to every detail, while pushing, pushing forward. All with a mind I still didn't entirely trust.

"Yet you hesitate," I said, "revealing your intent and wasting the valuable element of surprise. You're not a hundred percent sure this is a good idea."

In fact, he looked entirely sure it was a good idea, and was more likely driven by curiosity than fear.

"I don't like being threatened."

"Neither do I," I said.

"This ain't a threat, it's a sure thing." His face hardened and I could sense the gun moving under the table.

"Here's the thing," I said. "You know nothing about me, but I know a great deal about you. I know where you live, what you do during the day, the names of your friends and all your family and where they live. You're not the only professional I've spoken to. I've arranged things so if I'm killed, you and the people closest to you will be dead within a week." I sat back in the booth and used my open hands to point at the middle of my chest. "So go ahead. In the end, the world will be a better place."

A look of calculation on his face took the place of conviction. His eyes stayed fixed on mine, but the stiffness went out of his posture.

"Who the fuck are you, anyway?" he asked.

That was a good question.

"Not sure, to tell you the truth. The concept of identity has become an abstraction. I'm not sure I still have what you'd call a conventional mental state. And my behavior seems propelled more by veiled compulsions than conscious deliberation."

"Whatever the fuck that means."

"You asked," I said, and got up and left by way of the kitchen and out the back door, ignoring the chubby guys in greasy aprons who called out to me, and headed to where I'd left my car.

In another minute I was absorbed back into that twilight realm of barren hope, discontinuity and pain, observed as much as felt.

CHAPTER 9

When I got back to my little house, I booted up my computer and saw a note from Evelyn to MrPbody. It was a simple message: "Call me."

"How are you feeling," she asked when I reached her disposable.

"Hard to tell."

"How's the spatial acuity?"

"Still the same, but I'm getting used to it. Tiredness continues to be a problem. Have you heard from Maddox?"

"Nothing," she said. "But that's not why I called. You remember we were doing a valuation of the agency. Mr. Brandt had his auditors in all week."

"How's it going?"

"Great. They've been very complimentary of Florencia's management. Bruce says they'll be aggressive about getting a letter of intent on the table, but obviously not until they've done a thorough audit."

When it came to our respective professional pursuits, Florencia and I had a nearly perfect arrangement. I'd regale her with tales of my projects and occasional field exploits. She told me almost nothing about her work life. She said the last thing she wanted was to drag herself again through all the daily trials and tribulations. She loved the work, she'd say, but only because it never became an obsession. My work, on the other hand, was a delightful diversion for her, described with such narrative brio, that it became her favorite form of entertainment. So, for better or worse, this was the pattern we settled into. I did all the talking, she did all the listening.

"What kind of an offer?" I asked.

"Generous, I'm thinking. Brandt wants the place for his kid, he's got deep pockets and they're liking what they see. A decision could be on top of us very soon."

"I can't concentrate on this right now," I said. "I've got other things to deal with."

"That's why you needed to know."

"What happens next?"

"They finish up with due diligence. It's a process. Bruce tried to explain it to me, but I don't really understand. Financial stuff is seriously over my head."

"All you do is cut into people's chests and

137

perform quadruple bypass surgery. Couldn't expect you to have the brains to balance a checkbook."

"Speaking of which, I think I sold the house."

"Really. How'd that happen?"

"I lowered the price to fifteen hundred bucks. The offers flooded in. I got it back up to two thousand. Just kidding. I did a little haggling, but the buyers are basic Wall Street yuppies, and seemed willing to settle on eight-fifty."

"That's fine. Just keep the proceeds liquid," I said. "Things are complicated out here."

"If only I knew what 'here' meant."

"No. You really don't."

I exhausted the rest of the night trying to connect the name Chalupnik with anyone at Clear Waters Resort and Casino, a stunningly huge gambling and entertainment venue in the southeast corner of the state. I did capture the addresses of three Chalupniks who lived nearby, a bigger number than you'd think with such an odd name. I assumed relatives.

It was late when I finally gave up the chase, my eyes tearing to where I could no longer read the computer screen, and the limbs on my weak side nearly frozen with cramps and numbness. I brushed my teeth and lay down on top of the bed, breathing hard and gazing bleary-eyed at the ceiling. I remembered myself as a vivacious person, driven along by a jazz combo of curiosity, natural vigor and good cheer. While I'd lost large pieces of my essential nature, a version of that energy had been reincarnated as a malignant force, taking the place of the demolished joie de vivre. It was more than life had lost its meaning. The very idea of meaning, in the affirmative sense, was a forgotten concept.

Though still active, I was prone to moments of depletion so absolute I wondered if I could ever rise again. Even the relentless pain in my thigh seemed like such a weary thing it barely deserved notice. Amputees experience the cruelest form of torture — pain emanating from an arm or leg that isn't even there. For me it wasn't a phantom limb, but the destroyed elements of my self that was the greater agony. Indefinable, beyond language, yet tangible, solid enough to grasp, to clutch to my chest.

So when sleep came it was not so much a solace as a suspension of time, a bridge from the gloom of night to the eternal darkness that enveloped my soul.

■ ■ ■ ■

Clear Waters Casino rose out of the forest like the otherworldly phantasm it was meant to be. It was located on its owner's Native American reservation. The isolation from urban centers only added to the imaginary feel of the place, at once startling and seductive.

My disguise for the day was my current appearance, which looked nothing like I once did. Pale skin stretched over a shaved head, my luxurious moustache another distant memory. A pair of heavy-framed glasses. Haphazard eating and continual exertion had ground down my body, converting once fleshy folds into hard angles on which clothes looked more draped than worn. I could mostly forswear the cane, though I brought it that day, aware that the sheer scale of the casino would mean long walks often over hard surfaces.

The purpose of the trip was pure reconnoiter. I had no plans or expectations. I didn't even know if it was necessary, but the massive fact of the place compelled me to at least take a look. I was careful, though, to look around without appearing to look around. This was a place where nothing went unnoticed, by either living or electronic eyes. It was part of the deal, so to speak, and everyone knew it.

So I played the slots and a few hands of blackjack, bought a baseball hat and then lunch at a piano bar, tipping the piano player despite the effrontery of a Barry Manilow medley. The bartender worked for the owners of the franchise who'd leased the space, but once had a stint as a croupier at the roulette tables.

"Sounds romantic," he said of his former job. "Like everybody's in ball gowns and tuxedos speaking French. Actually, it's people no better'n me and you get tired of watching that little goddamned ball."

"Good place to work, though, eh?" I asked. "I'm thinking of applying."

He agreed there.

"Oh, yeah. They take good care of their people. What do you want to do?"

"Security," I said. "I was an MP in the Army. Computer jockey. Never left the little dark room, but somebody's got to do it."

"So, what, injured?" he asked, glancing down at my legs.

"Something like that," I said, slightly ashamed to imply I'd been in combat. "Who should I talk to about applying? Any ideas?"

He took a tattered book out from under

the bar and leafed around until he found the right page. Then he wrote a name on a cocktail napkin: "Ron Irving, AVP, Human Resources/Security."

"Good guy," said the bartender. "I'd tell you to say hello for me, but he doesn't know me from shit. I'm not as famous as I should be."

"A common complaint," I said.

As I moved through the wide corridors and out into the open spaces filled with sparkling, cacophonous machines, I scanned the faces of every man in uniform who passed by. Since anyone could be in security, I also scanned men in cheap casual wear, like Fred Tootsie's, men in plain suits, workout gear and polo shirts. When I realized I was studying everyone, I stopped for fear of attracting attention.

I wandered into a big area filled with blackjack tables. I picked one run by an attractive young Asian woman. There were already two guys there, but she folded me in seamlessly.

"How many points does a king get?" I asked. The other two guys looked at me like I'd just tracked fresh manure over to the table.

"Ten," said the dealer, in clear, accent-free English. "As many as a queen or a jack."

Then I won my first hand. My popularity among my table mates adjusted downward. Blackjack had been a good game for me growing up, since counting cards was something I did naturally, until my father pointed out that the skill could get my legs broken if practiced in the wrong venue. This should have no longer been an issue, given that I could now barely count my fingers and toes, though I still seemed to sense the flow of the cards. I followed that flow for the next hour, until I found myself up about $400.

The other two guys drifted away without comment.

"Beginner's luck," I said to the dealer.

"When did you begin?" she asked. "As a child?"

"I used to be good," I admitted. "I didn't know I still was."

"You want to go a few more rounds? I think the house can afford it."

I said sure and the two of us started to play.

"I have a few old friends who work here," I said, in the midst of innocuous small talk. "I was thinking of tracking them down."

"You know what they do?" she asked.

"One's in security. Don't know about the other one. You don't happen to have, like, an employee directory or something?"

I lost the next five hands, then I flipped over a five of clubs and laid it on a six of hearts and ten of spades.

"There's nothing published," she said, "though the guys on the help desk know everything. You should ask one of them."

I played well enough through the next hour to get the feeling I could play to near perfection for the rest of the night, which would have been a bad idea. So I lost a few to help curb the temptation.

The dealer didn't buy it.

"You're counting cards," she said, in a very low voice. I also noticed she was smiling.

"No, I'm not," I said back, as quietly. "Not intentionally. It's just happening. Must be some sort of weird calculation taking place on the subconscious level. I used to have a mathematical mind, but I was injured, and I thought I'd lost it all."

I didn't know why I was telling this to a complete stranger, but the confession, or revelation, felt good in the oddest way. She was a delicate person, with the palest skin and dark eyes filled with cheerful intelligence. Maybe that was why.

"I shouldn't play anymore," I said. "I don't want any trouble."

"No trouble from me," she said, still upbeat. "I don't care what you do. Though you should move around to different tables. Too much success in one place is not so good."

"Are they filming us?" I asked.

"Of course. It's okay, they'll just think I'm flirting with you," she said, sharing a radiant smile. "You could flirt back. It would help the act."

I experimented with a grin. It had been so long, the facial muscles wouldn't respond.

"Sorry," I said. "I'm still recovering from a bad accident. Not all the gear is in working order."

She cocked her head at me, then dealt two cards off her dealer's shoe.

"We have to play or you go someplace else."

I lost the next three hands, played at a leisurely pace.

"Did you crash your car?" she asked, as she gathered up my wasted cards.

"Somebody crashed into me. Is there an employee hangout here? An after-hours joint?"

She thought that was amusing.

"A place where customers can get to know dealers? Buy them drinks? Make friends? Security would really love that."

I flipped over another losing hand.

"Not here. Maybe near here. In town. I worked my way through college tending bar. There's always a joint."

She set us up again. I had a strong feeling about the next two cards. I went with the feeling and won the hand.

"There might be a place in New London where casino people go," said the dealer. "Not official or anything."

I gave back about two hundred dollars' worth of winnings and resisted the dealer's gentle encouragement to buy a cocktail. Or two.

"Can't," I touched my head. "Doctor's orders. Where would I find the name of that place?"

"You ask me. Or follow me after work, because that's where I'm headed."

I asked her, fearing the other approach was too logistically complicated. She gave me the name, the Sail Inn, and the address, which I wrote in a little notebook drawn from my back pocket. I thanked her.

"No problem," she said. "Another hand?"

I won a little more, then thought it best to move on. When I stood up I reached out to shake her hand. She shook her head, and I dropped the hand.

"John," I said, feeling oddly treacherous

for not using my real name, or even the new one, Alex, noting the absurdity in that.

"Natsumi. Be careful at the Sail. You're dealing with people who spot scams for a living."

"What scam?" I asked.

She looked at me for a moment, considering.

"I don't know. But something's going on. You don't fit."

I found that alarming. It must have shown.

"Not in an obvious way, "she said, recovering. "I better deal another hand." Which she did, covering the conversation. I sat back down. "I should shut up, don't you think? What a blabbermouth I am. My mother tells me that all the time, in Japanese, which doesn't even remotely translate, though I know what she's getting at."

I wanted to exude the opposite of whatever vibe she'd picked up, but had no idea how to go about it. Self-recrimination welled up within me.

"I was in a coma for a while," I said. "When I woke up, I had trouble connecting with people as I used to. I'm sorry if I seem a little odd. I seem a little odd to myself. That's the only thing going on."

She kept her eyes on the cards she was sliding across the green felt.

"That's a crummy thing," she said. "I'm sorry."

I thanked her again and left, overcoming a slight pull that held me to the table. At the same time, I felt as if a seam in the cloak of invisibility I'd been nurturing had slipped open. I took it as a cautionary moment, a warning to be more alert to my own manner. The feeling moved me out of the casino and back into the Outback, which I drove to New London. I found a coffee shop with broadband access to kill time before stopping by the Sail Inn.

I checked my two mailboxes, then embarked on a search for Austin Ott. There were a surprising number of them. I culled the list down to those living in and around Boston and Connecticut. I guessed at an age range between thirty and eighty-five. I found three Austin Otts self-important enough to include "the Third." They were evenly distributed among Boston, Connecticut and Rhode Island. I wondered if they got together for gin and tonics, and croquet.

Just as I was feeling daunted by all the undifferentiated data, a simple thought came to me. My Austin Ott, the Third was none of these. Because it wasn't his real name. This search was fruitless. I recorded all the information anyway, and moved on.

A young woman in a T-shirt and shorts, feebly contained within a loose apron, asked me if I wanted another plain black coffee with nothing in it. I said yes, even though I really didn't. Her bright response made it worth it.

I spent the remaining minutes forcing down the second cup of coffee and locating the Sail Inn via Google search and Yahoo maps. It was around the corner, within easy hobbling distance.

I was never much of a drinker. I'd tried, but usually fell asleep before I had a chance to get drunk. Florencia said I was the only person she knew who got more boring with every drink. Nonetheless, I'd cultivated a fine regard for the dynamics of bar life, discovering early on in my missing persons trade how useful it can be for gathering information.

The first rule when entering a new venue was to head directly to the bar and look eager for service. This established you as a common lush, and thus unworthy of extra scrutiny. I ordered a beer, which defined the limit of my capacity.

My alcoholic act broke down a little as I nursed the beer, though no one seemed to notice. I continued to look invisible — successfully, I think. Until I felt a hand on my shoulder.

"Well, hello there," said Natsumi.

"Hello back," I said. "I just got here. My friends aren't here, much to my relief. They aren't close friends."

That made her unhappy.

"So what's the worst that can happen?" she asked.

"I'd feel dopey. I have no social skills. Can I buy you a drink?"

She put her hand back on my shoulder.

"You just proved you have the first and most essential social skill. I'll have a shot of Jim Beam. Neat." I must have looked surprised and impressed. "Picked it up from my mother. Who picked it up from the sailor who brought us to America."

She climbed on the barstool. I waved to the bartender and completed the transaction. He looked at my nearly consumed beer, but I just said, "In a minute."

He left a wake of complete indifference.

"So," I said to Natsumi, "do you see many of your cohort in here?"

She looked around.

"A few. No one I know personally. There're thousands of people working at Clear Waters. It's one of the biggest casinos in the world, believe it or not."

150

"So you couldn't know anyone named Chalupnik. He's the one who works in security."

She shook her head.

"I only know one guy in security. They're mostly scary people, which is okay with me. You want them scary when they're on your side. I can ask a girlfriend on the help desk, if you want."

I didn't have to fake my appreciation.

"Boy, that'd be great. Truth is, my goal is to get a job here in the surveillance department. That's what I did back in the day, before the accident."

She seemed to be studying me.

"I thought you couldn't drink," she said.

"I'm nursing a single beer. Don't tell my neurologist. Or the bartender."

"You can buy me another Beam. That'll satisfy him."

"I've been to Japan," I said, for no good reason. "Kyoto. Spent two weeks and decided I could live there for the rest of my life. Have you been back?"

She looked at me again with that same scrutinizing look.

"No, but I have been to Philadelphia. I could live there, too. Why do I believe everything and nothing you say?"

I had another gush of nerves, fearing I was

losing control of my behavior. All I could do was smile, apologetically.

"I feel the same way about myself," I said. "Head injuries will do that to you. Though I think you can be reasonably sure that most of what I've said is substantially what I believe to be true. Except when I'm lying outright."

Her face actually lit up at that.

"If you be a bullshitter, you're the best there ever was," she said.

In the monologue within my mind, I felt no reason to disagree with her.

"You, on the other hand, display an alarming penchant for psychological analysis, however misguided," I said, handing it back to her. "Is this a job requirement for blackjack dealers?"

"No. Though it is for psychology majors, of which I am one. At Connecticut College. During the day. Up the road across from the Coast Guard Academy, which produces an alarming number of horny, patriotic cadets."

At this point, I felt secure scanning the room, covered by my proximity to Natsumi, with whom I was clearly engaged. There was nothing remarkable to be observed. No recognizable trench coat-fancying killers.

"You don't seem quite college age," I said to her.

"Ah, that social skills thing you mentioned. No, I'm thirty-eight years old. You think that's too old to get a degree?"

"Not at all," I said. "I'm merely making an observation. Learning at any age is the best thing you can do. I believe that more deeply than I believe any other thing in the world. I feel a perceptive woman like you would agree."

"Good answer. Buy me another drink."

I did just that. When the bartender came over and she placed her order, I had another chance to look around at the bar's clientele. Natsumi noticed, and tapped me on the arm.

"That guy over there with the sideburns," she said, giving her head a little jerk toward a booth against the wall. "He's security. The woman with him works in one of the dress shops. I like to go there and pretend I can afford to buy something. It annoys her."

"So I guess you wouldn't mind annoying her again."

She smiled.

"I'll gladly introduce you to the security guy. You just have to tell me your last name."

"Oswald," I said. "Like the assassin. No relation."

Her smile widened.

"Natsumi Fitzgerald. Fits me about as well as yours fits you."

"The sailor?"

"My adopted father. He's dead. Liked the Jim Beam a little too much."

"Sorry."

"Come on," she said, pulling at my shirtsleeve, "let's go annoy some people."

Natsumi led us over to the booth. I tried to shrink myself into the remotest possible threat. Natsumi ignored the woman and stuck her hand out to the guy.

"Hi, I'm Natsumi. I deal blackjack at Clear Waters. I've seen you on the floor." The guy took her hand cautiously. "My friend John Oswald is looking to get into security, so I thought you might tell him how to go about it. Come over here, John," she said to me, regaining her grip on my shirt. I offered my hand to the guy and he took it.

"I've had some experience in video surveillance," I told him. "I thought maybe you could use me at the casino."

The guy nodded. His features, too small for his head, merged seamlessly with his neck. A sparse moustache did little to improve the situation.

"They might. Not my part of the deal, but

154

it wouldn't hurt to apply."

"So just go to HR?" Natsumi asked.

I dug the crumpled napkin out of my back pocket.

"Ron Irving?" I asked.

"Yeah," said the guy, in the clipped way you often hear out on Long Island, not so much in Connecticut. "That's the guy. Retired state bull. You don't got any kinda record, do you? Anything more'n a parking ticket is an automatic disqualification."

"I'm good there," I said. "Drive like a senior citizen."

The guy and his companion, who wore a wedding ring that didn't match his, looked ready for us to retreat back to the bar. I thanked him, and he looked satisfied with himself for helping a fellow human being.

"Your friend?" Natsumi prompted me.

"Oh, yeah, I think I got a friend who works with you guys. Lost track of him years ago. Last name's Chalupnik."

The guy's eyes narrowed.

"We got three of them. Don't know 'em personally," he said. "What's the first name?"

"We just called him Munk, like in chipmunk," I said, stalling for time as I searched my battered brain for the names I'd found on the web. "It was a funny name I think,

155

like Bela?"

One in three chance.

"We got a Bela," he said. "And a Radek and a Dano, like *Hawaii Five-O*. Bela's the old man. Got the kids into the family business."

I ached to pull out the police sketch of the man in the trench coat, but discipline won out.

"That's great," I said. "Thanks. I'll ask Mr. Irving about him."

With that, I withdrew, Natsumi following. We reclaimed our stools, reserved by the half-consumed drinks on the bar.

"See, that was easy," I said, "and only vaguely disruptive."

"Chipmunk? You made that up."

"You don't have nicknames in Japan?"

"I don't know. We left when I was three years old. The kids here called me slopehead. But that's probably not what you mean."

"Do you think your friend in IT could get me a picture of Bela?" I asked. "That would nail it."

She narrowed her eyes in the same way as the security guy. Probably for the same reason.

"You really want to find this friend of yours," she said.

I tried to look nonchalant.

"Not really. It's just the way I am. Get on a mission and can't stop. And there's this social anxiety thing. Worse since the bang on the head. It was very generous of you to help me. A good deed."

"I try to do one a day. I'll get you his picture. Then how do I get it to you?"

I took a cocktail napkin out of a stack on the bar and wrote down an email address.

"You send it here. Which will give me your email address, and then we can communicate. Unless you don't want to."

"I think I do. Jury's still out. My mother tells me I think too much. Do you believe that's possible? What do you think she means?"

"I've been accused of the same thing. I used to call it hyper-analysis syndrome. Tell your mother you love her and to worry about something else, like the yield curve or invasive species."

Natsumi was very expressive, but I found her face difficult to read. Some of it was the nature of her features, different from mine and outside my familiar experience. I thought it would be easy to overestimate her bright-eyed congeniality, or misinterpret the occasional look of confusion, or marvel. I wondered if I could get her into an in-depth, one-on-one interview to better document her facial cues.

"What?" she said.

"What do you mean, what?"

"Why are you looking at me?"

"I have nowhere more productive to look."

"Is that a compliment? I'm not sure," she said.

"Since you've already admitted to thinking too much, I was trying to divine what those thoughts were by your facial gestures and body language. I think unsuccessfully."

"I'm trying to do the same thing with you, with about as much success," she said.

I felt the room close in on me, not the first time that evening. I felt exposed and intrigued at the same time. It was hard to trace the cause of the spatial disorientation, the potential uncovering of the man in the trench coat, or the likeable Asian woman, who seemed to possess a unique talent for dislodging my reflexive self-defense.

"I better get home," I said. "I'm getting really tired."

"Not the company, I hope," she asked.

"Hardly. You've been extremely helpful and kind. It's just getting late for me and that beer took a toll."

"The world's cheapest date."

I paid the bill and made to leave. We shook

hands and she repeated her intention to get me the information I was looking for.

"Not just for your sake," she said. "You could be interesting to have around. I like the people I work with, but I'm easily bored."

"I might be a lot more boring than you think," I said.

"Too late, John. You've already proved otherwise."

CHAPTER 10

As I drove back to my rental house, I pondered a paradox. Contrary to my claims of social ineptitude, I actually had extraordinary talents in that area. Though only when used as a professional tool, a way to extract information from the unsuspecting, preying on people's natural desire to help out the confused and befuddled. In essence, exploiting people's better nature.

It wasn't hard to see the ethics challenge, but it didn't matter so much when the quarry was identifying toothpaste preferences, or cable TV bundling options. This was different. This time the pursued was murderous and the pursuer no less inclined.

A complicating factor was an original truth. I *was* socially awkward when the intent was purely social. I never felt comfortable with the mating and networking dance, always the twitchy, hyperactive geek, and like Natsumi, easily bored by the mingling crowds I often found myself trapped within.

Florencia rescued me from all that. Took me under her wing, not to tutor so much as protect and defend against the vagaries of casual discourse.

Another reason for me to love her, as if I needed one.

The next morning, my computer woke me up with a gentle ping. It took a while to gather the significance as I slowly emerged from sleep, foggier than usual after the long casino and Sail Inn experience.

I looked through a dull blur at the computer screen. A dialog box was open. I put on my glasses and saw that MrPbody had an email message waiting. I opened the program. It was from EichenWrite.

"Thank you, but a week was pretty stingy," he wrote, "though you got him softened up. He was sure you were going to whack him. Inspired a confessional mood. When the cops showed up, he was part relieved, part annoyed, thinking he'd spilled too many beans. I got most of what I needed, and now there's another court case. My editor sent back the advance I had to give up, so I guess I owe you. Which is why I didn't share our contact info, namely this email box, with the retired cop. He's VERY VERY curious about you. Tried to lean on me. I said, hello? Ever heard of protected sources? Go ahead, subpoena my ass. First amendment is my middle name. I got the ACLU on speed dial. FYI, the cop's name is Shelly Gross, which you might already know. I told him the best I could do was relay a message. No guarantees, and that's the truth. BTW, who the fuck ARE you?"

After reading the email, I fell back in bed. I'll answer, I thought. But not right now. I had to figure out what I wanted to write, and anyway, never good to look too eager. And there was the matter of debilitating exhaustion. I needed at least another hour in bed, collecting myself. Assessing the situation.

Ten minutes later, the chime went off again. It was Evelyn.

"Things are moving quickly at the agency," she wrote. "Best to check in when you get a chance. Call me. Too complicated for email. Still nothing from Maddox. They're about to move you into cold cases. A little premature if you ask me, but he promised to keep his hand in, which doesn't mean anything as far as I know, but I appreciate the thought. I hope you're feeling okay, though I bet you're not. Don't push things too hard. Slows the healing process.

By official standards, the trauma is still pretty fresh. I know, I know, who cares about officials."

I turned off the alert sounds and fell back in bed once again. Evelyn's caution, as usual, was timely and directly put. Though sure to be ignored, after I had a chance to rest a bit and gather myself.

There's a difference, I said to myself, between feeling like hell and losing the ability to function. As long as I could operate reasonably well, the feeling-like-hell part would just have to stay out of the way.

The only treatment for fatigue that ever worked for me was generating more activity. So I forced myself into the shower and a fresh set of clothes and set out in the Subaru. The project I had in mind might have been premature, but it was foremost in my thoughts, and thus the easiest to undertake.

My first stop was the lumberyard. I bought several sheets of half-inch birch plywood which I had cut to tight specifications. I also bought some three-quarter inch poplar stock, hinges and some heavy wire mesh. I threw it all in the Outback and drove to Gerry's shop at the clock factory where I did an inventory of tools and fastening options, like wood screws and heavy-duty staplers. I went back out to a hardware store to fill in the gaps, then returned to the shop.

I wasn't much of a hobbyist, but I'd learned to use shop tools during a market research study for a company who wanted to downgrade material quality as a cost-saving measure. It turned out to be a fatal error on their part, but I got to generate a lot of sawdust and achieve another barely mastered skill without suffering serious injury.

I spent the rest of the day drawing out my idea and planning the optimum cuts. It was satisfying work, as Gerry promised it would be, using my hands and calculating skills, which seemed to have developed past arithmetic and into primitive geometry. A self-taught version, to be sure, as I had to draw multiple lines and make models out of cardboard in order to realize basic shapes and dimensions.

Luckily, it wasn't that complex a design, well within the capabilities of an ambitious thirteen-year-old.

In a few hours I had a rectangular box, approximately a foot wide and eighteen inches high, and four feet long. There were two doors in the middle of the box, one a solid piece of ply, and one Plexiglas, which you opened and closed by sliding it in and out of a slot on the top. The box was mounted on a two-by-four structure raised about four feet off the ground. A fairly primitive device, but there was little need for additional complexity.

By now, it was midafternoon. I had another goal for the day, but was unsure if I should try it in broad daylight. On the drive back to my rental house, I decided I would, and pulled into the driveway leading up to the empty gravel pit next door. What I saw would make an ideal movie set for the apocalypse. Rusted metal-sheathed buildings, rotting, partially disemboweled trucks, a cratered lunar landscape devoid of life. I found a building I assumed housed the original offices for the complex and tried to look through the translucent, pitted window glass, with no success.

I put on a pair of surgical gloves and worked my way around the building, testing doors and windows until I found a door with a smashed-in glass panel. The door opened into a dark hallway I lit with a small flashlight. The floor was covered in a tangle of weathered, dusty litter. I followed the hall to a large, open room I assumed was once the reception area for the offices. Now it was just an empty space, but for a mattress, scattered beer cans and pornographic magazines. It was windowless and black as pitch. The little flashlight was barely up to the task as I surveyed all the space. After I was satisfied with what I saw, I left and went back to my house.

I booted up the computer and placed rush orders for a few other components from several different suppliers. Thus involved, I forgot that Evelyn had asked me to call her. When I did, the first thing she asked was how I was feeling.

"Like hell, but it's manageable. I had a beer last night."

"You lush."

"If you really want to distort reality, I recommend a gunshot to the head. What's with the agency?"

"I think an offer could come sometime next week. Bruce can see I'm really uneasy about it, but he's been great. He assumes I'm feeling over my head and he's right. He doesn't know it's not really my decision. I'm half afraid hesitating will breed suspicion. I know that's paranoid, but I can't help it."

"I do keep putting you in untenable situations," I said.

"You think?"

"I just need to do some housekeeping. I'll

make it as quick as possible and let you know when I'm ready. Keep a close eye on your mailbox."

After hanging up, I went to the computer and dove back into web searches and online purchasing until I was too tired to stay awake, and thus successfully hammered my jittery brain into blessed unconsciousness.

During the night another ping from the computer woke me up. It was an email from Natsumi Fitzgerald with an attachment labeled "Chapulnik.Bela.jpeg." Before reading her note, I clicked on the attachment.

Could I know for sure? I asked myself. Probably not, but did it feel right? Absolutely.

I knew all the research on eyewitness testimony, on faulty memory, on the uncertain reliability of certainty. Yet, I felt I knew, without a doubt, that this was the man in the trench coat.

I took out the police sketch. Another person might not have seen the resemblance, which for some reason encouraged me. What I saw were the essentials — the set of his jaw, rigid, and slightly skewed to the left. The tone of his skin and blemishes on his cheeks. As a researcher, I also knew the power of the subconscious to capture and store information more dependably than the conscious mind, unimpaired as it was by the warp of cognition, the imposition of bias and preference. It was information you felt, rather than thought, a feeling that rarely let me down.

I fed the name into the people search programs and harvested all the necessary vital statistics — age (52), physical address, phone number, police record (none) and employment history. He'd been in security at Clear Waters for ten years. Before that had similar gigs at Electric Boat, the submarine builder in Groton across the river from New London, and before that in the U.S. Navy Shore Patrol.

I copied all the information into an email and sent it to myself where I could access it with my smartphone. Then I went back to my project, absorbed by the details of the plan, a continuous stream of if/then's running through my mind, waylaying whatever emotional distractions threatened to burble up from that helpful, but often nettlesome subconscious.

I started the surveillance several days later, after all the other preparations were in place. I made an educated guess that Chalupnik, a ten-year veteran at the casino, would have a shift covering peak periods of activity, roughly from midafternoon to ten at night. So I started to cruise by his sixties-era white ranch house in nearby Waterford at various times before and after ten-thirty P.M. It was a crudely imprecise approach, but I dared not push Natsumi to make further inquiries, however sympathetic she might be. I had written back to thank her, and she rather plainly expressed the hope that I'd stop at her table sometime, and that was that.

On the third night, I drove down the street in time to see the taillights of a generic Japanese sedan parked in Bela's driveway flick off. A man got out of the car, and as I passed by I could almost make a positive ID under the dim and shadowy outdoor lighting. I noted the time and continued on.

It wasn't until two nights later that I had another hit, this one more convincing. Still, I gave it another week to be sure I had the basic pattern established.

On the chosen night, I took the chance of pulling over to the curb to wait for the Japanese car to go by and pull into the driveway. Then, with my lights out, I pulled in behind just as Chalupnik was about to go down his front walk.

He spun around to face me, and I shot

him in the stomach with a police-grade Taser stun gun. He crumpled to the ground, and I left the car and reached his writhing body well within the allotted ten-second limit of the electric pulse. At the moment the spasms stopped, I stuck an air-powered syringe into the side of his neck and pushed the button. There was a little pop, and a sound that was part groan, part gurgle came from Chalupnik seconds before his struggling form went lifeless.

I gathered up the fabric of his jacket at the throat and grabbed his belt, and half carried, half dragged the dead weight over to the Outback. Using the rest of my reserve strength, I heaved most of him into the back of the station wagon's trunk. Then I went around to the back door and pulled him the rest of the way in.

I covered him with a packing blanket and gently shut the hatch, pushing till the latch clicked. Then I backed out of the driveway and left, putting my lights on only after reaching the end of the block.

The trip from Waterford to Wilton was uneventful and slow going, as I kept just below the speed limit; but I was in no hurry, and used the extra time to triple check the components of the plan, reminding myself of the virtues of careful planning in all endeavors great and small.

CHAPTER 11

When Chalupnik regained consciousness, he saw the inside of a wooden box. The wood surfaces were harshly lit by a recessed quartz halogen fixture in the ceiling of the box. His arms and legs were immobilized by the duct tape that secured him to the chair, which was in turn bolted to the floor with steel hardware. The box had barely enough ventilation to make breathing possible, if strained. The light, though dimmed, heated up the confined space.

From his restrained vantage point he couldn't see the two-way communication device mounted near his right ear, but he could hear me clearly, even with the filter that flattened out my inflections, turning my speech into a mechanized monotone.

"You're awake," I said. "Can you see?"

"What the fuck *is* this?" he said, with the nasally insinuation of the man in the trench coat.

"Can you see?"

"My gut's on fire. You shot me."

"I shot you with a Taser. Otherwise you'd be dead. Tell me if you can see."

"I can see," he said.

"Your name?"

"You don't know? You're kidding me."

"I do know. That's why I want you to tell me."

"Bela Chalupnik. How long I been out? My wife'll have the National Guard out looking for me. Never been late much less not shown up."

"They won't find you. Until I want them to. I have a series of questions to ask you. I know all the answers. If you lie, I'll know."

"Who are you?"

"You can call me George O. Where do you work?"

"Why should I tell you anything?" he asked.

"Because there will be consequences if you don't."

"What consequences?"

"You'll know when they happen. Where do you work?" I asked again.

"Clear Waters Resort and Casino."

We went through another dozen of these easy Q and A's, which he readily answered correctly. Then I asked him if working

173

security at the casino was his only profession. He said yes.

"You're lying," I said.

"What the hell does that mean?"

"You have another profession which you've practiced for some time. It's illegal. Tell me what it is."

He denied it. I asserted he was lying. We exchanged different ways of expressing these positions for the next two hours. I increased the intensity of the light, which also had the effect of warming the stale air in the box, but not past the bearable.

Finally I said, "So I guess there'll have to be consequences."

"Like what?" he asked.

"You'll have to wait to find out. Or you can tell me the name you use in your other profession. You have five minutes to decide."

"Goddammit, tell me who you think I am," he yelled through the little mike.

"No. You have to tell me. Otherwise, I won't believe you."

Neither of us said anything for the next two minutes, which I counted off for him. When I said "three" he tried to twist in his seat and banged his head around inside the box.

"What're you going to do?" he screamed.

I stayed silent and looked at the stopwatch

174

on my smartphone until it hit four minutes.

"Four."

"You motherfucker, you are so dead," he screamed again, nearly hysterical.

"Time's up," I said calmly. "Name?"

"Pally!" he yelled. "Pally Buttons, you miserable piece of shit who I am so going to kill as God is my witness."

I kept him in silence for another five minutes. I was disappointed that he stayed silent as well, braced for the fearsome unknown, but in control of his dignity. I was hoping for less courage.

"Good answer," I said. "Though I'm not sure you want God to witness the sort of thing you're threatening. Talk about consequences."

Getting people to tell me what's in their minds was at the heart of my professional life. I'd made an extensive study of accomplished interrogators and knew well the psychology behind their success. Rather than wrenching out the truth by force, they created the circumstances whereby the subject would just let the truth dribble out. All but the most skillful and committed liars have some compulsion, even unknown to themselves, to tell what they know. To brag, to confess, to succumb to the pleasures of seduction.

But the constant in these interrogations was time. Weeks, months, years — I knew for me this would be impossible. Not with this person. My hatred and revulsion was too great, too personal, to be restrained by the necessary discipline.

Physical force had long been proved the best way to extract false information. Or for creating martyrs, or people so deranged by pain they no longer knew what truths they possessed.

What was needed was a better motivator.

"Pally Buttons is well known in certain circles," I said. "What does he do?"

"If you know everything, why do you keep asking all these questions?"

"I told you. I need to know you're telling the truth."

"He's a gun. And a cleaner. Handles special projects. When do I get my head out of here?"

"When all my questions have been answered to my satisfaction."

"How do I know if *you're* telling the truth?" he asked.

"By the absence of negative consequences."

This was one of the ways Evelyn kept the incipient unruliness of her little brother in check. By darkly threatening the possibility of negative consequences.

"You think being taped up with your head in a box ain't negative?"

"In comparison? No. In comparison it's a tropical vacation."

I let that settle in for a while, then I asked him, "What're the responsibilities of a cleaner?"

"Jesus Christ, it's like being in fucking school. He cleans up after a hit, or after a fuckup that might lead to the wrong people being looked at. Pally offers a package deal. Lowers the overhead."

"So Pally must be pretty good at what he does. All that experience in the Shore Patrol and working security really paid off."

I liked the way Chalupnik preferred to talk about his alias in the third person. Made it easier to admit to things, operating under the illusion that he wasn't really talking about himself.

"Was that a question?"

"Not unless you want to argue the point," I said.

"No argument. The record speaks for itself. Who the fuck are you, anyway?"

I wished I was still able to perform regression analyses. They're highly useful tools for predicting outcomes based on a dance between dependent and independent variables. You learn when it's time to split off into a new analytical direction. Essentially identifying the critical forks in the road.

"I told you. I'm George. I represent one of your clients. They're feeling some unhappiness about a situation."

"Unhappiness? For Christ's sake, why do it this way?"

"They're very unhappy."

"No reason for this. No reason at all. Pally is Mr. Perfection. Never had a complaint from nobody. Ever."

"Really. So then would it surprise you that Pally the professional cleaner needs a cleaner of his own?"

I still couldn't read his thoughts, but I could somehow tell when he was struggling to form a response.

"Bullshit. Never happened."

"Names of the women Pally's capped over the last calendar year."

"No," he said without hesitation. "No fucking way. Bring on the consequences."

I stuck a straw into the box through a small hole lined up with his mouth.

"Want some water? You're getting hoarse."

"What is that, poison? Some fucking drug? No thanks."

"No. It's just water. I haven't heard all your answers yet. I have nothing to gain by killing or hurting you."

"There's a comfort," he said, but after a pause, sucked down half the glass I held for him.

"Here's what you should consider," I said. "I need to establish the context for the next part of this conversation. If I can't do that, then you have no way to free yourself from what could be a very unpleasant situation."

"You didn't tell me that before."

"There was no need," I said. "You've spoken the truth at every stage, so I've trusted what you say. But now you want to be stubborn. It's only fair that you appreciate the stakes."

He considered that.

"Let me get this straight," he said. "Something fucked up with one of the projects, sometime after the fact. I can be in the shit for it, but maybe not, depending on the facts of the matter. Is this what you're saying?"

It was a critical moment. I had to take a chance that giving him some hope wouldn't encourage deception now that I was running out of questions with verifiable answers.

"That is correct. Names of the women, last chance."

"Only one woman. Florencia Cathcart.

Fine-looking skirt, but Pally's a professional."

Something surged up from deep within me, heating my face and crackling in my ears. I slipped my hand into my jacket pocket where two more powered syringes were waiting. I fondled the one with a lethal charge. I saw myself jamming it into the back of his neck and ending everything right there. I got control of my breath and gave a moment for my heart rate to calm back down.

"You continue to show an admirable pragmatism," I said. "So now perhaps we can reach the end of these proceedings and both get on with our lives."

"I'm for that. I'm feeling like hammered shit."

"Very well. We're still validating, however. How many blanks did you ask Ms. Cathcart to fill out on the sheet of paper you gave her."

"Oh, man, that was a long time ago. I don't remember stuff like that. I'm not trying to dodge the question. I just don't remember. I get it wrong, you'll think I'm lying."

"Try."

He did. Then said, "Five? I think it was five."

"What were the answers?"

"Jesus Christ, Forgiver of Sins, I have no idea. I really don't. Just numbers, or letters and numbers together. That wasn't part of my job. I was just told to give her the paper and verify one of the answers. I forgot it the second I saw it and this was, like, a year ago. I'm not lyin'. I cannot answer that question."

The stress in his voice was unmistakable. What little mobility he had seemed to go rigid, braced for impact.

"They wouldn't expect you to," I said.

His body sagged to the limits of the duct tape restraints.

"You haven't told me what fucked up," he said, his voice hoarse with tension. "I can't help you if you don't tell me."

"There's money missing," I said.

"Missing from where? That's got nothing to do with me. I just handled the project with those two people, period. I got no idea what it was about and I don't care. None of my business. They think I had something to do with this? I never heard a thing. Never a peep in all these months. They can't just talk to me? You working for them?"

"For whom?"

"The clients on the Cathcart thing. You're not working for them?"

"You know the rules. You give me the names and I tell you the answer."

Even in his rising panic, he had the presence of mind to think before he spoke.

"What if you're not?" he asked. "What if all this is a setup on them? You know how long I'd last in this business if I sell out my clients? There aren't consequences negative enough to match what they'd do to me."

"Don't bet on it. Give me the names."

"No, that's it. This is bullshit. I've already said too much. Get me out of here. You hurt me you're a dead man. I got sons that'll track you to the gates of hell."

He went on like this for a while, stopping only when he noticed I wasn't responding. I allowed about five minutes of silence to pass before speaking.

"Okay," I said. "Fair enough. You've made your choice, and I respect that. I'm ready to get back home anyway. Let me just show you how this is going to work."

I reached up and slid the hard panel out of the top of the box. This left the other half visible through the piece of Plexiglas. Chalupnik immediately understood the implications. I waited for the screaming to stop.

"These big rats have to eat almost continuously," I said, "and it's already been a few days. So I think as soon as I pull up the

Plexiglas there won't be much hesitation. I'll give you a few seconds to get ready."

"Mother of God you're not going to do this," he said.

"I just hope it's not too much of a mess for the cleaner. Unlike you, I subcontract all that. It's amazing what some people will do for a living. Have a nice night."

I pulled up the Plexiglas. I had to pull the earpiece connected to his mike away from my ear it got so loud in the box. But I could still hear the thump, surprised how little time it took for the rats to ram into the piece of clear, hardened glass I'd installed a few inches from his face as a final obstacle. You could hear the frantic scratching as they tried to claw their way through to an overdue meal.

"Oh, that's right," I said into my mike. "I forgot this thing has another door. Sorry about that."

"Ott," Chalupnik screamed. "Jason Three Sticks. And some other shit he had on the phone. Didn't identify himself. Please don't do this."

"Tell me about the project."

"They sent me a letter with the stuff I was supposed to show the woman," he said in halting, breathless bursts. "Gave me a scheduling window, wired half the fee before, half after. That's it. Didn't tell me nothing else and that's the way I like it. Less I know the better. You gotta get them rats out of here. They're gonna break the glass. Mother of Mercy."

"Interesting that a man so devoid of mercy feels he can invoke that privilege for himself," I said.

"Fuck mercy. Put a gun in my hand, George. I'll do it myself. That glass is moving. I can see it move. They're gonna break through."

I knew they couldn't, so I waited another few minutes, then reached into my jacket pocket and chose the syringe with the nonlethal dose and stuck it in his shoulder. Then I used a combination of buck knife and industrial scissors to cut off and strip the gummy duct tape. After that, it was merely a matter of hauling his inert form out of the building with the same cart I'd used to get him in there, then pouring him into the Outback. I went back inside to free the rats and break down the box, hiding it for later disposal. Then I drove to the little park in Norwalk where I'd met Henry Eichenbach. I dumped Chalupnik out in the parking lot and drove home, already working out the calculations for the next

phase of what I now called the project,
courtesy of Pally Buttons.

CHAPTER 12

I spent the next morning in a library in Bridgeport trying to hack into the accounting system at Florencia's insurance agency. I had reasonable hope of success since I was the one who'd purchased and configured the system five years before. It was a web-based application, so I was able to do much of the work from my home office through remote access. In the first five seconds I learned the disappointing news that my password had been deleted or changed. I'd been careful to spec a system with the best security protections available at the time, so this was no small thing.

I was in unknown territory. In all the years of tracking down people and information, I'd never resorted to anything remotely defined as hacking. I never saw the need, nor sought the thrill of the hunt that drew many otherwise honest people into illegal cyber-invasions. So after a failed attempt, I spent a long time staring at the log-in screen, pondering.

To the best of my memory, there was no way for the system to trace a thwarted effort to log in. However, it was able to shut out further attempts after three failures, which meant the IP address of the potential invader was recorded somewhere within the application. Which was why I was operating from the library, where the only restriction to anonymous Internet access was the inability to find an empty seat.

The record of the offending IP address stayed forever. The block itself could be removed, though only by the system administrator. That used to be me. I once knew how to get around any of the security protocols and protections, but it had been a while, and in the intervening time the part of my brain most involved in quantitative pursuits, like computer automation, had been mashed up by a bullet through the head.

No excuse, I told myself. The memory was in there, extractable.

I conjured a mental image of my old self: reviewing options, developing tables with side-by-side comparisons, poring over hardware catalogs, effortlessly shooting down jet streams of swirling data, homing in on the ultimate solution.

It's too much, I thought. I'll never get it back.

But that's okay, I said to myself, I don't have to get it all back. I just have to get back enough to let me breach security and capture the data in the system. I remembered such a thing was possible, and hoped it wasn't a manufactured memory.

Since I was already at a safe workstation, I switched over to my renewed interest in Austin Ott, the Third, whom Chalupnik had also referred to as Jason Three Sticks. It wasn't much, but more than I had before.

I started with Google and went well past page 500 before giving up the chase. Then I tried to uncover paid databases on known criminals, but quickly realized the futility of searching for the criminal record of an alias of a man who likely had no record at all.

I tacked away from that approach and pulled up a Word document so I could put something down on paper.

Mr. Gross: The gift of Sebbie Frondutti was an act of good faith, albeit unsolicited, meant to demonstrate that I can be a reliable intermediary. I hope this gesture will encourage you to reciprocate. I'm seeking information on a professional killer who goes by the alias Austin Ott, the Third. He is also known as Jason Three Sticks. Any information you feel free to share with me on this person would be greatly appreciated. Should you and your former colleagues have any interest in apprehending Mr. Ott, the more complete the information you provide, the more likely this wish will be fulfilled. (I will find him eventually, but help from you will speed the process and assure your share of the benefit.) If you're agreeable, put a classified ad in the print version of the Sunday *New York Times* offering a "1965 Mustang convertible, four-speed, 289, insanely clean and meticulously maintained, sold to the best offer with assurances it will annoy your wife as much as it does mine." Further instructions will follow.

After putting on a pair of surgical gloves, I printed it out and left the library bleary-eyed from hours in front of the computer screen. I drove around Bridgeport until I found a little bodega, where, with the gloves on, I bought a tonic water in a clear glass bottle with a twist-on cap. I poured out the liquid and used my pocket knife to scrape off the label. Then I threw the empty bottle in the backseat and drove north. About an hour later I was in Rocky Hill. By now it was almost dark, night coming early that time in late fall, so I stopped to eat — killed time on the laptop — then drove the rest of the way to Shelly's neighborhood.

Before I got there, I stopped at a little strip mall and under the ghostly fluorescents, with a fresh set of gloves, curled up the note and stuck it in the bottle. I drove down Shelly's street and tossed the bottle in the middle of his front lawn.

After the tedious trip home, I brought up the computer for a final check before bed. The only unread email was from Natsumi Fitzgerald.

"What I meant was, I'd really LIKE you to stop by my table sometime. Then maybe we could go out for another wild night of drinking. I'll have my shot, you have your beer. You pay for mine, I'll pay for yours. Did you ever meet up with your friend?"

For some reason, I reread her email several times, and then answered in the affirmative, before succumbing to the usual late-night exhaustion, which drove me into bed for another night's sleep, strangely neither fitful, nor riddled with ugly, snarling phantoms or ephemeral reminders of irredeemable loss.

■ ■ ■ ■

Brain scientists will tell you there's no better way to solve a problem than to sleep on it. As the light of day joined with my emerging consciousness, the beginning of a solution crept stealthily into my mind.

I saw myself at the workstation of one of Florencia's employees. His computer had locked up and she needed to extract his data. Ordinarily, this wouldn't be a problem, because as system administrator, I could just waltz in there and take over; but for some dumb reason the guy had overlaid our security with his own private application, which was blocking me out. This would also be an easy problem to solve if he was in the building, but he was snorkeling in the Virgin Islands, and hadn't left the necessary passwords. Florencia was none too pleased. I offered to come in and figure out what to do, probably out of misplaced concern for her knuckleheaded employee.

I succeeded, but how, I asked myself.

I opened my eyes and saw the light, outside and within my battered brain. I suddenly knew then how to get into the agency's system. The only catch was I'd also have to get into the agency itself.

I called Evelyn.

"Does the agency still have a security system?" I asked her.

"It does. Why are you asking?"

"I need to get in there. Do you know the password? And do you have a key?"

"Yes and yes," she answered. "Why do you need to go there and what do you hope to find?"

"I need access to the computer systems. I don't know what part her agency might have played in this disaster, so I'm loath to let it go without at least having a record that I can refer to later on."

"What kind of record?" she asked.

"Everything. I want access to the whole operation. Current and historical."

"I don't know how to do that, and I can't ask without raising suspicion," she said.

"You don't have to. I just need to get to one of the workstations. Preferably Bruce Finger's. Is he using Florencia's office?"

"I don't know. The offices have nameplates. When are you going to do this?"

"Tonight. At two in the morning. Before you go to bed, drive over there and put a key under the mat."

"That's imaginative."

"It'll only be there a few hours."

"How are you going to know what you're

looking for with no math skills?" she asked.

"I've got a calculator on my smartphone. That's all I need. What's the security code?"

When I got off the phone I went right to the computer and wrote "boot disk" in the search box. There wasn't much about the process I remembered, but those two words were enough to get me going. Originally created to help techs troubleshoot corrupted files, or recover data from damaged machines, a boot disk application took the place of the built-in "boot up" program, overlaying its own mini-operating system and user interface. This essentially allowed the tech to hijack the computer, bypassing any and all security measures. You could do whatever you wanted with the computer, and once you shut down and popped out the boot disk, it was like nothing ever happened.

As with any application that could be adapted to proper or improper use, there were both officially sanctioned and outlaw versions. The outlaw ones were, of course, the best.

However, this wasn't something I could do remotely. I had to have physical possession of the computer.

It took the rest of the morning, but I found a program called MattBD that was written to match the agency's hardware and operating system, the precise description of which I still had buried in my archives. I downloaded the app, which only took a few minutes, and burned it to a disk.

The easy part was done. I had to wait until dark for the rest.

Florencia's agency was in one of the many faceless little office buildings that lined one of two major thoroughfares that led in and out of Stamford from the north. I parked several doors down and used a series of shared parking lots to approach from the rear. I wore a fake beard and a hat over one of the long-haired wigs. If a security camera picked me up, they'd record a cliché of a disguised man.

Though I couldn't know what security measures the new management might have added to the original system, I thought it unlikely things had changed. Insurance agencies just weren't the type of places people typically broke into. Though millions of dollars passed through the computers, the only cash on hand was barely enough to pay for a pizza delivery.

The entrance to the building, conveniently off to the side away from the street, was shrouded in darkness. I crouched down and pulled up the big mat that was still in use, and retrieved two keys. One for the building, the other for the agency. I went through both doors without hesitation, bringing along a laptop and a few other handy devices.

The heat had automatically dropped back for the night, so the air was cool and smelled of carpet and human industry. Guided by imprecise memory and a pen-sized flashlight, I felt along a hallway until I came to Florencia's office. The bracket that once held her nameplate was empty. I went to the next office and saw Bruce Finger's name. I let myself in.

In defiance of the stereotype of the tidy, meticulous financial expert, Bruce was an inveterate slob. Mountains of paper and periodicals not only rose above his desk, there were stacks on the floor and in the middle of a small conference table. His computer keyboard and screen had safe haven on a little platform that slid out from the desk. The CPU was on the floor where I'd placed it five years earlier. I turned it on and put the CD in the slot. Moments later, a screen with the MattBD logo appeared with a little dialog box that said, "Press any key."

I hit Z and waited. After a few minutes,

the ghost was in the machine. The look of the interface was different from the official software, but all the same folders and files were there.

The first thing I did was copy the software that ran the accounting and financial system, operations and email to an external hard drive. Then I went into Bruce's folders and started copying everything there. It was a lot of data, but well within the terabyte of storage I had available. It just took a long time, made longer by crouching in the dark with a tiny flashlight and ears tuned to the slightest sound.

Which is why I heard someone moving through the office before I saw the sliver of light under Bruce's door. I looked over at the window, but knew it was for naught, since it was a solid slab of glass with a vent at the bottom too small to squeeze through. There was no closet to hide in, no curtains or couch to slip behind. Trapped.

For a second I was tempted to switch off the computer screen, but didn't know how that might affect the downloading. I heard doors opening and closing, and a clattering sound that proved the invader was unafraid of being caught. I almost stopped breathing as I strained to hear, but the thump of my heart was the only thing that got louder.

Until the vacuum cleaner started up, which was the definition of good news, bad news. I moved the wastebasket from the back to the front of the desk and put a box in the way to discourage the cleaning person from putting it back in place.

I heard the door to the office across the hall open, and the fading sound of the vacuum as it moved inside. Then I shoved myself under the desk and prayed for a tired, lazy or negligent person to be at the helm of that vacuum cleaner.

The door latch jangled and the room was suddenly filled with sound and light. My view consisted of the drawers in Bruce's credenza and the base of the chair. I sent a little word of thanks for his slovenly nature, which I hoped would inhibit easy progress into the room.

The desk shook when the vacuum hit one of the stubby legs. An involuntary jolt of alarm shot through my heart. Another thump came from another part of the desk. It was a woman, and I could hear her saying something to herself, though not clearly enough to make out the words. I imagined it to be a regular lament about vacuuming around Bruce's piles.

The machine suddenly appeared before me, knocking the chair out of the way as it made deepening forays into the space behind the desk. I saw a thick white woman's leg, sheathed in heavy support hose, above black high-top sneakers. I pulled in my feet and strained against an agony of apprehension.

The woman grunted something in an unknown language and the vacuum started to retreat. It moved back out to the hall. Then the emptied wastebasket dropped to the floor, the chair was pulled back in place, and a second later, it was dark again.

I stayed under the desk, feeling my legs go numb from lack of circulation, until well after the light along the bottom of the door flicked out.

Only then did I start to breathe normally and begin to appreciate just how undignified my position was. It made me smile inside, not because I could make fun of myself, but because I cared so little about what constituted proper dignity.

The episode did serve to distract me from the tedium of the download, long enough for it to have run its course. I checked the files on the external hard drive to make sure I had everything, then moved on to the final task of the night.

It was a long shot, but if Finger was anything like most top executives, he had little regard for proper computer security at the personal level. I opened up Microsoft Word and started searching, beginning with "password." The word itself appeared in dozens of documents, but without any specific codes. I moved on to other possibilities, such as systems administrator or just plain administrator. Lots of mentions within documents, but no passwords. I began to compliment Bruce's good behavior when a search for "Important Agency Numbers" brought up a remarkable document. It was a single double-space page listing the access codes and test questions for all the agency's online banking, payroll service, group medical, 401(k), the premium trust account (a holding pen to manage the flow of client money through the agency and out to the carriers) and investment accounts at two brokerage houses. And right there, near the bottom of the page, under the heading, "In case Ethan gets hit by a bus," the administrator username and password. The keys to the realm.

I printed out the document to Bruce's private printer, shut down the computer and removed the boot disk and external drive. I followed the dark hall down to the temperature-controlled room where I'd installed the servers that lived at the heart of the agency's automated systems. As hoped, the administrator's workstation that I set up was still there, and likely still the subject of daily check-ins. I turned on the computer, logged in and went to a place called the domain controller. This is where every employee, laptop or external computer authorized to connect from the outside was logged and labeled with their own security code. I was pleased to see Administrator One and Administrator Two listed, me being Administrator One with my access rights turned off. All I had to do was switch them back on and provide a new password. It felt unlikely a guy like Ethan, lazy enough to leave most of my original ID intact, even providing a new username, would have the presence of mind to notice a subtle change within such a large field of data.

I had one more change, also well disguised amidst the rows of names and numbers — the registration of my laptop as an authentic workstation. This gave it a name and security ID that would allow me to log in to the network and connect to any computer from a remote location.

After that last alteration to the active directory, I inserted a little flash drive into the USB port and downloaded a different, but related piece of treacherous code.

Going by the rather banal name of monitoring software, the application would record everything the administrator did on his computer, every keystroke he made, every email that went in or out, every application opened and every server managed. And most importantly, every password typed into every log-in dialog box. Without him ever knowing it was taking place.

More than a nuisance spyware virus, this one lived deep in the nether regions of the operating system, quietly and innocuously going about its business of reporting everything to the PC at my little house. Virtually undetectable as long as no one thought there was something malevolent in the system in need of detection.

When the program was installed and the initiating command established, I pulled out the flash drive and shut down the computer.

I walked out of the agency with the entire operation in my pocket, past and present, with a direct feed into all that would happen in the future. A decent harvest of information, and only my nervous system the worse for wear.

CHAPTER 13

The next morning a little alert from my computer woke me up as it often did. It was telling me that the agency's system administrator had logged on. I watched with oddly little satisfaction as he ran through a series of checks on the agency's servers. I turned away and let the spyware carry on with its relentless surveillance.

After showering and eating a breakfast of yogurt and granola, I went clothes shopping. This was something I truly knew nothing about, having been an awkward geek my entire life, a status that thoroughly excluded any gift for sartorial aplomb.

I was on the hunt for two types of outfits. One casual, yet sophisticated, the other baldly pretentious and predatory, extravagantly expensive, yet in a way that only the fashion cognoscenti would know.

So it was no charade for me to walk into a small shop in Westport that stank of wool, silk and leather, and completely give myself over to the predacious attentions of a tiny white-haired man named Preston Nestor.

"Imagine a roomful of investment bankers who can also claim advanced degrees in classical languages and ancestry back to the Mayflower. No one is better, nor more appropriately, dressed than I," was basically how I put in my order. "Two versions."

"So that would be two shades of grey," said Nestor.

"If you say so."

Having set clearly defined criteria, the process was fairly brief and efficient, especially after I told him not to bother describing the clothing's physical properties and pedigrees. He wasn't offended. Armed with precise measurements of my body, we moved from custom-made to off-the-rack casual wear and accessories. I accepted every recommendation and rationale, in whole cloth if you will, with the exception of a yellow cashmere sweater.

"It'll be too distracting," I told him, "and I'll probably end up dribbling Coquilles St. Jacques down the front."

A little over two hours later I left the store with the only items not in need of fitting and tailoring, and a renewed appreciation for the power of pretension in the confiscatory pricing of luxury goods.

It was time to sell a few more guitars.

I drove to a music store in South Norwalk I'd noted back when I was stalking Madame Francine de le Croix. It was a small shop, but the window was filled with vintage instruments, and thus an ideal prospect. I always carried in my back pocket descriptions of select items in the inventory, just in case an opportunity arose. So I entered the shop prepared.

A balding man with a curly black and grey beard looked to be in a death struggle with a floor stand for some sort of electronic keyboard.

"The perfect road rig for the piano-playing PhD in mechanical engineering," he said, without looking up from within a contortion of black metal tubing.

"This is why I never bother with assembly instructions," I said.

He looked up at me.

"What can I do you out of?" he asked.

"Vintage guitars. Wife says to cut down on the collection."

He picked up a piece of the floor stand, then used two hands to toss it on the floor.

"Assemble thyself," he said to the black tangle.

We retired to a desk at the back of the

shop. He pulled a chair up for me and introduced himself.

"Aloysius Cooper," he said. "I prefer Al. Not the famous one."

I handed him the sheet describing five very different guitars, from an exotic clear plastic Danelectro to an early twentieth-century Martin acoustic.

"Pretty eclectic," he said. "You looking for consignment?"

"Straight purchase," I said.

"I'm running a store here," he said. "I gotta have some margin."

"Generous terms," I said. "Especially on cash sales. Just not stupid."

There was a well-thumbed copy of the Elderly Instruments catalog on his desk. I waited quietly while he looked up current pricing ranges for each of the guitars.

"Wait here," he said, getting up from his desk chair and disappearing into the back room. It wasn't hard to imagine a phone call to a collector to arrange a little pre-sell. I'd seen it before. He came back ten minutes later.

"The Les Paul and pre-war Martin," he said, noting the two most expensive guitars on the list. "Let the haggling begin."

After telling me he wouldn't insult me with a lowball offer, he tossed a ball whose elevation barely cleared the ground. I explained I had plenty of other options, and had only stopped by because I was in the neighborhood, and thought he might help expand my distribution. He noted the declining state of the vintage guitar market, about which I expressed some sympathy, while pointing out that we'd only just crested the peak. This genial thrust and parry went on for another ten minutes, after which I was ready to shake hands and depart friends, when he floated a respectable range for each instrument.

"Depending on condition," he added.

"I'll be back this afternoon," I told him, and left.

The drive up to Danbury and back was uneventful and almost unnoticed by me, as I was utterly absorbed in my thoughts, fueled by a growing anxiety over Austin Ott, III. He was teaching me my limitations, a check on over-confidence after the encounters with Sebbie Frondutti, Fred Tootsie and Pally Buttons. Contributing to the feeling was his M.O. — an intermediary between clients and field men, brokering rather than executing. It suggested excessive caution, or paranoia, or both. And thus a far more elusive quarry.

This clinched my decision to draw in

Shelly Gross. Risky, but essential to forward motion. Shelly could do things I couldn't do, even in retirement. He still had plenty of relationships that could give access to official channels and police prerogatives, and if I properly read his personality, he was bored and ripe to be drawn back into the game.

When I returned to the music shop, the keyboard and its unruly floor stand had disappeared. In its place were two stools and two guitar stands, as if waiting for a pair of performers to arrive.

I set the guitar cases on the counter and opened them up. He snatched up the Martin and looked inside the sound hole.

"Son of a bitch," he said. "Welcome home." He looked at me. "This is my guitar. Was my guitar."

"Really."

"I sold it to Gerry Charles. How is that old wood freak?"

I knew I was better than most at keeping my emotional state from leaking into the observable world, but this time the shock of the unexpected showed.

"What's the matter?" said Cooper. "Is he okay?"

"Don't know him," I said. "I bought it online. Never checked the provenance."

"Don't worry about it," he said, putting his hand on my shoulder. "I never do either. Not the first time one of my chicks has come home to roost."

Self-recrimination took the place of alarm. I should have anticipated that happening. Gerry had been a serious collector in the area for decades. He probably knew every dealer. A nauseating sense of vulnerability surged through me, somehow conflating with my fears over Jason Three Sticks. The room tilted, and I sat down in one of the performance chairs before I fell over. My heart began to race, and I nearly asked Cooper for a paper bag to breathe into.

"Sorry. I'm still recovering from an injury," I said, using the easiest and least challengeable cover.

"Sure. Take your time."

While I sat in frustrated examination of my sudden failing, Cooper went over the two guitars, playing a lively bluegrass riff on the Martin and the opening bars of "Smoke on the Water" on the Les Paul.

"You never go wrong with the classics," he said, before throwing out a number for both. I bumped it up to where it belonged. "Okay," said Cooper, "can't blame a guy for trying."

He went to the bank, which was a block

away, leaving me in charge of the store. Luckily no one came in, giving me time to compose myself. Evelyn had predicted lapses in cognitive acuity and sudden mood swings, most of which I'd avoided, especially in recent weeks. It was a reminder that I still had a functioning brain, though it wasn't entirely the same brain I used to have.

When Cooper got back to the store, he handed me a fat white envelope, insisting that I count it while he watched. It was all there.

"I do love that old Martin," he said. "Maybe explains why it came back to me. The prodigal dreadnaught."

It wasn't until I was back in the Subaru that I felt the world reassemble itself into its former, mildly distorted state. I breathed slow, deep breaths, bringing down my pulse and easing the clenched muscles in my neck and upper back.

"You're not a machine," I could hear Evelyn telling me, the day before I left her house, "you're a human being. It takes strength to understand your weaknesses. Not to capitulate, but to cope."

I felt again the gratitude and defiance her words engendered, and then I coped the only way I knew how.

I threw myself into my work.

Before leaving Norwalk, I stopped at a deli and bought a copy of the *New York Times.* It was the first day Shelly had a chance to place an ad in the classifieds. And there it was.

"1965 Mustang convertible, four-speed, 289, insanely clean and meticulously maintained, sold to the best offer with assurances it will annoy your wife as much as it does mine. Call now. Car goes off the market in two days."

He included his phone number in Rocky Hill. I bought another disposable cell phone and drove down I-95 toward New Haven. I called him as I went through Bridgeport.

"Shelly Gross," he answered.

"I have zero interest in that Mustang," I said in my Clint Eastwood voice.

"So that's not why you're calling."

"I'd like to have a conversation, but I don't know how to do it safely."

I got off the highway and drove toward the harbor, winding my way toward the dock area where they built icebreakers and mega yachts.

"You could trust me," he said.

"I can't. Not yet."

"We appreciate the tip on Sebbie. I'd like to know how you did it."

"Some people are mind readers. Do you know Austin Ott, the Third?"

"Not personally. Do I know you?"

"You might," I said. "What are the chances you could just tell me where he lives?"

"About the same as you inviting me over to dinner."

"I just need a hint. Point me in the right direction."

"What do I get in return?"

"You get him, and the evidence for a conviction. And maybe a few of his fellow rats in the bargain."

"Why don't we just team up?" he asked. "Why all the cloak and dagger?"

"Personal preference. I was hoping to avoid a Mexican standoff."

"I can't discuss this over the phone."

"Okay," I said, and hung up. By now I was standing at the top of a breakwater holding a piece of brick I found by the side of the road. I used duct tape to attach it to the disposable phone, then dropped it in the harbor.

As a way of celebrating my unwanted bout of disorienting paranoia, I decided to do something guaranteed to engender more of the same. I drove across the state to Clear Waters Casino to visit Natsumi Fitzgerald at her blackjack table.

"Hey, mister," she said as I sat down. "You're back."

"I am," I said, and that was all the conversation we had until I won enough to encourage my table mates to find their luck somewhere else.

"So, was that guy your old friend?" she asked.

I shook my head.

"Didn't look like him at all. Sorry for the trouble."

"No trouble."

"I'm not ready to go back to work anyway," I said. "I have another month of disability, I should take my time."

"Still getting over that beer? You drank the whole thing."

"The wages of sin. I'm thinking of having another one tonight. Build up my immunity."

"I have to study," she said.

"Of course. You should do that."

"I have to study some time. Not necessarily tonight. What do you know about Münchausen syndrome by proxy?"

"Sounds complicated."

"It's the subject of my term paper. If we

talk about it, I can deduct the time from my study budget."

"We've done the Sail Inn. Where else would you suggest?"

She picked a spot in Groton favored by submarine workers from Electric Boat and rarely patronized by casino people.

"They make a lot more money, so the tips and wait staff are better," she said. She gave me the name and address. "I'll meet you there in about an hour, okay?"

For the first time since waking from the coma, I was on a mission with no hope of furthering my objectives. That in fact, might even threaten the initiative itself. There was absolutely nothing, based on logic and reason, that could justify this impulse.

Except that I was lonely.

This does not deserve complex analysis, I said to myself. She's an attractive young woman. She's flirting with you. You're not a machine, I could hear Evelyn say, you're a human being. Accept your humanity.

Which didn't mean I missed my dead wife any less. If anything, the time with Natsumi had driven that repressed ache to the surface. As if the pain and the palliative were one and the same.

These thoughts were still fresh in my mind when Natsumi slid into the booth across

213

from me at the restaurant in Groton, which likely explained my first words to her.

"That day I was injured," I said to her, "my wife was killed."

She folded her hands on top of the table and bowed her head.

"I thought there was something like that," she said. "I'm sorry."

"I'm still not myself. In fact, I'm not sure what I mean by 'myself.' I'm different from how I was before, but I'm not sure in what ways. I'm discovering as I go. So it's not surprising if you think me a little odd."

"Not odd. Just inscrutable."

We drifted off from there into a meandering conversation with no references to either of our pasts. And though potentially sensitive areas were left untrodden, I felt that a basis for a legitimate friendship had been established — in defiance of my trepidation — yielding to the need for simple company with a kindred soul whose only motive was precisely the same thing.

The next day I began to stalk Shelly Gross. I'd been cautious when chasing down the hoods, but I'd imagined Shelly to be far more watchful and vigilant. A wily old G-man with eyes behind his head and prescience crackling through his nerves. I had no particular basis for this romanticization, but it was good discipline to pretend I did, especially given the recent lapses and cautionary moments.

This is why I only drove by his house twice — once in daylight to get a photo of his across-the-street neighbor, and again at night to stick a remote, battery-powered webcam under the neighbor's yew.

The camera was originally designed to capture wildlife. It was remotely controlled and only switched on when a passing creature triggered a motion detector. Camouflaged, weatherproof and rechargeable by the sun, I hoped it would survive long enough to get a fix on Shelly's patterned movements before his neighbor peered under the bush or an errant ray of sunshine lit up the lens.

The wireless signal from the camera was picked up by a video receiver hidden within a tangle of roadside brush several blocks away. The receiver uploaded to an Internet service that asked for very little in the way of identification beyond a credit card number. This was still an exposure, even though I'd acquired one for the exclusive purpose. The card was issued to Alex Rimes, but the address was an empty storefront in Bridgeport, Connecticut. Again, not perfect, but

215

probably good enough.

The next two weeks featured a satisfying tedium. Through most of the days and nights I re-familiarized myself with the insurance agency's finances and operations. It helped that I was the one who set up the folder structure and files, and the day-to-day bookkeeping, including how every transaction was tied back to the general ledger. I eventually discovered that I'd missed some important blocks of data from Bruce Finger's computer, but that was easily remedied by logging in as Administrator One and helping myself. This I only did late at night as a mild precaution when the activity logs rarely saw anyone else on the network. Many would find this activity a brutal slog, but even with my compromised quantitative skills, I felt tremendous comfort in the presence of long columns of numbers and the puzzle-solving reconciliation that was inherent in double-entry accounting.

It was little wonder that Elliot Brandt was eager to close a deal. Florencia ran an unadventurous but profitable little ship — disciplined, orderly and strictly adherent to the most conservative interpretation of generally accepted accounting principles.

"My goal is to bore the auditors to tears," I remember her saying.

This happy work was often interrupted by alerts from the webcam that there was activity at Shelly's house. I was able to review the video, which was time stamped, and either go live or let it slip back into standby. After two weeks, I'd harvested a lot of information on Shelly's comings and goings.

As important, I got a good look at Shelly himself, a short, fit, white-haired guy who moved very briskly for a sixty-eight-year-old. He always wore running shoes, and lighter outerwear than the increasingly cold weather should have called for. He drove a late-model, silver Chevy Malibu.

Every evening, seven days a week, he left the house at six-thirty carrying a gym bag, returning exactly three and a half hours later. I made a study of the health clubs in the area, choosing one that offered a discount to Rocky Hill residents, that was well-equipped and within easy driving distance. I drove there and parked in the lot near the entrance and waited with a newspaper conspicuously open on the steering wheel.

At the predicted time, Shelly arrived and parked in a slot within eyeshot of where I was waiting. I recorded his location, and after he left the car, I left the lot. I came back a half hour before his estimated departure, but he was already gone.

I repeated the process the next night, returning with an hour to spare. Shelly's car was still there, so I waited again. He came out soon after and drove off. I tailed him as long as I dared, finally turning into a shopping strip and pretending to use a drive-up ATM.

Over the next several nights I used rented cars to pick up the hunt further down the trail each time, until he finally led me to his destination — a homey-looking bar and grill in Old Wethersfield called the Powder Keg.

I went home to more financial study, waiting until two nights had passed before going to the next step. I also used the time altering my appearance into something both natural and easy to maintain, yet still transformative. This began with growing out my beard, which surprised me by displaying a fair amount of grey. I had to buy a new wig to match, one long enough to sprout out from beneath a baseball cap. I also put in some time at a tanning salon, then further darkened my skin with some cream out of the makeup kit.

The crowning touch was a pair of color-altering contact lenses, a deep brown that completely disguised my natural hazel.

Even given my overestimation of Shelly's

perceptive powers, I thought I looked thoroughly disguised, and not merely a darker, more hirsute version of myself.

I picked a Tuesday night, when restaurants were neither too busy, nor too empty. Old Wethersfield was an ancient American suburb, and the inside of the Powder Keg was eager to uphold that status, deploying Revolutionary War armaments, including muskets lining the walls and a full-sized cannon, as the decorating motif. In keeping, it was a dark place with lots of weathered wood and phony lanterns barely penetrating the gloom. The brightest spot was the bar, discreetly set off in a room of its own. It was just big enough for the bar itself, with a narrow aisle, and a row of wooden, high-backed booths, one of which contained Shelly Gross eating his meal and drinking a tall glass of draft beer.

I sat down across from him.

"Do you still have that Mustang?" I asked.

He looked up from his plate but continued to cut into a cheeseburger that he'd ordered without the convenience of a bun.

"You didn't read the ad very carefully," he said. "It's off the market."

Shelly had a narrow, pinkish face with an aquiline nose and close-set eyes. His full head of white hair was on the long side, suggesting a hint of vanity. His eyes were grey-gold, not unlike my own natural color, and also likely fitted with contacts, since he didn't wear glasses.

"That's what negotiations are for," I said.

"What are we negotiating?"

"Continued post-career success for Shelly Gross."

"I've already had plenty of success."

"Partly thanks to me. And if you don't care about that, do it for the general well-being of society."

"Vigilantes aren't good for society," he said. "It's one of the first things you learn."

"Then call it a public-private partnership. You set the rules."

"How do I know you'll follow them?" he asked.

"Every successful partnership is built on trust. I didn't have to hand you Frondutti."

"That was your choice, not my request."

"This is not a good negotiating technique," I said. "It won't yield results."

"What technique?"

"Playing hard to get. Pretending you aren't interested in what I have to offer, thinking that will cause me to turn supplicant, giving up more than I want just to earn your acceptance. I don't care that much about your acceptance, and you're not my only option. I picked you because of your record in Connecticut, but you have successors, and they're still on the job."

He took another bite of his burger.

"So what technique would you suggest?"

"Give me something. A crumb. I don't need much."

"So why me?" he asked. "Like you said, I'm not even on the job."

"Right. Which means you have more time to focus on the project. And you probably know more about the people I'm looking for than any current agent. And you're keeping yourself in great physical shape. What, so you don't get tired pushing the buttons on the remote while sitting by yourself in the living room?"

He pointed at me with his fork.

"Don't get personal," he said. *"That* doesn't work with *me."*

"Yes, it does. That's the first honest thing you've said."

He went back to his meal, this time with his eyes cast down at his plate. A waitress finally realized he had a booth mate and came over to take my order. I asked her to bring me whatever he was having.

"You won't blame me if I wonder just who the hell you are," he said, finally.

"I won't blame you for trying like hell to

find out. But I'd rather you put that time and energy into helping me find Jason Three Sticks. He might not be the most wanted man in this area, but I bet he's the most elusive. What do you got to lose?"

He finished off his beer as mine was arriving, but didn't order a second.

"He's in Connecticut," he said. "Somewhere in Fairfield County, though his operations spread across the whole Northeast. He's gone by a variety of aliases over the years, Austin Ott is only the most recent. Contract murder is a featured product, but he's into a lot of other things, what the Bureau quaintly calls criminal enterprises. Hijacking, prostitution, cyber-fraud, money laundering. Not as a principal, but as a backer. This guy is at the top of the region's crime syndicates, and has at least two or three layers of security between him and the action. That's expensive and time-consuming to maintain, but it's working for him. Don't let the fancy name fool you. This guy's as evil and merciless as the worst of the lowlifes he deals with."

He waved the waitress back over and asked for his check, with my beer thrown in.

"That's all you know?" I asked.

"No. That's all I'm telling you. Bring me

something I don't know and we'll see from there."

We sat in silence as the waitress cleared the table and went through the credit card ritual. I worked slowly on my beer. He took a newspaper out of his pocket folded to the crossword puzzle.

"I usually do these before I head home. Go ahead and finish your beer," he said.

"No, you don't. You do them when you get home," I said, standing up and walking out of the restaurant with the beer in hand, my fingerprints and DNA still within my sole proprietorship.

On the way home, I retrieved the video transmitter, assuming Shelly would waste little time discovering the camera across the street, which I left with the serial number scratched out. I imagined him setting up a camera of his own, hoping to catch me pulling mine out of the bush. His friends at the Bureau would tell him about the transmitter, and probably try to track it down in order to follow the signal back to me. Or maybe he'd assume I'm smart enough to stay ahead of them and not bother with any of that.

"Big assumption," I said out loud. "Don't start making it yourself."

CHAPTER 14

"They want to give us $8.6 million, with twenty percent held in escrow for a year as a reserve against undisclosed liabilities, meaning things they didn't catch during due diligence," said Evelyn over the phone the next day. "It's a lot of money, Arthur."

"What does Bruce think?"

"He gave me a four hour lecture on all the pros, cons, considerations and ramifications. He's my counselor, that's his job. Net, net, he thinks I'd be crazy not to say yes."

"Of course you'd be."

"But it's your agency," she said. "It isn't up to me."

I'd never thought of the agency as anything other than the place Florencia went to work every day. By law, shared property, but never in my mind. It was all hers to benefit from in any way she saw fit. Its ultimate disposition so remote a prospect, the topic was never broached even in the vaguest terms. Even now, fully accepting that Florencia was gone forever, I couldn't separate her business from her corporeal being, as if a part of her lived on.

"It's surprisingly hard for me to let it go," I said.

"They want an answer in a week. I don't know if I can stall beyond that. But I'll do whatever you want."

I looked over at my computer. It was alerting me that Ethan, the administrator at the agency, was logging into the system. It presented an interesting quandary. Technically, I owned the place, so stealing all that data and maintaining surveillance over the operations wasn't illegal. That would all change as soon as possession changed hands. At least in the matter of the spyware. On the other hand, would they bother to tack corporate espionage on to identity theft and document forgery, to say nothing of kidnapping and torture? I'd already chosen my path. There was no point in splitting hairs.

"Give it a day and say yes. Just be sure Bruce hires an experienced M&A attorney. Brandt's not naïve. He's only throwing you a big number to guarantee he closes the deal. For his kid's sake."

"The money will be waiting for you," said

Evelyn. "And don't tell me you're not coming back. If I think that, I'm not sure I can keep doing this."

I had no response to that, so I wrapped up the call with a cornball joke from our childhood, and when she laughed, she became a co-conspirator in the deflection. There was nothing else we could do.

I wanted to sneak up on Henry Eichenbach the way I did with Shelly Gross, but that proved a challenge. No addresses for Henry, past or present, showed up anywhere, and no phone numbers were listed on any public database. Google gave up dozens of bylined articles, but that was it. Most of the articles, including the most recent, were run by his former employer, the *Connecticut Post*. The editor was a woman named Marion Bertz, who'd been in the job since the mid-nineties.

I bought two more disposable cell phones and sent one to Ms. Bertz with a note asking her to forward it on to Henry. I signed the note, "A Confidential Source." I'd pre-programmed the phone with the number for the other disposable. It only took a few hours for him to call.

"I'd like to have another conversation," I told him.

"Sure. It's been lonely lately. I miss our old times sitting by Long Island Sound."

"That's not a good idea. Here's what we do," I said, then told him the plan.

"Pretty James Bondy," he said when I was done.

"Interesting perspective for a guy who's erased from the Internet all evidence of his existence."

"I'm big on privacy."

"Use the clock on your cell phone. It's the most likely to be synchronized with mine."

After hanging up, I spent the remainder of the day on basic research and my appearance, trying hard to match the last getup I'd exposed to Henry, which was unfortunately my first attempt and thus the most amateurish.

After night fell, I left the house in a rental car left over from stalking Shelly Gross. It was so innocuous I had to check the rental receipt to confirm it was a type of Hyundai. Not that it mattered. It drove well and suited the purpose.

During one of my general explorations, I'd identified restaurants and bars in the area that had restrooms and rear exits in close proximity. The one I'd selected that night was by far the best, a dive bar in Stamford with the men's room only a few feet from a door that led to a parking lot connected to the street behind. It didn't seem feasible that the police or FBI would have Henry followed merely on the basis of a barely believable story of an anonymous character who'd singlehandedly tracked down a notorious fugitive. But I couldn't know everything, and there was no reason to risk it when I could take a simple precaution.

Though no precaution could protect me should Henry decide to betray me to the cops; there was nothing I could do about that. I didn't necessarily trust him, but I trusted his professional self-interest and journalistic pride.

Enough to take the chance.

As I waited in the parking lot, I visualized Henry getting off the barstool, leaving a half-consumed beer and enough cash on the bar to cover his tab. I saw him walking down the narrow hallway past the women's room to the men's, opening the door so it blocked the view to the back of the hall, then strolling out to the rear parking lot. I was already moving when the door opened and he stepped out, so it only took a few seconds to snatch him up and disappear into the night.

"I'm going to be really irritated if this is a

hit," he said, pulling on his seat belt.

"Hadn't occurred to me. Should it?"

"Ha-ha. No way I'm giving you up, pal. Way too much fun. A name would be nice, though."

"Peabody will do."

I flipped the lights on when I reached the end of the block and dove deep into the labyrinthine streets of outer Stamford. No one was following, as far as I could tell.

"I'm screaming along with this big piece on the Eyeball. I'm grateful, I admit it. I told Shelly I'd embargo it until his old outfit was done interrogating the creepy old bastard, or after four weeks, whichever came first. I need the time anyway to gin up the advance. I'm hoping the *Times* will like it, though they got a hard-on about anything Connecticut. Spent too much time in grad school jerking off to John Cheever. Mansion-envy is my interpretation, though if they ever dragged their precious asses out of the city I'd show 'em around some of the rat-hole neighborhoods in Bridgeport. Makes Bedford-Stuy look like the Botanical Gardens."

"What do you know about Austin Ott, the Third?" I asked.

"Whoa, quick left without a turn signal. Three Sticks? What do you want to know?"

229

"Everything."

"That's too bad, because nobody knows anything. Compared to Three Sticks, Sebbie Frondutti's been living in Macy's window. I'm not entirely sure he's a real person, if you want to know the truth. Criminals are just as likely to create myths as regular civilians. Maybe more so."

"That's okay. I need to know, one way or the other."

Henry shifted his bulk around the passenger seat, causing a faint sway in the ride. I used the GPS in my smartphone to get back on to a major commercial strip along Route One to look for a place to stop.

"What's the plan, Stan?" he asked.

"Burgers and beer."

"Those are the two things in the world with which I am most familiar. If we can find a game on, it'll be a trifecta."

We did find all three not soon after, and once ensconced at the end of the bar with the array before him, Henry nearly glowed with contentment.

"I can tell you, without reservation," he said, biting down on a giant wad of beef that leaked condiments back on to the plate, "that none of my other confidential sources ever showed this level of generosity. Though don't expect special consideration. Okay, maybe a little."

I let him gorge for a while, then asked, "Who's the new Sebbie?"

"Say what?"

"Who's the most serious organized crime figure in Connecticut not currently in jail?"

"You're asking me? I should be asking you."

"I wouldn't know the answer. I've researched it on Google, but I need greater certainty."

He kept his eyes on me while taking the last bite of his burger, chased down with the beer.

"I would surely love to know what your story is," he said.

"Give me another name," I said. "It worked out for you last time. It might again."

"Unless you believe in fairy tales like this guy Ott, the best candidate for local boss would be Ekrem Boyanov, in my not-so-humble opinion. He and his organization got forced out of Bosnia during the war. They call him Little Boy. Works out of the South End of Hartford, where a lot of Bosniaks are taking over the old Italian neighborhoods, appropriately enough. I haven't done much on him, which is probably smart. I don't think guys from that part of the world have the same respectful regard for the Fourth Estate that we've enjoyed with our traditional Mediterranean professionals."

I remembered that name from my research on Sebbie Frondutti. There was little about him in the press, which spoke to his success in evading unwanted attention. I noted that to Henry.

"Sure, he's not only scary, he's good. The gang is into all the usual things, drugs, girls, chia pets. Kidding. Extortion, rackets, probably grand larceny — boosting stuff out of warehouses, hijacking trucks full of booze and cigarettes. I don't know if they're techy enough for cyber-crime, but it wouldn't surprise me. They must love it here. Land of opportunity."

I bought him another beer and told him about my encounter with Shelly Gross, without going into details.

"He might want to talk to you again," I said. "And it's not beyond the realm of possibility that they'll be keeping an eye on you."

"Hence the out-the-back-door routine."

"Should make sense to a paranoid like you."

"Just because you're paranoid doesn't mean people aren't out to get you," he said, clinking my water glass with his beer mug.

An hour later, I dropped him off at another parking lot near the bar where I'd picked him up. I thanked him for the tip.

"I would truly love to know what the fuck your story is," he said, after opening the car door.

"Understandable for a reporter," I said. "But do us both a favor and concentrate on someone else."

"That kind of talk always makes me try harder," he said, getting out of the car.

I waited until he made it to the street and disappeared around the corner, then I drove back to my house, resisting the urge to check my rearview mirror every thirty seconds and mulling a theme of the evening: where is the line between paranoia and precaution?

If you want to evade an Internet search engine, have a name like John Smith, not Ekrem Boyanov. In a few seconds I had his address off Franklin Avenue in the South End of Hartford, and a home phone number. His profession was listed as stonemason, and he had a wife and two kids. There wasn't much else in the public record. He had one criminal charge, for allegedly stealing some heavy equipment off a construction site, but the case was dropped for lack of evidence. When he was arrested, some in the Bosniak community spoke with alarm about possible police persecution, a charge the leadership, and the police themselves, vehemently denied.

Nevertheless, Little Boy's name did pop up a few times on lists of notable Connecticut underworld figures, and in a memo from Shelly's old outfit leaked to the *Hartford Courant.* The question was whether they had enough on Boyanov to launch deportation proceedings, deciding later they didn't, especially given his status as a political refugee. Again, a robust defense by community spokespeople also played a part, raising the potential for some nasty PR for the State's Attorney. The writer of the memo noted that Little Boy never inflicted his illicit activities on his fellow Bosniaks, an opinion that in effect caused some of the bad PR they hoped to avoid.

I spent the next three days deep in the convivial land of Internet research. And though I almost believed there was nothing you couldn't learn online, it took until the third day to settle on the right strategic vehicle.

A food truck called "Grub On The Go."

It was owned by a man named Billy Romano, who expressed a keen interest in selling the business so he could move to Florida and fulfill his wife's lifelong dream, if not his own. He went on to note, that the reasonable cost of the truck and nonperishable inventory was just the beginning. The real value was in the route, earned over many years of intense competition and negotiation with some of the biggest manufacturing operations in the Greater Hartford area.

I had to agree, though I didn't drop for the first price he put on the table when I called him on his cell phone.

"Sorry, bub," he said, after hearing my number. "We got to do better than that. Florida real estate ain't that cheap."

"I haven't seen the truck," I said.

"The truck's mint. But that don't matter. It's the route you're buyin'."

We batted the ball back and forth a few more times, and I finally settled on a price contingent on inspection of the vehicle. We set a time and place to meet.

I wrote Evelyn and asked her to wire the money to one of my accounts, with promises to explain when I got the chance. Then I packed a duffle bag, filled up the Outback

with boxes of electronics and drove to Hartford.

I'd been to Hartford frequently enough to
have a general idea of the layout. The city
itself was a tight cluster of office buildings
surrounded by mostly poor African-
American and Hispanic neighborhoods.
Across the Connecticut River was working-
class East Hartford. West Hartford was
principally an affluent reserve, though along
the border with the city there were several
blocks of wood frame, multi-family housing.

I headed there first.

Two of the apartments had either too
many stairs, or not enough parking to accommodate the Outback and the food
truck. A third was close, but a kid on the
first floor was practicing a tortured rendition of "Foxy Lady." The rental agent forced
a smile and we moved on.

The fourth stop was an ordinary house
with a grandmother apartment above the
garage in the back. There was plenty of
parking, with a small, privately-owned
convenience store — what in New York
you'd call a bodega — within easy walking
distance. The apartment had two bedrooms,
one of which I could use for the computers.
The agent warned me it was a little over my

budget, but she knew I'd like it. Thus explaining why it was the last one we saw.

She confirmed that one of the garage bays was available, though for another hundred bucks a month. I wrote her a check for the security deposit and six months in advance. She looked at me like I'd swindled her.

"There are some even nicer places on the other side of Farmington Avenue," she said, hopefully.

"This'll do."

I'd already moved in the computer equipment and miscellaneous gadgets, unpacked my growing wardrobe and filled out a shopping list when someone knocked at the door. It was a short woman, swarthy and broad of beam. She stuck out her hand.

"I'm Louisa Colon-Cordero, the owner of this little house."

"I'm Alex Rimes," I said, taking her hand. "The happy renter of this little house."

"I want no noise, no crazy parties, no trouble requiring the police," she said. "The rental people tell me not to say this, but I think it's good to lay down the rules of the road."

"I want the same thing. I hope you will honor my wishes," I said to her in Spanish.

She looked confused, then lit up with a smile that seemed to extend past her face.

"Very good joke," she said in English. "We will be fine."

"I only know Castilian."

"My father was a professor of biology," she said in Spanish, struggling to maintain proper Castilian usage and inflection. "We had many fine people from Spain in our home. My grandfather rode a white horse in the Mexican Revolution," she added, probably out of habit. "He brought it over from Spain. In a boat. He owned a ranch, but gave it to the people. This is the type of people my family have been. It's too bad Marcelino, my husband, was so jealous of them. He died unhappy. Leaving me this house," she added, with a sweep of her hand, as if to both define and celebrate her good fortune, despite the intervention of great tragedy.

I thanked her again for the privilege of renting her little apartment, the charm and cleanliness of which she spared no effort to go unacknowledged, after which she left me, reluctantly it seemed, her proclaimed defense of my privacy notwithstanding.

Señora Colon-Cordero's pride in her apartment was justified; it was a very charming and comfortable place. Especially after months of subsistence accommodation, I couldn't help but notice. I wondered what

238

that meant — if I was getting healthier, or simply more alert to my surroundings.

Either way, I didn't care. I had things to do.

Billy Romano was true to his word. The truck and onboard equipment was in perfect condition. Every surface was sparkling clean and the cab was like a cozy living room.

Billy himself was just as tidy. Short, well put together and defiant.

"So what did you think," he said, for no good reason, "a piece of crap, right?"

"I never thought that," I said. "I'm not thinking that now."

He was only partially satisfied with my answer. Trust was likely hard-earned with Billy.

"Okay, so what else do you need to know?"

I asked about the route and permissions from the various manufacturing outfits and construction sites. He pulled an iPad out from where it was tucked into his belt and swished his fingers over the touch pad. Then he held up an Excel document.

"It's all here," he said. "Read at will."

As he said, all the routes, addresses, arrivals and departures, the names and birthdays of security people — a complete dossier elegantly laid out on a series of spreadsheets.

"Didn't expect that from a dumb gumba, eh?" he asked. "I've got a degree in accounting. Tried it for a few years, hated getting stuck behind a desk. Plus I'm a people person. The kind of interaction you get when you're auditing somebody's books isn't what I'm lookin' for."

"I never make assumptions about people. Unlike what you're doing with me right now," I said, in as light a way as I could.

He smiled at that.

"Touché. Which leads me to ask, if you don't mind, why the interest in this business?"

"I also hate being stuck behind a desk. I'm not a people person, but I'm very polite."

From there we did a little more gratuitous haggling, and eventually came up with a figure we could agree on. Though he tried to hide it, Billy looked happier and happier as things progressed.

"It's physical work," he said. "Just so you know. In and outta the truck, tossing donuts and sandwiches around, pouring coffee. And all the time talkin' it up with the customers. There're a lotta sites, and you're competing with other trucks. You can't be a surly asshole and go alienating people, no matter what you're feeling at the time."

He spent another hour sharing tricks of the trade, eventually drifting into oft-told anecdotes, which I listened to just as carefully. As a researcher, I knew this is where some of the most valuable information was revealed.

"So, Collingsworth Machine Tool and Metals Company. The security must be pretty tough," I said.

He made a sour face.

"Tough? There's more gold stored there than they got at Fort Knox. But once you're in, like me, it's no biggy."

"So no background checks."

He looked at me with a careful eye.

"Got a few skeletons in the closet?" he asked.

"Something like that."

He shrugged.

"Don't we all. No, no background checks for the roach coaches. We never get past the parking lot."

Not long after, we settled on a time and place to make the transfer, and by then Billy had evolved beyond hostility to outright bonhomie.

"Hey, you wanna go get a drink?" he asked. "Celebrate the beginning of your new life?"

I demurred, citing an AA pledge and a

commitment to early bedtime. He honored my choice.

"I respect that, man. You're a man of integrity. Serve you well in the food truck industry."

We parted in a fog of mutual good will.

CHAPTER 15

I spent most of that night working out money transfers with Evelyn, researching the various industrial plants served by "Grub On The Go," and reading up on food truck cuisine.

I wasn't much of a cook, always deferring to Florencia, the daughter of Chilean political refugees who were also passionate gourmets. But this didn't look all that hard. Strategic procurement was the most important ingredient, and coffee the prime mover.

As part of the deal, Billy Romano rode with me for a few days, showing me where to park and introducing me to people. It was brisk work, but manageable. The biggest challenge was making change, greatly facilitated by the use of a calculator, which drew some faint derision from Romano. I told him with practice I'd get better, which was true, as my brain continued to rewire itself.

Once on my own, I slipped easily into a steady routine, the only hindrance being the weather, which surprised me with a series of snowstorms. It was indicative of my complete indifference to external circumstances. I recognized the mental state: back in my old life I'd often lose myself when engrossed in a project or mental exercise. In this life, I was so oblivious to the natural world that a volcano could erupt in downtown Hartford and I wouldn't notice. I'd often wander off on a mission in my shirtsleeves, despite freezing temperatures, or find myself standing in the rain, hatless and drenched to the bone.

I had no idea what was going on in the world at large. I never read or listened to the news, never took note of an advertisement or paused on any web site with no relevance to the task at hand.

That I didn't disappear into obsessive oblivion was owed to regular trips south to meet Natsumi for dinner. Oddly, with every encounter, the urge to reveal more and more of myself grew. As if my mind was fracturing into two parts — the reclusive and the confessional.

Natsumi's perceptive nature was a contributor.

"You work very hard at keeping the focus

of our conversations on me," she said one evening. "What I did today, my mother's health, what I think of the political situation. I like the attentiveness. You do it so well. But I only get the tiniest glimpses of you before you pivot away. Most adeptly, I should add."

"My life isn't very interesting," I said.

"You should let me be the judge of that. And anyway, that's what people always say when they don't want to tell you about themselves."

"How do you know that? You've met so many of these people?"

"See. That's how you do it. It's very tricky. But don't feel bad. I like you anyway."

"You do? That's so interesting."

"You really miss your wife," she said, matter-of-factly. "What was her name?"

I felt something twist in my chest, a reaction to the unholy stew of grief, paranoia, guilt and regret.

"I can't speak her name," I said.

She reached across the table and took my hand.

"You don't want to make something up. But you can't tell me her real name. Because then I'll know who you really are."

"I'm John Oswald."

"No, you're not. There's no one in Connecticut named John Oswald who looks or sounds like you." I tried to pull my hand away, but she held her grip. "Bela Chalupnik has disappeared. The guy from security we talked to in the bar reported it to HR. Ron Irving called me into his office to ask about you. My friend told him she'd sent me Bela's photo. She's not my friend anymore."

I gripped her hand back.

"What did you tell Irving?"

"That I just met you that night at the Sail Inn and never saw you again. This is why I wanted to meet up in Old Saybrook tonight. It's why I tried to find you online."

"Why didn't you tell him the truth?" I asked.

"What truth? I don't know what the truth is," she said, somehow managing to keep accusation out of her voice. "But really, I'd rather see you than make you talk to me. It's okay, I just don't want you to think I'm too dumb to notice you probably aren't who you say you are."

"You are anything but dumb," I said, sitting back in the seat and pushing away my meal.

"Not that I'd mind," she said. "If you let me in a little. Women don't like it when men don't share."

"You learned that in psychology class?"

"No. Our mothers teach us from birth. By the way, finals are next week. After I finish a big paper, I'll have my degree."

At that point I again demonstrated my skills at deflection, or more likely her willingness to be deflected, by chatting about psychology. And thus the night continued in an agreeable fashion, ending as it always did in the parking lot where I escorted her to her car. She pushed the key remote as we approached and I opened the door for her.

Before she got in, she took my head in both hands and pulled me to her face.

"Someday you need to invite me home," she said in a near whisper. "Consider that an incentive."

And then she drove away, leaving me with a whole different stew of conflicting emotions.

The Collingsworth Machine Tool and Metals Company had been established in 1854, and was therefore well entrenched in the Hartford area, a sober place that put a high premium on longevity. Originally a large-scale smelter, they'd evolved through the years, slowly shedding their tool business and drifting into recycling, specializing in

247

exotic metallurgy. So by the late twentieth century, they'd made the logical transition into salvaging precious metals from used electronic gear, which eventually became their sole business.

The CMT&M plant just inside the West Hartford border was not only my most lucrative stop, it was where I most wanted to spend my time. Billy Romano had been a popular attraction out in the parking lot during the four o'clock coffee and fattening treat break, so the CMT&M troops were grateful that losing Billy didn't mean an interruption in service. With fears assuaged, I quickly developed an easy rapport. Billy was clearly happy about this, thinking that any personality clash would wreck the whole concept, a possibility he assiduously sought to avoid.

"You got a way with people," he said to me. "This is the key to success in the food truck industry. There's a lot of flexibility in terms of food and drink quality, but if the personal touch isn't there, it's not happening."

And so after about two weeks serving sandwiches, donuts and coffee at CMT&M, I'd begun to learn people's names and what they did at the plant. Of particular interest was a guy named Leo Dunlop, who worked as a billing manager.

"I admire that," I told him. "Anybody who can work with numbers. Never my thing."

"Not me," said Leo. "Never met a number I didn't like."

"Plus I could never sit in the same place every day," I went on, after pouring out his coffee. "You can tell, I'm a run around kinda guy."

"These days you can work anywheres," he said. "Have laptop, will travel."

I showed no more interest, so Leo had little idea that there was nothing more interesting to me than him.

I was in Hartford over a month when Evelyn called to say the purchase of Florencia's agency was only a signature away.

"I don't think I can delay this anymore without messing up the deal," she said. "What do you say?"

"Do it. Have them wire the money into an online account you're going to set up using a laptop I'm going to send you. I'll include a return label. After you establish the login and security information, send the laptop back to me. Then start using your desktop to log on, and they'll have both MAC addresses assigned to you. Don't be alarmed if big numbers move in and out over time."

"It's your money, Arthur."

We talked some more, mostly about my physical condition, which on the whole had been greatly improved by the rigors of running a food truck. Even my math skills had evolved to where I could give up the calculator. And I was developing a taste for my own ham and cheese croissants. I shared the general story with Evelyn, leaving out the specifics.

"I wish I could tell you the police have made progress on the investigation. Young Mr. Maddox is sticking with us, but that's about it."

I told her not to lose touch with him, for no other reason than the contact might come in handy someday. I said not to interpret that as an optimistic prediction.

"I'm not much of an optimist, Arthur, except on this issue. I have faith that I'll see you again as your old self."

"I'll never be my old self," I said, then added quickly, "but you might like the new version better."

Before sending out the laptop, I used one of my spare names to set up a mailbox account at the UPS Store as an extra precaution. A week later it was back, effectively making me the only independently wealthy food truck operator in the Greater Hartford area.

I only had to wait another week for luck to strike. I was tossing sandwiches and soda, and pouring coffee at CMT&M, when I saw Leo Dunlop standing in line with a laptop case over his shoulder. Before handing him his usual tall iced coffee, I sprinkled in a special kind of artificial sweetener from a special package long reserved for the purpose.

As my research indicated, the onset period was nearly instantaneous.

"Oh, Christ," he muttered, staggering back into the waiting line.

"You okay, Leo?" the woman behind him asked.

"I don't know," he said. "Really dizzy."

He started to breathe heavily and went down on one knee. I knelt down with him and held his shoulder, taking the iced coffee off his hands. He was shaking.

"My arm's going numb. Jesus."

"Somebody call an ambulance," I yelled.

"I got it," yelled a woman with a smartphone. When all eyes turned toward the caller, I stuck a gas-powered hypodermic into Leo's side and pushed the button. Moments later, he fell the rest of the way to the pavement with both hands clutching his chest. His eyes were wide and spittle was forming on his lips.

"Chest pains. I think it's a goddamn heart attack," he croaked out.

I looked up to see the ambulance caller with her hand above her head, yelling out the address. With all eyes watching her, I picked up the laptop case and placed it in a slot next to the fresh fruit section and directly behind the cab.

Then I braced for a voice raised in protest or alarm, but the whole crowd was now circled around Leo, offering comfort and encouraging words. Leo wasn't buying it.

"I think I'm fucking dead. Somebody call my wife," he said, skidding his phone across the pavement. "She's on speed dial."

Everyone quieted down while another woman made the call. There was some back and forth, then she yelled, "Which hospital?"

"UConn," the original caller yelled back.

There wasn't much else for us to do but wait and hector Leo with well-intended questions and condolences. Through it all, I was able to dispense drinks and meals to the unfortunates who were behind Leo in line. They all spoke quietly and had a vague look of shame, though none thought the occasion demanded they go hungry. Still, I was glad no one said, "Leo would have wanted it this way."

The ambulance showed up soon after, and after they hauled away their ashen-faced patient, the parking lot cleared and I was left with Leo's laptop and the next phase of the process.

I took the laptop into the cab and turned it on, slipping in the boot disk as soon as I could open the little CD tray. Once inside the operating system, I installed the same spyware that now infected Ethan's server room workstation at Florencia's agency, and did a quick search for passwords, but Leo was far more security conscious than my last victims. It didn't matter. As soon as he was back on his machine, which would be in a few days if my research held, I'd have it all.

Minutes later, I shut down the computer and wiped it down with diluted bleach. Then I took it to the parking lot entrance and turned it over to CMT&M plant security.

"In all the confusion, I didn't realize I still had Leo's briefcase. Hope he's okay," I told the guard.

He took the case from me and stuck it under his desk, as if it was in imminent danger of further unauthorized possession.

"Makes you want to give up the donuts and start jogging," said the guard, whose enormous pot belly I had the good sense not to look at.

"We'll be lightin' candles," I said, and left him with my digital Trojan Horse safely ensconced beneath his desk.

CHAPTER 16

Natsumi woke me up at three in the morning screaming into the disposable phone I used to communicate with her.

"Oh my God, John, I'm so afraid," she squeezed out between hacking sobs.

I sat bolt upright.

"What happened?"

"A man. He had a knife. I thought he was going to kill me. Oh, God. He was in the backseat of my car. He grabbed my hair and stuck the knife into my neck. It cut me. He whispered in my ear. It was horrible."

"Are you bleeding?" I asked.

"It's a little cut. I'm in my car at the casino. I took a late shift for another dealer. The doors are locked. I don't know what to do."

"Drive away. Now."

I heard the faint sound of the car starting. Then she came back on the line.

"He asked about you. He called you the

guy who was looking for Bela Chalupnik. I told him your name. I thought that was safe since I don't believe it really is your name. What is going on?"

"I'm so sorry," I said, closing my eyes in the dark and cursing my foolishness.

"I told him the same thing I told Ron Irving. I described what you looked like. I said I hadn't seen you since that night, but you promised to get in touch with me sometime, thinking that might stop him from killing me. I guess I was right."

"You didn't see him."

"He told me to lie down across the console, and that he'd shoot me if I tried to look up. Then he just left. What do I do?"

I played a little movie in my head, on fast forward.

"Go home and pack the most important stuff you have that you can fit in a suitcase you can handle. Computer, meds, jewelry, passport. One change of clothes. Then drive to New Haven and park in the train station parking lot. I'll arrange to have the car towed and stored when I get the key. Take the train to Hartford, and walk to this hotel." I gave her the name and directions from the station. "Take the elevator to the fifth floor. I'll meet you and we'll take it from there."

"I'm frightened."

"This is all my fault. But I'm going to make good on it. Right now you need to trust me and do exactly what I tell you to do."

"I trust you. Even though my mother says I shouldn't."

"Where is your mother?" I asked.

"Kyoto. We talk on the phone."

"Does the casino have her address?"

"No. I told them she wasn't in the country and that's all I said. I didn't want the background checkers invading her privacy."

I thanked God for the one bit of good luck embedded in all the bad.

"No other relatives?" I asked.

"No. You have to tell me now. You can't pretend anymore."

I finally relinquished, with a strange rush of pleasure, all my reticence before Natsumi.

"Florencia."

"Who is that?"

"That was my wife's name. Her real name. The rest will have to wait. Call me when you're on the train."

When she hung up, I felt a familiar rage surging within me, a feeling that was effective in dousing its corollary, raw fear. If there was any way I could be driven to greater effort, this was likely it. I gave voice to that, loudly, alone in the room, then went about the proper preparation.

The hotel was in easy walking distance to the train station. I rented a room to legitimize my presence, and used the time to case the layout. As hoped, there was a separate service elevator that worked without a key, accessible from the utility room that stored sheets and towels and tiny bottles of shampoo and body lotion. I'd asked Natsumi to call me when she was on the train heading north, which she did.

"Do you think anyone followed you to New Haven?" I asked.

"That's a frightening thought."

"Sorry. Do you?"

"I can't tell. I'm a psychologist, not a spy."

"So you passed your exams."

"I did. Now it's just the thesis. I'm changing my topic to 'Effects on the Nervous System Resulting from Knife-Wielding Attackers.' "

Her next call came as dawn was creeping up from the horizon.

"I'm on the move," she said. "Rolling suitcase in hand."

"Is anyone you recognize from the train behind you?"

"No. And stop saying things like that. It's freaking me out."

"Sorry. When you get to the hotel, go to room 535. Knock on the door and I'll come out."

"If this is just an elaborate ploy to seduce me, I'll kill you."

"I'm not that imaginative."

"Maybe you should be," she said. "I might like it."

"What room am I in?"

She confirmed it, and we hung up.

I couldn't bear waiting in the room, so I went and stood by the elevator. As soon as she cleared the doors with her rolling bag, I grabbed her free hand, ignoring the startled look on her face, and pulled her down the hall to the freight elevator. I asked her not to talk. As we waited for it to show up, I could feel my pulse thumping in my ears. The doors slid open. Empty, thank God.

I pulled her in and hit the button for the bottom floor. We went down and the doors opened on a gloomy, shadow-laden concrete world. I held the doors open and listened. Nothing.

I pulled her out of the elevator and toward the loading dock used to load and unload convention displays. There was a security guard sitting at a little desk, reading by a task light that barely illuminated the cavernous space. I waved at him and said it was a long story as we zoomed by, and he never budged, having been charged with keeping unauthorized people out and given no guidance on those passing the opposite way.

I hit the button for the big loading dock door and we slipped out as soon as we had the headroom.

The Subaru was waiting at the curb. I opened the hatch and told her to crawl under the blanket that lay there waiting. I put her suitcase in the foot well of the front passenger seat, got in and started the car.

No one followed as we drove down the street and on to the entrance ramp to the highway. Unless they were invisible. I shot the car up the ramp and into the waking day. I let Natsumi know it was now okay to talk.

"Well, that was a first," she said, pulling the blanket off her head.

"Can I just say I'm sorry one more time, or do you want me to spend the rest of my life apologizing?"

"I don't like apologies. The Japanese do it so much it's hard to believe they really mean it."

"Would you describe the voice of the guy

who attacked you as high, low or in-between?"

"In-between."

"Did you detect an accent?" I asked.

"You say detect, which means any accent he had would be subtle. I'm guessing a borough of New York City, but I'm not sure, having only lived in Connecticut, so all New York accents sound the same to me. Where are we going?"

"To my apartment. I have a room waiting for you."

"With room service, I hope."

"Of course."

"I need your real name," she said.

"Arthur. But I'd rather you called me Alex. That's the name I usually use. Most of the time."

"I'm Natsumi all of the time."

"Not anymore. You'll need a new name."

"You're going to explain all this to me, right?"

"Yes. As soon as we can get to a place where I can look you in the eye so you can see I'm telling the truth."

"That bad?"

"That bad."

I drove directly to the apartment above the garage and carried Natsumi's rolling bag to her room. I apologized that she didn't have her own bathroom, and she reminded me that we'd abolished apologies. I asked her to meet me in the kitchen as soon as she felt ready to do so.

She showed up a half hour later freshly showered and wearing a dark blue sweat suit.

"Is it too early for wine?" she asked. "Just joking. Coffee would be nice, though."

As I worked on the coffee, I started in on my story, beginning with Florencia's murder and the attempt on me. I told her everything, deciding there was nothing to be gained by doing otherwise. Now that she was in, she needed to be in all the way. I told her that.

"Thank you," she said. "I think."

I told her about my sister Evelyn and how she faked my death, and my friend Gerry Charles and his guitar collection. About Henry Eichenbach, Madame Francine de le Croix and Sebbie "The Eyeball" Frondutti. I described my meeting with Fred Tootsie and how it led me to Clear Waters Casino, and with her help, Bela Chalupnik, aka Pally Buttons.

"And thereby stupidly connecting you to me by talking to that security guy at the Sail Inn," I said. "And by asking you to get

262

Bela's photo. I don't know why I wasn't thinking more clearly."

I spared nothing in describing my interview with Pally at the abandoned gravel business, and my subsequent chat with Shelly Gross. And finally, the sale of Florencia's insurance agency, my journey north to Hartford and the purchase of Billy Romano's food truck.

"For the purpose of?" she asked.

"Breaking into organized crime. It's the only path to Austin Ott."

She took it all calmly, her face neutral, her head nodding at the right times to signal she was following the narrative.

"I knew there was something up with you," she said.

"You're a perceptive person."

"But you kept coming back, even though I was suspicious."

"I did. I knew you were a good person who wouldn't hurt me. I'm also perceptive. At least I used to be."

"Though I never imagined anything like this," she said.

I booted up one of my laptops as I was telling her my story. I did a search for "Arthur and Florencia Cathcart" and set the computer in front of her so she could pick through the material. She looked up at me a few times as she read.

"You're a lot skinnier and balder, but I see the resemblance," she said. "Your wife was very beautiful. I can tell she was a very good person. I'm so sorry." She read some more, then looked up at me. "What does all this mean?"

"It means I have to find the people who did this thing. And now it's no longer my private enterprise. I've involved you, so there's an even greater need to follow this through to the end."

"What do you mean 'this'? What is 'this'?"

I didn't have an answer, because I'd never had anyone but myself around to ask the question.

"I don't know," I said. "I'm figuring it out as I go along."

"What's wrong with going to the police? Why do you think you have to take this on by yourself?"

Another unanswerable question.

"No one will try as hard as me or care as much about the outcome. I'm dead anyway, so who's better suited to the job?"

She frowned.

"You're not dead. You might be a little nuts, but you're not dead."

"You should go visit your mother for a while. You'll lose your job, but I'll compensate you for your lost salary. You can be on a flight tomorrow."

"You want to get rid of me," she said, in a tone that belied the harshness of her words.

"I want you to be safe. I put you in this situation."

"Enough with the guilt. Crap happens. I'm staying with you. I make $45,000 a year. Feel free to write the check. What happens next? I'm signing up."

She got off her chair and started to clean up the kitchen, not a difficult task, since I kept it impeccably clean. I watched her for a while, then realized I was on the verge of falling asleep, the night's frenzy having finally taken its toll. Natsumi told me to go ahead, that she'd occupy herself studying my larder and filling out a shopping list.

"This is really going to cost you, buddy," she said. "You've never seen my monthly mascara tab."

"I've got boxes of makeup in the other room. You can probably help me with that."

"I can help you with a lot of things," she said. "More than you know."

Soon after, I was out cold, allowing mercifully little time to absorb another massive, irredeemable shift in the nature of the universe.

■ ■ ■ ■

Leo Dunlop survived his ersatz heart attack, to my relief, since that wasn't a fore-
gone conclusion, as careful as I was with
the dosage. I knew he was okay because
forty-eight hours after collapsing he logged
back on to his computer. I didn't bother to
copy down the log-in information. It would
all be there when I wanted it.

He started out by returning emails telling
more or less the same story, thanking people
for their concern and explaining it was
probably just something he ate. He didn't
directly blame my iced coffee, which was
also a relief. He noted that toxicology tests
showed traces of Dobutamine, which can
induce arrhythmia and angina, but no one
knew how that could have gotten in his
bloodstream.

He spent a long time with his correspondence, the story growing in drama with each
email. Then he went to a web site that
featured bikinis, with the innocuous name
Sun and Fun that probably just squeaked
by the corporate censors.

Eventually, his voyeuristic ardor slacked,
he actually started to do some work. I was
glad to see he'd been truthful about his du-

ties at CMT&M, as the enterprise financial management system came up and he went right into accounts receivable. He was one of five billers, the work divvied up based on the size and geographical location of the customer. Fortunately, for my purposes, Leo's customers were among the largest, and his territory was the lower Great Lakes industrial region.

He was also impressively productive once he actually got under way. His keystrokes were fast and sure, and far more precise on the first pass than mine would ever be. Probably allowed for more time with the bikinis.

As with most industrial businesses, about a third of the customers accounted for most of the sales, the other two-thirds a long tail of small, infrequent orders. Each had been vetted and approved by the comptroller's office, and given the same credit terms, a tolerant and leisurely sixty days before interest was applied.

I left the spyware running in the background, gathering and recording all the incoming data, and searched for services that allowed you to open a small sales office, or merely create a mailbox that expressed the dignity of an actual street address. Part way down the first Google page was a site called spacejockeys.com that stopped me immediately. I'd seen the name before, when I was burrowing around Florencia's personal financial file which she kept in a walled-off subaccount within the general agency system. I took a break from the current task to go back into those files to find the reference.

It was an entry in accounts payable covering the lease of five hundred square feet of office space at an address in Scottsdale, Arizona. The service gave you a discount if you paid twenty-four months in advance. The issuer of the purchase order, Florencia Cathcart, chose that option. Based on the date, the lease had six more months to go. I copied all the information into a Word document for later examination, then went back to my original endeavor.

The spacejockeys site allowed you to choose from a menu of vacancies, with specifications, and to pay with an ordinary credit card. I deployed one of my rarely used, dead guy Visas, burning up nearly the entire credit limit.

I chose Evanston, Illinois as the location, and leased a simple drop box in an outlying industrial park. I called it First General Metallurgy Associates, LLC.

Part of the spacejockeys service was

logistics handling. You could have packages and mail shipped to the site, then forwarded on to another location. So I opened up another operation, this one a warehouse near Gerry's shop in the clock factory where you could lease small storage cages.

Natsumi came in the room and looked at the screen over my shoulder.

"Do you mind?" she asked.

"Why would I deny my partner in the purchase and distribution of industrial precious metals?"

"Sounds expensive."

"Not if you steal them."

"Okay. Noted."

Leo worked past closing hours, but eventually logged off. I waited another hour, then logged back in and started exploring.

The financial management system at CMT&M was nicely tied together and nearly unsecured. Leo had access to every subprogram but corporate finance and human resources, which was the barest minimum protection. It was also child's play to get behind the reports and functional screens to the application itself, where I could make adjustments at a deeper, less noticeable level.

The first thing I did was provide First

269

General Metallurgy Associates with the highest credit level, with notes that our Dun & Bradstreet ratings were impeccable. I backdated the entry by a year.

Then I checked the CMT&M inventory for available product and was pleased to see a nice supply of palladium, iridium and gold, all high value per troy ounce, the standard unit of measure. Heavier than hell, but still shippable.

It wasn't hard to pack several hundred thousand dollars' worth of merchandise into packages no bigger than a few cigar boxes.

There was a hot link directly to purchasing on the inventory page, so I went there and placed my order. The confirmation, sent to First General Metallurgy's new email account, said the metals would be shipped the next day.

Natsumi sat with me through the whole process, transfixed.

"I never believed you could actually do things like this," she said. "I thought it was all Hollywood baloney."

"Hollywood doesn't know the half of it."

We went out after that on an expedition to buy food, as well as clothing and other necessities Natsumi left behind. My role was to follow her around and express enthusiasm for her purchases. I'd never really done this before, since Florencia greatly preferred to shop alone, citing my poorly restrained impatience.

It wasn't something I'd want to do every day, but I had to admit there was a certain thrill of exploit to the experience, a satisfying cycle of search and discovery. I shared this with Natsumi.

"Maybe tomorrow we'll introduce you to another activity common to twenty-first-century civilization," she said.

We had dinner at a pleasantly underlit restaurant connected to the shopping mall. It was late, and the place was drifting toward the end of the day. However, we felt attended to and unhurried, and slipped easily into the rhythm of our evenings out, oddly unaffected by recent tumult and revelation.

I fell asleep that night with emotions that would have once been inconceivable. And as such, too novel to bear close examination, and thus fortunately, not of an anxious and sleep-depriving nature.

CHAPTER 17

Over the next few weeks we fell into a general routine. I'd get up early and run the food truck around the Hartford area, Natsumi would get up late and work on her paper until I showed up again in mid-afternoon. Then we'd sit together in front of my computer and she'd watch me perform a variety of tasks, including the purchase of industrial precious metals.

My goal was to get near, but just shy of $5 million worth of product before suspending operations. I wanted to stay well inside the maximum purchase limits and sixty-day aging on my account to provide leeway for future contingencies. I supported this strategy by paying for the first shipment, thus showing good faith, and buying another two weeks before anyone took note of any unpaid bills.

Once I hit my number, it was time for a field trip.

"You've been in too long, you need exercise, and this can't be outsourced," I said to Natsumi when I got home from my food truck route. "How are you at weight lifting?"

"I'm small, but game," she said.

"Good enough."

We drove the Outback to the spacejockeys warehouse in a drab, nearly forgotten New England industrial park. I checked the inventory of very heavy little boxes and was relieved to see it was all there. I wondered if the handlers guessed what they were handling — if any of them had taken basic chemistry in college and remembered the periodic table of the elements, where each element was ranked by mass. Which, when within the earth's gravitational field, translated into weight.

"Oh, my God, these things are heavy," said Natsumi, when I handed her the first box.

"The only things that pack more value in a smaller package are gemstones," I said, "and that's a different scam."

It took about fifteen minutes to load the Outback, whose valiant springs took the weight remarkably well. We drove it to Gerry's shop at the clock factory and unloaded. The springs held up better than we did.

"I hope I didn't wreck anything in my back," said Natsumi, after the last package was secured in a room behind Gerry's dust collector. "I'm too young to be hobbling around."

"I've been hobbling around for months now," I said. "You get used to it."

"You hauled more than me. I feel bad about that."

"I don't. I was merely hauling my share. As were you."

"Sounds collectivist," she said.

"Buddhist."

I kept one bar of gold, the heaviest and most valuable of the metals by troy ounce. Then I laid out for Natsumi the next phase of the plan. To her credit, her voice carried none of the alarm I could see in her eyes.

"This sounds a little dangerous," she said.

"It is, but only a little. I always do everything I can to stay safe. My objective is to move forward, not to perform derring-do."

"I know. The world itself is pretty dangerous. What's the difference?"

I explained the upcoming steps in the process, the first of which was driving to the FedEx retail outlet to send this note to Little Boy Boyanov:

Mr. Boyanov:

I have engineered a means for acquiring a large quantity of gold kilo bars that a buyer of the proper stature could obtain at a price seventy-five percent below market value. You are that buyer.

Given the sensitive nature of this transaction, I have strict requirements for how we engage.

The first meeting will entail a proof of product. I will bring a single kilo bar. You will bring the means for confirming product purity of the sample, which will be twenty-four karat. Please be careful that your test is precise. This is in your interest.

We will meet in the sauna at the Capital City Gym on Trumbull Street at ten P.M. Thursday night the twenty-sixth of this month. The gym closes at eleven, so the sauna is mostly empty at this time. Towels only, please.

I will come alone. I request you do as well. I will be carrying a gym bag. I will be able to identify you.

If you agree to the first meeting, please move the flowerpot next to your front door from the left side to the right by Wednesday the twenty-fifth.

I signed the note Auric G.

"You're going to be essentially naked, alone with a murderous gang leader while in possession of a gold bar," said Natsumi, summing up the situation.

"It's hard to stow a gun under a towel," I said. "Anyway, there's no percentage in stealing the bar when he could get his hands on a truckload for twenty-five cents on the dollar."

"Good point."

It was a little out of my way to drive the food truck down Little Boy's street off Franklin Avenue, but I fit it in. The flower-pot moved well before the deadline, which would have been less encouraging if I'd known better what Little Boy actually had in mind.

The Capital City Gym was in a rehabilitated industrial building just north of the divide between Hartford's downtown office cluster and the edge of the busy, though impoverished North End. It was in a sort of no-man's land of bombed out commercial relics and hopeful revitalization.

The club was expensive to join and had the feel of an old-time athletic club, meaning it was mostly men, mostly middle-aged and mostly wide around the middle. I had bought a two-week trial membership with cash, and visited often enough to be fairly certain the sauna would be vacant from about nine o'clock on.

I left my watch in the locker room, so I didn't know exactly what time it was, but it felt as though I'd been sitting there well past ten o'clock. I was about to abort when a very large man accompanied by two slightly less enormous men — one carrying a gym bag of his own — entered the sauna. All were in towels, exposing massive torsos festooned with ugly scars and tattoos. The sauna suddenly felt a lot smaller. They sat down across from me, and the biggest of the three, Little Boy, said in a pronounced accent, "Sorry, I brought company. I get lonely when I'm by myself."

Little Boy had a head about the size of a medicine ball, exaggerated by a rebellious wad of curly brown hair. His cheekbones protruded like fleshy hemispheres, and his eyes, in deep wells, were a glassy, pale green. He maintained a vague, somewhat unhinged smile throughout, which I eventually realized was the natural set of his face.

"What kind of deal can I make with someone who doesn't follow simple directions?" I asked.

277

"I got another friend standing guard at the door. So nobody bother us. Nobody hear us beating the shit out of you and taking that thing out of your dead hands."

"So you'd settle for a single bar when you could have a truckload? I thought Little Boy was smarter than that," I said, presenting the same hypothesis I'd floated by Natsumi.

"I don't like people driving by my house. I don't like them claiming to know my face. I especially don't like people dictating terms," he said. "That's my job."

"Not terms. Just precautions," I said. "You would do the same if you had the keys to a gold mine. Quite literally. I know you're a smart man, Boyanov. I wouldn't be talking to you if you weren't. So please don't fuck this up by getting all aggressive with a guy who could make you richer than you could ever imagine."

Little Boy seemed somewhat persuaded by that, though it only showed in his eyes.

"I got a pretty good imagination. But I'm listening."

"Did you bring the test gear?"

Little Boy nudged the guy with the gym bag, who pulled out a cordless drill, a rubbing stone and a rack of little bottles of acid, calibrated to assess common degrees of gold purity, from ten karat up to twenty-four. He handed all this to Little Boy who put it on the bench. I was happy to see this array, since it both determined the karat and proved the purity held straight through the bar. You could achieve the same end by doing a specific gravity test with a tub of water and a good scale, but I figured rightly that drills and bottles of acid were more Little Boy's style.

I took out the gold bar and set it down next to the gear. He secured the heavy bar easily with one mammoth hand and used the other to drill straight through, extracting a slender core. Then he took the stone and rubbed the core across the stone's rough surface. The final stage was dropping two large drops of acid from the acid bottle.

We all stared at the wet blobs, which were still wet five minutes later, indicating that the gold in the center of the bar possessed the highest possible purity — twenty-four karat. Little Boy looked up at me.

"How much of this can you get?" he asked.

"Volume isn't the problem. It's time. The scam has a shelf life. You want in, you gotta say yes, like now. I don't know why you wouldn't. I take all the risk, you just take possession, realizing an automatic seventy-five percent profit by simply selling on the open market."

The two guys sitting to either side of him stared at me like a pair of catatonic pit bulls. It would be hard to hide weapons under their towels, but I was sure they'd found a way. They never joined the conversation, and you could tell they didn't care what we talked about. Their job was to watch me and keep Little Boy safe.

"Payments and transfers could be difficult," said Little Boy, hitting on an element of the concept in least supply. Trust.

"I have zero incentive to cheat you," I said. "My profit margin is only twenty-five percent. That's good enough for me. You could try to cheat me. You could steal from me. You could kill me. But then, that's the end of the project. Because only I can bring you the goods. It's my angle, and it dies with me."

Little Boy tried to project skepticism, but his eyes betrayed a different intent.

"Okay. We give it a try," he said. "What happens next?"

"Before we get to that," I said, "There's one other thing."

Little Boy looked up from the gold he had sliced off the bar. His eyes were the iciest I'd ever seen. At the same time animated and inert.

"What is that?" he asked.

"I have other types of product. More unusual stuff like iridium, palladium and rhodium. Much harder to move than regular gold, which I also have in more common purities, like eighteen and ten karat. For this I need a different kind of organization, no offense to you. I need Austin Ott. You can introduce me. It's no skin off your back. You get all the pure gold you can handle."

Little Boy looked suddenly less energetic, less like a little boy than a cautious, middle-aged man.

"Ott is made-up," said Little Boy. "There is no such guy."

"Bullshit, I say respectfully. Like I told you, there's a window on this operation. We move fast enough, everybody wins. Word to Ott is part of the deal. No word, no deal. Kill me if you want, my people will just move on to the next potential partner, with you cut out forever."

Little Boy sat back and put his arms around himself, as if imitating a hug.

"Okay, we tell a guy, who tells a guy and maybe the next guy can get word up the food chain. I'll do my part. But no guarantees."

"Why all this fear of Ott?" I asked. "Everyone else in the world is afraid of you. I'm

281

afraid of you."

Little Boy frowned. Few know how to process an insult, even if it's indirect, when it's packaged with a compliment.

"It's not fear. We just don't know if the guy really exists."

"Maybe it's not a guy. Maybe it's a bunch of guys. Maybe it's a woman. Who cares? There's somebody with a very sophisticated operation out there calling himself Austin Ott. People are dead because of him. This I know."

I hadn't meant for my real life experience to comingle with the character I was playing, but it was probably for the best. The sincerity apparently cut through.

Little Boy rolled his head around in the way strong men do to stretch their overdeveloped neck muscles. His companions leaned out of the way.

"Okay, Mr. G.," he said, breaching a layer of reserve by using my name. "We can send a message and ask for a reply. But we can't make the reply happen. I write you a letter, you don't write me back. What do I do? I go to your house and point a gun at your face and say, 'Write back, you son of a bitch.' But I don't know where this man, if he's a man, lives. So this is not an option."

I nodded, joining in the new level of congeniality.

"Fair enough. Let's split the difference. We do a deal. Say, worth a hundred thousand to you in expenses, four hundred in revenue. You put out the message, but the deal goes through no matter what. Then we see if this phantom Ott steps up. I'm thinking he will when he sees the numbers, backed by your good name. And by the way, when you secure Ott, you're in line for a commission on every deal that happens after that. I'm talking deals worth hundreds of millions apiece. Maybe you should see at least five percent per. And that's on top of our separate arrangement. Pure gravy."

It was pretty obvious that Little Boy was starting to enjoy the hook in his mouth, even though he tried hard not to let it show. I sat back and waited for his response.

He held up the test sliver.

"I don't worry about this one being okay. I worry about all the rest," said Little Boy.

"Bring a metallurgist and all the testing gear you want to the exchange," I said. "I won't let something as stupid as product quality mess things up."

"What gets messed up is your face," said Little Boy. "Then we move on from there."

I tried to look disappointed.

"Successful relationships do not involve

all these threats," I said. "I have ways to do you terrible harm. But why constantly point that out? Better to just be civil and get on with business."

Little Boy looked at me as if I'd recited some poetry in ancient Greek. Yet somehow the sense of my proposition leaked through.

"Alright. Fair dues. How do we communicate? Transplant some more shrubbery?"

His buddies thought this was funny, as did I. We all laughed. I gave him a disposable phone, the best friend of the felonious.

"Call me on this. My number's already programmed in. Tell me what you're willing to invest, and I'll bring the appropriate product to the meet. You bring cash and a way to confirm product quantity and quality. This is not complicated. Metal is metal. Your kids could test for karats. The price is set by international markets. You pay a quarter of the number we look up on the Internet. We all go away happy."

He agreed, though still exhibiting a stubborn suspicion. I was pleased with Little Boy, whom I'd figured for a common breed of thug. A certain evil craftiness was apparent, but also subtlety of thought. Yet he could be led, and snagged by simple suggestion.

After they left, I sat in the sauna until closing time, then showered and got dressed, and left the gym by a back door which led to an alley, which led to the remote parking lot where I'd left the Outback. The night was pitch black, with no humans or vehicles in sight. If Little Boy's people were following me, they were the best stalkers in history.

I drove out of the parking lot and went home. Natsumi looked relieved when I walked through the door.

"Oh, good. You're not dead," she said.

"Not yet, though the possibility was raised. Ekrem Boyanov is a very big person."

"Did he agree to the deal?"

"I don't think he was completely sold, but close. But it's a good start."

"I made dinner," she said.

"You did?"

It was such a strange moment for me. To have a person living with me make a meal, and then wait for me to eat, was an entirely alien concept. Even when I lived with Florencia, I cooked all the meals, the default position of the partner who worked at home versus the one who worked late and usually arrived after a grinding ten-hour day.

"What, I shouldn't have?" Natsumi asked.

"No, I'm just not used to it. Too long a

feral man."

"It's not a banquet. Chicken pot pie and mixed greens. And wine, at least for me. You can drink tap water."

While we ate I told her more about my meeting with Little Boy and his two muscle heads.

"How are you going to manage the exchange?" she asked.

"I'm still working on that. Any ideas?"

She thought about it.

"Make the switch in the parking lot of the Balkan Bakery. You told me Little Boy never commits crime in his own neighborhood. By the same token, no one will interfere with his transactions, or even acknowledge anything's going on. It's also an assurance to him. You'd be beyond crazy to pull any crap right in the heart of Bosniak central.

"Isn't this committing a crime?"

She shrugged.

"It's a business deal. Try it out on him. See what he thinks."

I had the chance to do that the next day when Little Boy called me on the cell I'd given him. He told me he was willing to invest $100,000 in the first go 'round. To test the concept and to work out the downstream market. I proposed Natsumi's approach for the exchange, with an honest

286

description of the rationale. He surprised me by buying the whole argument.

"For sure, we're not going to kill you in our own backyard," he said. "So maybe we can later have a little more trust, eh?"

We made arrangements for me to meet him at eleven P.M., an hour after the Balkan Bakery closed. He'd bring the $100K in cash, a scale and testing gear. I'd bring the gold.

When I got home, I was able to tell Natsumi that she had a future in criminal transaction logistics. She looked proud of herself.

"When you add that to professional blackjack dealer, I sound quite sinister."

We didn't talk much more about the plan since there wasn't much to say. I was going through with it, and we'd done all we could think of to keep me safe, so there was little point in belaboring the obvious concerns. Instead, Natsumi went back to her paper, which had grown from ten pages to nearly fifty, prompting her to ask if she was reinforcing stereotypes of the Asian overachiever.

"Thirty-eight years old, and you're finally graduating from college?"

"Point taken."

■ ■ ■ ■

For myself, I went back to my favorite evening pastime, reviewing Florencia's financials. That night, I remembered the lease on the property in Scottsdale she'd arranged through spacejockeys.com. I went in other private files and saw the address was 358 Jacaranda Boulevard, Suite 35. I pulled up a Google map and pegged the spot as deep within a heavily commercialized area of the city. Google asked if I wanted a street view, and I thought, sure, why not.

It was a fairly new brick building in a complex that included a Marriot Hotel and Morton's Steakhouse. Florencia's space was on the top floor at the end of a long hall. I googled the building's address, and got the leasing agent — a commercial real estate firm — and three other businesses connected with the location: an advertising agency, geological surveyors and a brokerage house. None were at Suite 35.

I wrote the real estate agency and asked who was leasing Suite 35. I was surprised by the nearly instantaneous response, apologizing that such information was confidential, but there were still many highly desirable vacancies in the building which she'd be eager to show me. Would tomorrow at ten be convenient?

She included an attachment with photos and specifications. The smallest space in the building was five hundred square feet, and thirteen out of twenty units were empty.

I went back to the spacejockeys contract and dug deeper into the language. I saw that the lease amount was contingent upon which additional services the renter required. The ones Florencia selected were listed by a number code. So I went back to the spacejockeys web site and opened the screen where you picked through your options.

Her number codes corresponded to security alarm, monthly janitorial and mail forwarding services. The same three I'd chosen for my office in Evanston, having no need for incidentals like furniture, phone service, broadband access or receptionist. Why get all this when the address is just a pass-through?

Since the financial program I'd installed for Florencia was web-based, and built on a browser, it was searchable, a feature I really liked when I was weighing different packages. You just had to be within the broad functional category, like AR/AP, aging, balance sheet or general ledger. I went through all of them, pasting the address into the search box, and racking up "no results" at each one.

That left only two other possibilities, Florencia's personal account and the premium trust account. I started with Florencia's account and the spacejockeys contract came up instantly. There were no other notations, so I moved on to the premium trust account.

As with her personal records, the premium trust account was bolted to the floor. Only one other person, the comptroller Damien Brandt, had access, though only to make deposits of clients' premium payments, not withdrawals. These could only be done by Florencia, and only she could do the monthly reconciliation, essentially balancing the account. In addition to accounting for deposits and disbursements, this segment of the software listed all the carriers who held the policies the disbursements funded. Most of the carriers were fully set up to handle the flow of premium funds through electronic transfers. Routing numbers and bank codes were contained within the program, so she could simply point and click to take an appropriate action.

Five of the carriers, four with names I recognized, still required paper checks. The

fifth was an outfit called Deer Park Underwriters, located at 358 Jacaranda Boulevard,
Suite 35, Scottsdale, Arizona.

I needed all the time I had left to retrieve
the gold and meet Little Boy. I told Natsumi I'd call her when I was on the way
home with the money.

"If you don't hear from me, don't call the
police. There's always the possibility they'll
grab me and try to force me to give up my
source. It may take a while to work that
out."

"Okay," she said, "I understand. Don't
tell me you're sorry in advance or any of
that. We've already talked about it."

It was a very cold night. Without a moon,
and the air crisp and brittle dry, the stars
were clean little pinpricks and the Milky
Way a black cloth sprayed with iridescence.

I brought along my own scale to Gerry's
shop. Before I left the apartment, I pegged
the price I looked up on the web to the
amount of gold I needed to load. The resulting cardboard boxes filled with bars took up
remarkably little room in the trunk.

With no traffic to contend with, the trip
to the Balkan Bakery only took about
twenty minutes. In the lot were two big
SUV's and a step van. All black. Men were

standing around and leaning against the van under a dusky floodlight, hunched against the cold and smoking cigarettes. I flicked off my lights before I turned into the lot.

"Hey, Mr. G.," said Little Boy, "I gotta admit, you got guts."

"I also have your product. Do you have my compensation?"

"That's why we're here. Come into my office and we get this over with."

He walked over to the van and opened the rear doors, inviting me in. Since there was really no way to guarantee I'd have the money in my hands either before or immediately after delivering the gold, I just popped the trunk and told the nearest Bosniak to bring it to the van. I watched while he and another transferred the heavy little boxes. They stepped back when they were done and I followed Little Boy into the van.

It was a remarkably pleasant environment. There were two low, soft leather seats along one side of the vehicle. On the other side was a long couch in the same material. In the middle was a big round coffee table. The carpet on the floor and the wood paneling were elegant and understated.

Little Boy unpacked the gold and stacked the bars on the table. He took the scale and testing equipment out of a compartment at the front of the van and set up shop. I sat in one of the leather chairs, which swiveled, and watched him work.

"I've been paid in gold plenty of times, but never really thought about getting into the business itself," said Little Boy, in a convivial mood. "But why not? Sure, it's heavy, but you can stuff a lot of money into a very small package." He looked up at me. "And who's it going to hurt? Not like drugs, or girls, or numbers, or even boosting trucks filled with cigarettes. These are all not only sinful things, but bad for people."

"I agree with you," I said. "I'm hoping for a long-term relationship. As soon as this connection expires, I'll open another. There's no limit here. And for you, very little risk, if any at all."

We continued to make small talk, which found its way into a discussion of professional basketball, a subject I knew nothing about. Luckily, Little Boy was so loquacious the conversation was really more pontification on his part. He only relented when the last bar had been analyzed. He looked at me with a hard face.

"Mr. G., I'm very disappointed with you."

I felt my heart begin its involuntary ascent up into my throat.

"Why do you say that?"

"This isn't the amount we agreed upon," he said, waving his hand dismissively at the stacks of gold bars. "What do you take me for?"

"It is the amount. You must have missed something. That happens. You need to check again."

"I spend all this time and you expect me to spend it again?"

I showed him the piece of paper on which I'd tallied up the total weight loaded into the Outback.

"That's what's sitting there," I said, in an angry but even voice. "Give me your scale and I'll prove it to you."

Little Boy's perpetual grin broke into an all-out smile.

"I'm not saying it's not all there. It is. I'm saying that amount is worth at least a thousand dollars more than the current price per ounce. You give me too much, Mr. G."

I sat back in my seat. I'd forgotten I'd thrown in a little extra just to be sure I wouldn't be under, depending on whatever price fluctuations might have occurred since I last checked. My plan was to throw in the overage as a gesture of goodwill. Instead I'd handed Little Boy the perfect excuse for scaring the crap out of me. I told him just that.

"Thank you, Mr. G. So you weren't just testing me, eh?"

"No. Though that might have been a good idea."

He laughed and swatted my chest with the back of his hand. It stung, but I pretended it didn't.

"Very good. I like that. So now I suppose you want your money."

"That's customary."

"You don't talk like a person who steals gold," he said, as if informing me of something I might not have known myself.

"I think people who steal come in all varieties. It's a universal human affliction."

"See. There you go again."

"So, the money," I said.

He stood up and got a small leather bag out of the same compartment that held the testing gear. He dropped it in my lap.

"American dollars," he said. "Real, not counterfeit. Unmarked hundreds. Count away."

Count I did, not that I thought he'd short me. Not counting would have been a sign of weakness. He waited silently until I was finished, which I confirmed with two thumbs up. He smiled another of his wide smiles and reached out his broad hand. I took it.

"I need some time to replenish supplies," I said. "I'll be in touch. And don't forget to refer me to Austin Ott."

He continued to shake my hand after I released my grip, increasing his.

"It's not exactly fair you know where I live and I don't know where you live," he said.

"It's not fair you have a family to love, a brotherhood to embrace you, an entire community to keep you safe. I have only myself. If my life isn't secret, I'm defenseless."

He dropped my hand and pursed his lips, a telltale of complicated thought.

"I'm starting to like you, Mr. G., despite my better instincts. Take your money and get out of here before you disappoint me. I don't get over disappointments very well."

I did as requested, acknowledging in the privacy of my own mind that I was starting to like Little Boy as well, for no good reason on earth.

CHAPTER 18

I woke up about five the next morning and, after making a big pot of coffee, returned to the computer. I went back into the premium trust account at Florencia's agency and started adding up the premium payments to Deer Park Underwriters. I went back seven years, when the trail ended at the point I brought the new system online. The records for the prior eight years were on magnetic tape stored in a warehouse somewhere, out of reach of the World Wide Web.

Still, the tally had hit $6.5 million over the last seven years.

I left the financial system and moved into operations, tracking the clients who'd been sold policies covered by Deer Park Underwriters. There weren't any.

I once worked for an insurance company that sold directors and officers liability coverage. Built into the policy was protection against employee fraud and embezzlement, which could result in a suit against management for failing to enforce adequate controls. My job was to research and document the various ways employees could dip their hands in the corporate cookie jar. Some were very clever and elaborate. Some bold and brilliant in their simplicity. I immediately recognized where this fell. Somewhere in the middle.

I called up the contract with spacejockeys and asked for a review of the account. In particular, I wanted the destination for all the mail forwarded out of the Deer Park Underwriters address.

The answer was immediately forthcoming: Blue Hen National Bank of Newark, Delaware, lockbox services. Contained in the forwarding information was an account number and access code. I jumped into the Blue Hen online banking site and spent a tense two hours cracking into the account. The trickiest part was sending an email from Florencia through her personal email system requesting a new username and password. Once I finally broke through, the result was as expected.

The paper checks made out to Deer Park Underwriters were deposited in a Blue Hen lockbox account labeled Claims Clearance. Every three months, the account was swept clean and the money wired to another bank in the Cayman Islands.

I'd seen it before. I knew what it was. A fissure opened up in the floor beneath me and I nearly fell through. My heart seemed to catch fire as it clawed its way up into the upper reaches of my chest. No, no, no, can't be, I whispered to myself, while the cold, calculating animal at the center of my mind was saying, oh, yes it is. It's exactly what you think it is.

I knew then what it meant when people said their world had turned upside down. They meant it literally. It was only after I slid off my chair and lay supine on the ground for a half hour that equilibrium returned.

I went out to the kitchen where Natsumi was tapping away at her laptop, books open all around her on the kitchen table, kitchen chairs stacked with papers, CD cases and other books. She looked up happily, then changed her expression when she saw mine.

"What's the matter?" she asked.

"Not sure. It's too fresh. Need some processing time."

"Okay. Can I get a headline?"

"I'm not sure, but I think I've slid into a parallel universe."

"Really."

I squeezed my eyes shut and pulled my shoulders in, as if braced for a blow.

"I wish I could trust my own brain," I said.

"I think you can. It's a good brain."

"Was."

"Tell me about this new universe," she said.

"It's a place where Florencia was stealing money from her own company."

"Really?"

"Really."

I left her and went to my bedroom to lie down. I tried to go limp, releasing my frame from the painful pull of gravity, assessing the grip of knotted muscles and inflamed joints. The sun was starting to come up, but the shade was down, leaving the room in brooding shadow.

I played a movie in my mind. The opening: it's the end of the year and a big client wants to use leftover budget to pay their premium well in advance of renewal. Florencia graciously accepts their check to hold in an escrow account. When another big client sends in their premium payment, half their money goes to Deer Park Underwriters. The other half goes to the legitimate carrier, with the balance made up from the other client's escrow account.

The next month, some of the premium

money coming in covers the deficit in the escrow account, some of it goes to fully fund other coverage, but a bit of it slides into Deer Park Underwriters, eventually working its way to the Caribbean. Month after month, year after year, the performance is repeated. Over time, Florencia's commercial insurance business grows until significant amounts are moving through the premium trust account. Good fortune allows all policies to be in force when needed, while some of the froth is steadily drawn off and sealed up in a vessel that makes Switzerland look like a colander.

Natsumi came in and sat next to me on the bed. I opened my eyes.

"You don't have to tell me anything you don't want to tell me," she said.

"Yes, I do. I got you into this. It would be unfair to withhold anything that could have an effect on you."

"There's something you don't understand," she said. "And maybe that's because I haven't spoken the words. So I guess I'm the one who's withholding."

I sat up on my elbows.

"What is it?"

"I'm glad I'm here. I wouldn't have prescribed the way things happened, but there was something predestined about the way it

301

did. I loved working at the casino. I loved going to school. But now I'll have the degree, and I can't go back to my job. I understood it was time for my life to move into something new, but I needed a big bang to make it so."

She took my hand. "When you sat down at my blackjack table I was almost knocked over by your urgency and grief. I could feel your battered, calculating mind. Don't ask me how, but I'm not a psych major for nothing."

"I let down my guard," I said. "I couldn't help myself."

"Because this had to be. It wasn't up to you."

I had spent my life in the pursuit of empirical, quantifiable, verifiable truths. There was never room for mysticism or spirituality. Random occurrences, yes. Mathematics would be nonfunctional if happenstance wasn't factored into the equations. Yet even math was ruled by probabilities, and repeatable results. The only hand that guided the outcome was the blind hand of inexorable logic and reason.

Yet as you feel the certainties upon which your life has been anchored shift like tectonic plates, never to be returned to their original state, logic and reason can seem entirely inadequate adjudicators of reality.

I sat all the way up, took her face between my hands and kissed her full on the lips. She didn't resist.

It wasn't until later that day, when I got home from my food truck run, that we returned to the subject of embezzlement.

"It's called skimming and lapping," I said. "A classic scam where you essentially divert a modest percentage from a revenue stream, covering the shortfall as you go with new revenue as it comes in. If you don't get greedy and over-skim, and if nothing happens to call attention to the irregularities, it can go on for a very long time. Forever, if you're the one who controls all the information and manages oversight."

"So who was that in Florencia's agency?"

"Florencia."

Natsumi looked at me intently.

"It was?"

"No one else could have done it. She had full control over the premium trust account. She was the only one authorized to make withdrawals, directing the payments to the appropriate carriers. She did the monthly reconciliations, manipulating the numbers to stay below the auditor's radar. She set up a shell company made to look like one of the agency's carriers. She established a lock-box account to clear the checks that ran through the shell, then established that numbered account in the Cayman Islands to hide the money."

"Why siphon money off your own company?" Natsumi asked, a question that was large enough in my mind to become a physical thing.

"I don't know," I said. "But I do know that payments to the fake carrier stopped the month she was killed. Anyone taking over the books would find everything in proper order. The only way the scam would be revealed is if a client needed to make a claim, but the policy had lapsed for failure to pay the full premium. Essentially, caught in the middle of the float, because Florencia wasn't there to skim fresh revenue. But that obviously didn't happen. The only other way would be to confirm the legitimacy of every carrier the agency ever engaged with. There are hundreds of them; many are specialty underwriters brought in to cover a unique exposure. Most are now dormant. There's no good reason to check."

"What does this mean?" she asked.

"That's a question I want to ask Austin Ott."

■ ■ ■ ■

Little Boy Boyanov called me again in the food truck on our private cell connection.

"You're gonna like this," he said, when I answered.

"Okay."

"Guess who I sell my gold to?"

"The Pope?"

"Austin Ott," he said.

"Get out of here."

"Not him directly, of course, but to some flunky who comes to see me after I put the word out I want to speak to his boss. They don't usually work this fast, so I'm thinking you made a big impression."

"What's next?" I asked.

"The flunky's called Jenkins. He wants a sit-down with you, one-on-one. I don't suggest this. Too dangerous. Even if you're only wearing towels."

"What do you suggest?" I asked.

"You make the arrangements, but we're the ones who show up. Then we all take Jenkins for a ride in the van."

"Ott probably won't like that."

"It's just a protection. He'll understand."

"And you protect your investment," I said.

"Nah, we just like having you around,

Mr. G."

He gave me the name of a diner on the Berlin Turnpike, a classic four-lane commercial strip that had been the area's north-south highway before they built the interstates. Though showing signs of revitalization, it was still the favorite home of cheap motels, gun shops and the sex trade. Little Boy designated the time of the meet and the booth Jenkins should sit in, the one next to the swinging kitchen door, with a guarantee it would be empty and waiting.

I accepted his plan as proposed, since I had none better, and though the same hazards were there, so were the reasons for trust. Anyway, I'd long ago learned the folly of secondguessing people with obvious professional expertise.

Before hanging up, Little Boy gave me Jenkins' cell number.

A silky young male voice answered the phone, "Yeah, what's up?"

"Jenkins?"

"Speaking."

"Mr. Boyanov asked me to give you a call."

"Indeed. We have some mutual interests to discuss."

"We do," I said. "Though I'm only interested if a certain party, name unsaid, will be involved."

306

"That depends on how beneficial any arrangements will be to this party we aren't naming."

"He knows the potential. I'm guessing he's looking at it right now."

"Guessing is not advised, brother. We need to talk."

"How safe is your phone?"

"Don't go insulting me."

"Though we're not naming names."

"That's what sit-downs are for," he said.

I gave him Little Boy's explicit instructions, saying I'd only approach him after he was comfortably seated for at least ten minutes.

"That's cool," he said. "I'd be afraid of me, too."

When I got home, I filled in Natsumi.

"You're making progress," she said.

"I am. Someday I'd like you to meet Little Boy Boyanov. We could have him and his wife over for dinner."

"Do you trust him?"

"No. But I trust his self-interest."

"And I trust you," she said.

"I'm glad, because I'm trying hard to keep you informed of everything," I said. "Though I left something out."

"Really."

"Wait here."

I went into my bedroom and retrieved a selection from the nice casual wear I'd purchased from Preston Nestor — a pair of tan silk pants, a cashmere blazer and a blue-and-white striped pima cotton shirt.

"You're a closet fop?" Natsumi asked.

"It's part of a longer-term plan. I wasn't trying to conceal, I just hadn't figured out which direction things were heading."

I told her what I was thinking to make happen. Natsumi was skilled in controlling her facial expressions, but something akin to wonder, or more likely incredulity, lit up her eyes.

"In other words, you're going to put everything you've done since coming out of the coma in reverse," she said.

"More or less, yes. I know very little about Austin Ott, but I have my theories. He has a model that is working for him. At its heart is personal anonymity. He won't deviate, no matter how enticing the opportunity. However, he will find ways to engage via higher level intermediaries if he's convinced it's worth it. But I can't afford a lengthy process. With every passing day, I leave behind little scraps of vulnerability. These will build on each other over time, increasing the probability of a bad breach. I need to speed up the process, but it's difficult to operate aggressively without putting my own anonymity at even greater risk."

"It's a conundrum," said Natsumi.

"I need to reconfigure the operating strategy, both strategically and geographically. Shelly Gross told me he's no better than any other ruthless thug, so why the fancy name, why the affectations, why the affinity for Fairfield County? Because he's Jay Gatsby. A big-time criminal who's irresistibly attracted to the blue-blood elite, the socially refined and exclusive. Not for love, like Gatsby, but for the status it conveys. At least in his own mind."

"So you want to take the battle to him, on his own turf," she said.

"It's time to move Mohammed to the foot of the mountain."

"I thought you were a Buddhist."

While Natsumi made our evening meal, I changed into the nice clothes and spent some time researching on the computer. As was often the case, the subject was something with which I had only glancing familiarity, so most of the time was spent learning the basics.

"Wow, I'm feeling underdressed," said Natsumi, after calling me to the table.

"After we eat, you can help me with the wig."

As suspected, Natsumi had an artistic bent that did much to enhance my nascent cosmetic skills. She selected a light brown wig with distinguished white patches at the temples. Then, with the careful application of a skin toner, gave me a subtle tan, as if I'd recently returned from a golf holiday in Arizona.

I mentioned that when I looked in the mirror.

"Next time, take me with you," said Natsumi.

"We'll need new names. I have the Social Security number for a dead guy named Henri Grenouille. It works with Mr. G., the name Little Boy used in front of Jenkins, based on how I signed my note — Auric G. Henri isn't Auric, but it's close enough."

"Did you know Grenouille means frog?"

"No offense intended."

Before I left, I showed her what I was doing on the computer, and asked if she could keep up the search for a while.

"Does that mean I can pick what I want?"

"Absolutely. Think big."

I called ahead on the way to meet Little Boy and his coterie.

"I won't look the same," I told him. "Don't act surprised. I'm doing it for

Jenkins' sake."

"I hear you," said Little Boy. "We're getting ready for the snatch."

He reminded me of the van's location, which I would reach well in advance. He said he'd brief the guy waiting there on my appearance.

"Otherwise, he's liable to shoot you, which would really put a foot up the ass of the plan."

The van was waiting where promised, the parking lot of a strip club and motel complex on the Berlin Turnpike a few miles north of the diner. I knocked on the door and one of Little Boy's taciturn Bosniaks let me in.

"Nice threads," he said, sitting back down in one of the leather seats and returning his attention to a copy of *Elle* magazine.

We waited in silence for the rest of the gang.

Jenkins, who was the first to enter the van, looked to be in his early thirties, though some hard lines had already formed around his eyes. African-American, with long, loose limbs and a toothpick in his mouth, he seemed perfectly at ease with the situation. He fist bumped my babysitter and plopped down on the couch. Little Boy and a third

Bosniak joined him.

"Sorry about the switch-up," I said to Jenkins. "Just a precaution."

"I know about that shit," he said. "First meet and all that."

"He laughs when we come out of the kitchen," said Little Boy. "Knew right away. Smart guy, Jenkins."

"That's right. Smart like your boys here who know any serious fucking with me will bring an avalanche of serious shit down on your heads."

Little Boy looked slightly offended.

"No reason for any serious shit," he said. "We're all adults here."

"We are," I said, capturing the group's attention. "Here's the scenario. I have the means of acquiring a vast amount of precious metals at incomparable prices. Namely, for free. This allows me to offer it to committed buyers at ridiculously discounted rates. I am interested in stable, ongoing relationships, and so will happily forego greater potential margins in return for the consistency and security these will provide."

"Little Boy here explained all that," said Jenkins. "Tell me more about the product."

"I have gold, of course, and silver, but also platinum, palladium, iridium, rhodium, osmium and ruthenium."

Jenkins fished a pen and a small notebook out of his jacket.

"You're gonna have to run that by me again. I got the 'ium' part. Spell out the rest of it."

After doing that, I said, "The distribution of these metals at the quantities I'm contemplating requires an operation with an international footprint. I'm obviously thinking of Asia and Latin America. Growth economies with a hungry industrial base."

"That's right," said Little Boy. "Our footprint is basically between New York and Boston. Otherwise, we'd be snatching up all the 'ridiums we could get our hands on."

Jenkins looked at him sideways, then went back to jotting down notes.

"I understand Mr. Ott's desire for anonymity," I said. "I desire the same for myself. But I need assurances that I'm engaging with his organization and not a group of poseurs."

"We be the real deal, man," said Jenkins. "Nobody posin'."

"With all due respect, I need more than that. A gesture of good faith. I'll let Mr. Ott decide what's appropriate."

We concluded the meet soon after that. Jenkins already had one of my cell numbers from our earlier call, so the link was there. I told him the next move was theirs, but I sincerely hoped we could quickly come to a satisfactory arrangement.

"I prefer to only deal with the best of breed," I said, as we shook hands. "As evidenced by my association with Mr. Boyanov. Please convey that to Mr. Ott."

One of Little Boy's men drove Jenkins back to the diner so we could recap the meeting.

"I like that thing about best of breed," said Little Boy. "No matter we're the *only* Bosnian breed in town."

"There's another $100K's worth of gold coming your way," I said. "With a fat overage. You earned it."

"Then maybe I can afford the new dress code."

Natsumi had a bottle of Jim Beam and a beer waiting when I got back to the apartment. She was wearing the skirt from her casino uniform and a lamb's wool sweater. Burning candles stuck with paraffin to small plates and saucers were placed around the living room. The radio was tuned to a college station playing jazz.

"It's the best I could do on short notice," she said, kicking off her heels and sitting on the couch with her feet pulled up beneath her.

"What's the occasion?"

"I finished my paper."

"Congratulations," I said.

"It belongs to this apartment. It felt wrong to bring to another place. It was the right time."

"You're going to have me believing in cosmic confluences."

"To be honest, I was getting pretty sick of the whole thing. How much does an under-grad need to know about Münchausen syndrome by proxy?"

"A lot less than you do," I said.

"And how was your evening, dear?" she asked. "How're your Balkan criminals?"

"I'll know in a few days. But no matter how the meeting turns out, we're making the move."

"That's good, because I think I found the perfect thing. To die for," she added, with a studied upper-crust inflection. She put her shoes back on and went into her bedroom. She came back with her laptop, which she handed to me.

On the screen was a photograph of a furnished, 10,500 square foot, limestone mansion on thirteen landscaped acres in Greenwich, Connecticut, built in 1928 by an investor who didn't know a year later he'd be broke. A fate shared by the current owner, a descendent of John D. Rockefeller, who'd had the considerable misfortune to put much of his financial fate in the hands of a guy named Madoff. The offer was rent with an option to buy.

"You specified Gatsbyesque," she said.

"I like it."

We committed the rest of the evening to eating finger food and planning the next few days' activities. In the process, Natsumi put a large dent in the Jim Beam with no apparent effect, and I went hog wild and had two whole beers. The second one having the impact of pre-operative sedation.

"You look like you're falling asleep," said Natsumi.

"Because I am. I haven't your experience drinking motorcycle gangs under the table."

After saying our goodnights, I carefully dealt with all the cashmere and silk I was wearing and fell into bed as if pulled there by a whipcord. I turned off the bedside light and was about to roll over and pass out, when the door opened and Natsumi came into the room. She swatted me and said to give her some room. The bed was a double, so there was just enough to give.

She slid under the covers. I felt bare legs,

panties and a T-shirt.

"Only to sleep," she said.

Which we did, until later that night, when I swam up from the deep well of sleep and into her arms, clothes gone and futures irrevocably altered, a cosmic confluence, a consummation realized, not only devoutly to be wished.

CHAPTER 19

I promised my landlady Señora Colon-Cordero a thirty percent commission on the sale of my food truck. I suggested she call Billy Romano, in the event he'd had second thoughts about that retirement in Florida.

"That's a very big commission," she said.

"I want you motivated."

"Maybe I buy it myself."

I thought that was a great idea.

"Only I can't break you in like Billy did for me. I have pressing business elsewhere. With the deal I give you, you can afford to fly him back north to consult."

"So the food truck business not turn out like you hoped," she said.

"Frankly, I liked it. But it's not my destiny. I think you'll find, however, that I've left the route in good order."

I didn't tell her about Leo Dunlop's simulated heart attack following a slurp of my iced coffee.

■ ■ ■ ■

It only took a few hours to clear our belongings out of the apartment and pack up the Outback. I also used the time to contact the real estate agent for the big house and make arrangements for a viewing.

"It's a faaabulous property," she told me. "You'll just love it, love it, love it!"

We stopped at Gerry's shop on the way to Greenwich to pick up a sample of each item in the inventory. Though remarkably valuable on a pound-for-pound basis, the boxes were also remarkably heavy.

"Next time we deal in exotic down comforters," said Natsumi.

I rented a room in the best hotel I could find in Greenwich, just to get a start on proper appearances. It wasn't that burdensome a decision.

"The Presidential is available," said the desk clerk, "though we've been having some issues with the Jacuzzi."

Natsumi expressed disappointment, but we acquiesced after the clerk dropped the price-per-night to slightly below extortionate.

The suite was twice the size of our apartment in West Hartford and far better equipped.

"Did you know you could perform aromatherapy and pick your teeth at the same time?" Natsumi asked, bent over a woven basket of specialty comforts.

We ordered in food from a local restaurant, and suffered the rest of the night in a bed that managed to be firm and fluffy at the same time. Over breakfast we planned the upcoming day, focusing on seeing the house and building out our wardrobes, two prospects Natsumi was honest enough to say were less than daunting.

"And we need a nicer car," I said.

A few hours later, we drove down the long driveway to the big house in a new Mercedes E-class station wagon. A sedan version of the same car was waiting for us. A short, somewhat overweight woman in a luxuriant hairdo and white suede, floor-length, fur-lined coat got out of the car and greeted us.

"Like I said, faaabulous," she said, grabbing my hand and then lurching into Natsumi to apply a bear hug. Natsumi spun her nature in an opposite direction and gave her twice the hug back, nearly squeezing the wind out of the idiot woman.

"Well, nice meeting you, too. Shall we go in?"

The interior of the house was both grand and intimate. It was spotlessly clean, with not a whiff of mothballs or disinfectant. Stained oak paneling covered the walls, also festooned with traditional, representative art. Orientals on the oak and tile floors, rooms filled with sturdy, comfortable furniture smelling of embedded lemon oil. Lamps sprouting from oversized Chinese vases on the side tables. A massive three-foot frond encased in a glass frame above the fireplace. A library lined with bookcases stuffed to the gills and reaching to the sky. I didn't bother to see the rest.

"We'll do six months in advance," I told the agent. "Is tomorrow too early to sign the contract?"

As we floated down the million-mile, tree-lined driveway, Natsumi said, "I know this all has a strategic purpose, but it's fun, you gotta admit."

"I admit."

As if the day weren't extravagantly materialistic enough, we slipped into New York and spent the rest of the afternoon and early evening harvesting clothes and accessories from midtown department stores.

After a leisurely, overpriced dinner in Soho, we made it back to the hotel a little before midnight.

"Okay, that was another first," said Natsumi, sprawled on her back on the sitting room sofa.

"All this does have a strategic purpose," I said.

"I assumed so."

"I don't want to be a wet blanket."

She picked up her head.

"Then don't. I know the score. Just let me wallow in the fantasy a little. You don't know how much of a fantasy this is."

Recovering from a momentary lapse in compassion and understanding, I walked over and brushed her silky black hair out of her face.

I spent most of the next day trying to crack into Florencia's numbered account at the bank in the Cayman Islands. The problem was devilishly simple. I had the bank's routing code and account number, but not the user ID and password. Without these, nothing short of an armed invasion would provide access to the account.

I could have guessed at a few combinations based on my knowledge of Florencia, but the odds were long, and after five failed tries, the bank's security system would lock out my computer forever. I could get another computer, but the outcome would likely be the same.

The elegantly cunning Grand Cayman banking system anticipated these occasionally orphaned accounts, some bursting with illicit funds. They'd let plenty of time elapse, then swallow up the money. Should injured depositors or their heirs eventually turn up, things got worked out, usually yielding to the supplicants a generous percentage on the dollar. Another fine example of honor among thieves.

It wasn't until I remembered Florencia's home computer stuffed in the Subaru with a bunch of other computer gear I'd been hauling around, that it came to me.

I retrieved the computer from my car and set it on the desk, turned it on and slipped the MattBD boot disk into the CD slot. In a few minutes, I had control of the machine.

Florencia wasn't much of a tech head, but I didn't think she'd leave access to a secret numbered account in Grand Cayman simply lying around her hard drive. I could start searching for alphanumeric combinations, but that was another slog.

I went to my own computer and pulled a list of routing numbers for all the banks on Grand Cayman Island. I copied the list onto a flash drive and copied it into Florencia's computer. Then I put all the numbers into a query box that searched the entire hard drive.

Twenty minutes later it showed up in a folder called "Recipes," in which there was a Word document named *"Receta para estofado de cordero a la ostra."*

I opened the document. The bank number, which correlated with the First Australia Bank (Cayman) Limited in George Town, was at the top. Then the account number, then the words, "Eagle House."

I stood up from the desk and walked to the end of the room where I could look out over the side yard. Eagle House was the dreary apartment block just off the University of Pennsylvania campus where she lived while attending Wharton. My circumstances were little better, living with three roommates in a squalid walk-up in South Philly, which I barely took note of, so absorbed was I by my graduate work in advanced statistical analysis.

Here again, I was confronted by an impenetrable puzzle. With a brain that had lost the language of solutions.

Or maybe not.

The account code had to be of some length. There were ten characters in Eagle House. If A was one, and Z was twenty-six, the code could be 51712581521195. But that seemed too long, and too easy, even for Florencia.

Ten digits. The length of a phone number.

The phone number at her apartment in the Eagle House. Damn, I thought, what the hell was it?

I went back to my computer and started writing emails, continuing well into the night.

The last email I wrote was to Evelyn telling her substantial funds would be flowing out of the shared account, just as I'd warned.

I didn't tell her why, or much of anything else, aside from reporting that I was feeling better than ever physically, and that I was making progress. She didn't deserve so much ambiguity, and I was ashamed of that, but if I started to tell the full tale, I wouldn't know where to stop. And there was always the matter of making her an accessory before, during and after the fact.

I was sorely tempted to tell her about Florencia's skimming operation. But then again, I didn't know for sure — the matter still wasn't totally settled. I decided to hold back the shock and disappointment until I was sure I had the whole truth.

So I stuck with empty assurances and fell into bed feeling dishonest, but well-meaning.

Proving the maxim that people have a tendency to expand the amount of junk in their possession to fill the amount of available space, it took us almost a week to move ourselves and what we thought were our meager belongings into the giant house.

All the clothing delivered on our doorstep was part of the problem, though the larger issue was the disposition of my computer gear and related electronics, once spread across Gerry's shop, the little house next to the gravel pit in Wilton and the apartment in West Hartford. I had twelve rooms to choose from to effect the consolidation, though surprisingly, this abundance made the selecting that much more difficult. I finally settled on the poolroom above the three-car garage, mostly because of the absence of a pool table, opening up space for a row of folding tables and a rolling office chair to flit from workstation to workstation.

I put all the precious metal up there as well, in a small stack of cardboard boxes shoved into the corner. There was too much for a safe; and anyway, a safe was the best way to tell the world you had something to hide.

Natsumi set about domestic arrangements, in an unapologetic reinforcement of gender stereotypes. Confronted with a kitchen twice the size of her prior living space, she stocked the cupboards, filled in the china cabinet and decorated the counter space with all manner of modern gadgetry.

She interviewed cleaning and landscaping services — the latter at that time of year confined to plowing the driveway and hauling broken limbs from the yard — eventually settling on a husband/wife team from Colombia to manage the entire place.

We installed a tanning booth in one of the spare rooms, where I spent some relaxing time obviating the need for daily makeup. The wig was a necessary annoyance, made less so by Natsumi's deft handling.

It was a decidedly agreeable interlude, and I succumbed to its pleasures in defiance of my abiding weariness and angst.

One of the delights of research is it often takes you into stunningly unfamiliar terrains. To say that my knowledge of Greenwich, Connecticut high society was rudimentary was to grossly overstate the situation. As with any anthropological study of a human subpopulation, one first had to gain some knowledge of their habitats, exclusive parlance and patterns of association.

So I went to a good primary source — gossip columns — steeling myself against the natural revulsion this form of commentary spawned in me. I cross-referenced New York and Connecticut sources, developing a list of keywords that helped narrow the search, and after several hours of concentrated study came up with a short list of names.

Then I wrote Henry Eichenbach and attached my list: "We know your proficiency with organized crime, how're you on philanthropists? I know, they're often one and the same. (Sparing you from having to make the joke yourself.) How would you rank this list, and who would you add or subtract?"

An hour later he wrote back: "All in Greenwich? Interesting. Your list is fine. I can add a few, but the top spot is undisputed — Esme "Nitzy" Bellefonte and Aidan Pico. Pico's a big money guy — surprise, surprise. Nitzy's family founded the Bellefonte Gallery in Greenwich, based on a collection of Abstract Expressionism hoovered up by her grandfather back in the fifties, when the rest of the world figured those guys for a bunch of drunks throwing paint around the Hamptons (a fair description, in my opinion). It's now a public museum, but the endowment barely covers expenses. Nitzy has greater ambitions than that. She's constantly raising funds to buy contemporary works, believing she's the rightful heir to her grandfather's legendary taste. Which, to be fair, she mostly is. I don't suppose you're going to tell me why you ask."

I wrote, "I want to throw a party. You're invited."

"Of course," he wrote back, "I'll pick out my party dress."

I went back online and read about the dazzling Nitzy and Aidan, their museum and ongoing fund-raising activities. There was very little to distinguish one event from another, though themed events, such as, "Come As Your Favorite Villain," "Night at the Opera" or "Meet Me at the Forum" seemed to attract larger crowds and deeper engagement with the cause. I shared these insights with Natsumi.

"Absolutely brilliant, Alex. You've totally diagnosed the socio-ritualistic group dynamic of American wealth-class philanthropy."

"I detect a bit of sarcasm."

"Though I've never thrown a high society fund-raiser, I've been witness to some really cool events at the casino. So it's right up my alley. Even if I think such things are the height of the superficial, the banal, even reactionary and decadent."

"Okay. Remember, you have to pick a new name. A pseudonym."

"I've always liked the name Eiko, though not as much as Charlene."

"Charlene?"

"I grew up in New London. Whatcha expect?"

"Charlene it is. Charlene Grenouille."

"So we're married," she said.

"Better to uphold the artifice."

"I'll need a ring. And so will you."

"We can do that," I said.

"And an engagement ring," she said. "Can't have the artifice without it."

"You're really running up the tab."

"You told me already, if you're going for a con job, you gotta go all in."

"Would you mind doing the buying?" I asked.

"I'd hate it, but oh well."

Natsumi's willingness to take on these onerous tasks just made me appreciate her that much more. Better yet, it allowed me to refocus my attention on a matter even less within my specific area of expertise: contemporary art.

Bias is the enemy of research. People like

330

me are not only trained to have an open mind, we are priest-like in our devotion to impartiality. You can't do the job any other way. I had never studied a single subject without coming away filled with surprises. This taught me that you just don't know until you learn. So be open to any and all possibility. There was no better preparation for an exploration of the art world.

Having recently ranked professional assassins and Greenwich philanthropists, I felt well prepared to accomplish the same with living fine artists. A few hours later, I determined the only reliably agreed-upon criterion was gross sales, though financial success seemed as sure a way to attract derision and condescension as praise. After poring over countless images and representations, I could see the problem. While competition between artists and their patrons was undoubtedly fierce, constraints imposed by external authorities — like the nineteenth-century French Academy — were in little evidence. Variety of form and content, style and subject matter was limitless, and to my innocent and untrained eye, spanning the utterly absurd to the heartbreakingly sublime.

Many of these works had found their way to the Bellefonte Gallery, and thus provided me some focus. One artist in particular seemed favored, a North African living in Milan named Joshua Etu who created sculptures from woven strands of electrical wire. I liked these quite a bit. Less so the cartoon versions of historical figures a woman named Shree made from fabric recovered from people who had died in homeless shelters. On the other hand, Englishman Wilson Franklin's photorealistic paintings of blank-faced children, in color within black and white scenes — riding the underground, grocery shopping, watching the Royal Family's motorcade — were strangely compelling.

"I think you should come with me," I said to Natsumi.

"Where?"

"To see Nitzy Bellefonte and her husband Aidan."

"I know nothing about art."

"You don't have to. I'll carry that burden. You can stick to social climbing."

"I know less about that."

"I'll send you some links. You just have to memorize a few names."

The day before I had a messenger hand-deliver an engraved note to Nitzy at her home requesting an audience at the gallery.

The note said my wife and I were new to Greenwich, that we were renting the old Rockefeller place in town while we looked for a place to buy, and were hoping to find an appropriate introduction into the local community. I proposed we hold a significant fund-raising event with the gallery as sole beneficiary. Naturally, I would seed the donations with a six-figure gift of my own.

The messenger left with a return note that somehow seemed eager and respectfully restrained at the same time. The appointment was for the next day at three in the afternoon.

"What's going to happen when everyone starts googling us?"

"They won't find anything."

"And that's not suspicious?" she asked.

"Sure it is. It's also intriguing and suitable to the purpose."

"Which is?"

"To attract the attention of Austin Ott, the Third."

"It's a big risk," she said.

"Big risk, big reward or big bust. It's the kind of thing that happens in Greenwich every day."

The Bellefonte Gallery, identified by a discreet brass plaque, was in a neighborhood of old mansions captured behind hedges and thick brick walls. A few of the places had been subdivided, sprouting more modern, but no less grand examples of the form. The land surrounding the gallery had remained intact, a matter of pride for Nitzy as revealed on the museum's web site.

Before we stepped out of the Mercedes, Natsumi asked, "What's my budget?"

"For what?"

"The party."

"Less than five million dollars," I said.

"I don't need that much."

"How much do you need?"

"Two hundred and fifty thousand," she said.

"Okay. Spread it around. We need the friends."

The gallery officially closed at three, which explained the meeting hour. The door was open, and we were greeted by Nitzy Bellefonte in a small room with a ticket counter and a hardwood rack filled with art books and histories of the gallery.

Her hair was such a perfect blend of black and grey it seemed impossible to be artificially colored, though I knew from my Google search that she was thirty-nine years old. Her features looked larger than in my memory of her photographs, and her skin

had a more olive cast. Her face was youth-
ful and brightly alert, like a terrier on the
hunt. She wore a plain sweater dress and
flats, though it was hard to miss the cluster
of diamond rings when she held out her
hand to Natsumi.

"Charlene, you are darling."

Natsumi, unfazed, gave her a little bow.

"Thank you. That means a lot coming
from you."

"And you're Auric," she said, giving my
hand a sturdy shake.

"It's a pleasure, Ms. Bellefonte."

"Nitzy, please. Would you care for a brief
tour before we chat?"

What could have been brief turned into
nearly two hours as Nitzy shared with us
not only the significance of each work, but
the circumstances surrounding its acquisition. Much of this involved cagey negotiations and some dazzling escapades on the
part of her grandfather, and then subsequently Aidan and herself. It was hard to
call this outsized pride since her delivery
was so charming and unburdened by self-
awareness. Natsumi and I did little to
discourage her, since with every step
through the museum she became warmer
and more loquacious. By the time we
reached the comfortable leather seating in

her office, all of us armed with a delicate glass of light white wine, the atmosphere positively glowed with good will.

"So, please, you must tell me what you're thinking about, event-wise," she said as she perched on the edge of her seat, giving the hem of her skirt a symbolic adjustment, leaving plenty of shapely, bare thigh for all of us to enjoy.

"Fire and Ice," said Natsumi, after allowing the suspense to build for a few seconds. "Of course it will be optional, but we'll ask each couple to dress in either fiery gold, or icy silver. Jewelry will naturally be optional."

She and Nitzy shared a giggle over the absurd notion that any woman would come unbejeweled, given such a blatant excuse.

"Inside the house," Natsumi went on, "we'll have the big room with the walk-in fireplace just ablaze in gold and red décor. Here's where we'll have drinks and chitchat before moving to the banquet room for dinner. I think if we run two tables, we can comfortably seat fifty. The red and gold theme continues on — did you know you can burn torches that are absolutely nontoxic? Then, after dinner, we retire to this gigantic glassed-in room. We'll open all the doors and the ceiling vents and have ice sculptures on a big center table, plenty of aperitifs and gelato — I know a place in the city that delivers direct from Venice. So what do you think?"

She looked at Nitzy like a candidate for the junior high cheerleading squad.

"Oh, Charlene, I just love it to death. You are so clever."

I breathed a hidden sigh of relief. Whether she meant it or not, the local society's chief arbiter of taste had to be behind the concept.

"You are such a lucky man," she added, looking at me. I tried to look modestly prideful.

Nitzy went on to discuss a host of logistical details I wouldn't have considered in a million years. Natsumi did a brilliant job engaging in the discussion without betraying her own bewilderment. I just hoped she'd remember it all.

We wrapped up with a celebratory glass of wine, and Nitzy escorted us to the door and the darkening evening. She took me by the elbow as we walked, and in a voice drenched with apology, asked me, "What should I tell people you do, Auric?"

"Strategic commodity trading," I said without hesitation. I stopped and turned to her. "It's important for Charlene's sake that we're welcomed into the community. But I strive for privacy in business matters. There is very little public information. I have people who do a daily scrub."

Nitzy seemed relieved by the first part of my answer, and captivated by the second.

"Of course. I completely understand."

As soon as we passed through the open gate and out to the street, Natsumi let out a sound somewhere between a whoop and a laugh.

"We're in the club, Alex. We're in the secret club."

"Not yet. We need to get through the party."

"No prob. She told me everything I had to know. Gave it to me on a silver platter. Silver and gold. Hey, what was that?" she said. "I think I saw a little smile. I did. Don't try to deny it. I made you laugh."

"I'm practicing a repertoire of responses appropriate to the party environment."

"No, you aren't. I made you laugh. Ha."

It felt odd to be infected by Natsumi's good cheer, her natural lightness of being. But there it was. Despite all my best efforts, she persistently disrupted my standard internal dialog, my relentless drive for focus and calculation.

I didn't know what constituted the bigger surprise. That she had that effect on me, or that I liked it so much.

Though perhaps the biggest surprise of all
— I didn't care.

CHAPTER 20

Before we got to the big house I called Little Boy.

"Sorry, Mr. G., he don't want to deal direct. It's Jenkins or nothing. This doesn't surprise me. Three Sticks is one private dude."

"Thanks for trying. You might hear from him anyway in a few weeks. Just a heads-up."

"You got some kind of scam in mind?"

"I might," I said.

"You want some help?"

"Maybe. Don't take this the wrong way, but why would you want to help me?"

"This Three Sticks, he piss me off. I stay out of his way, he stay outta mine. But I put myself out there in the world. There's risk in that, but it's the honorable thing to do. So he's too good to meet with me, to sit down and talk? It's insulting. You, Mr. G., you watch your own ass, but you have respect. I can see it. Maybe I'm too sensitive, but you try being a Muslim in Bosnia, part of a people almost wiped out like the Jews in the big war. You don't know how disrespect can turn into death so fast you never see it coming."

"I know how death can surprise," I said, despite myself.

"So that's that. Call me if you need anything. And more of that gold would be a nice thing. It's got my distribution all hot and wet."

At ten in the morning the next day, Nitzy called to ask if we'd stop by her house that evening to meet her husband.

"I've told him all about you. He insists."

"Of course," I told her. "What could be more delightful?"

We filled up the rest of the day drafting a plan of attack for the party. It was a month away, leaving precious little time for such an ambitious event. Even so, it felt like a dangerous expenditure of time. Natsumi was helpful in assuaging these fears, showing herself a fine party planner, even with no experience, as well as a woman of firm, steady resolve.

Our Colombian caretakers, Jorge and Adelita Costello, pressed into extra service by Natsumi, were of priceless value. Neither of us had ever managed employees, so we played it by ear, applying a strategy of excessive appreciation enhanced by overcompensation. The Costellos responded as one would hope.

This is why they were still there in the big foyer on tall stepladders — working well into the evening stringing a giant woven red and gold boa along the crown molding — when we left to meet Nitzy Bellefonte and Aidan Pico.

I used the onboard GPS in the Mercedes to find their house. It was up in the northern, wooded region of Greenwich at the end of a long, intentionally curvy driveway. The house itself was a loose collection of square, white boxes with vertical siding and vast picture windows.

Nitzy greeted us at the door in either a very big sweater or a very short knit tunic, black leotards and black, fur-covered boots. Behind her stood a tiny balding guy, at least three inches shorter than his wife, in a silk T-shirt and sport coat, both perfectly color coordinated with Nitzy's reddish-brown sweater thing. Both held huge wine glasses containing barely an inch of wine.

"Aidan, allow me to present the Grenouilles," said Nitzy, as she herded us into the house.

He bowed as he shook our hands and spoke a line of French that I didn't quite understand. Something about being honored to have fellow countrymen visit him in his humble home. I answered in kind, though far more crudely, explaining that I was second-generation French, which my terrible accent must surely make clear.

He smiled and said, "What is an accent but a manner of speaking? My parents immigrated to Lyon from Mexico City when I was ten years old. I grew up having Frenchmen constantly answer my questions in Spanish. *Vin?*" He held up his glass and named the label, another demonstration of his linguistic acumen. "It's one of our winter favorites."

Before they could escort us toward the living room, I took a moment to compliment the twelve by twelve Wilson Franklin hanging in the two-story foyer. It depicted a young girl watching a boxing match from the front row of the stadium. Nitzy stood behind Natsumi and held her by both arms as we all looked up in veneration.

"Some of them you just have to bring home, don't you think?" said Nitzy. "If I couldn't have beautiful things surrounding me, I wouldn't feel like life was worth living."

"You home is very beautiful," said Natsumi.

"Everyone thinks it's Le Corbusier, but it's actually Willa Petersen, one of his students," said Nitzy. "I frankly think she's head and shoulders better, but who's objective about their own house?"

As with the rest of the place, the walls, floors and ceiling of the living room were a satin white, better to display the paintings, fabric hangings and sculpture that filled the space. Some of the artists I recognized from the gallery or my own research, though most were unknown to me. A situation duly remedied by another hour's lecture on the origins and intricacies of contemporary art. Nitzy did all the work. Aidan focused on the wine and sustaining an admiring and admirable silence. When she seemed nearly spent, he said, "Nitzy tells me you have some hell of a party in mind."

Nitzy gestured at us as if bestowing permission to speak.

"We do," said Natsumi. "It's so exciting that the Bellefonte Gallery has agreed to be the beneficiary."

"No less exciting for us," said Aidan. "It takes a great deal of money to collect at this level. And lately, with the Russians and Chinese and Brazilians all getting into the act, the price pressure is getting nuts."

"We're only too happy to help," I said.

"You know something about price pressure in your work, Auric," said Aidan. "Commodities is it?"

"It is."

He waited for me to offer more, and when I didn't he said, "Commodities scare me, I have to admit. I don't have the nerve for it. Too much like the wild west. I'm just a dull old securities trader. So your dodge is oil, wheat, pork bellies . . . ?"

"Precious metals," I said, "though not in the open market. I prefer to call it strategic trading."

"That sounds interesting," said Nitzy, looking over at her husband as if to say, see, there's something intriguing about this guy.

"It's pretty esoteric, and frankly, really boring when you get down to it," I said. "You're right, this is excellent wine. Charlene, tell our hosts more about your party plans."

Which she did, lavishing appreciation on Nitzy for having contributed to both the concept and the planned arrangements. Nitzy took it all in with "but of course" written all over her face.

345

"So the theme is 'Gold and Silver, Fire and Ice,' " said Aidan. "Seems appropriate for a precious metals trader. Will you be giving away some of your product?"

"Well, we're prepared to do just that," I said, as conspiratorially as I could. "Maybe the rumor of such a possibility will assure a good turnout."

Causing even a brief moment of speechlessness in Nitzy Bellefonte wasn't an easy task.

"Oh, my," she said, finally, "what absolutely delicious fun. I will definitely get the word out. I'm sorry — the rumor."

She stretched out the last word in a loud whisper, then sat back and clapped her hands. Natsumi clapped hers as well. I looked at her adoringly and Aidan looked at me with narrowing eyes.

"Auric Grenouille is a fascinating name," he said. "And unusual. In fact, Google's never heard of you."

"That's on purpose," said Nitzy. "I told you that."

"You'll have to give me the name of the people who keep your privacy," said Aidan. "There's too little of that these days."

"Charlene, you must love vintage clothing," said Nitzy, jumping out of her seat and grasping Nitzy's wrists. "Come along, you have to see what I have stored upstairs."

Natsumi went docilely and I was left alone with Aidan Pico. He leaned closer to me, as if he could be overheard by his wife.

"Enough of this wine shit. How 'bout a real drink?"

I shook my head.

"Sorry. I have the capacity of a five-year-old. But please, you go ahead."

"I will."

He went across the room to what looked like a raised-paneled wall, pushed one of the panels and it swung open, presenting a shelf with a tiny ice chest, a few chunky glasses and a bottle of Makers Mark bourbon. He poured himself a stiff one.

After he settled back into the opulent white couch and drained off about a third of the drink, he said, "What level of trade are you into? Can't help it, just curious. What sort of numbers? And tell me to stick it up my ass if I'm getting too nosy."

"Seven to ten figures. Depending on a lot of variables. This crappy economy is warping the spreads, which isn't all bad if you know how to play it. Most of the product comes out of bad places, so there's another wild card. But that's manageable. And I'm not going for the home run. Too easy to strike out. Don't get greedy, keep a low

347

profile and ignore crazy run-ups. They're always followed by blow-ups."

"Interesting."

"Profitable," I said, then asked him to tell me all about his business, which he did in great detail, helped along by my well-worn interview techniques. He was so engrossed in his own story, he almost missed the return of Nitzy and Natsumi, who were wearing different clothes from the ones they left in.

"We had a fashion show," said Nitzy. "I have all these vintage and designer things from the last fund-raiser. I have to give it away to get the tax break, but it's so hard to let go, even though one of the bedrooms is floor to ceiling. At least your gorgeous wife has a few new outfits to honor your visit."

Natsumi was wearing a relatively modest white camisole under a red jacket that barely reached her waist, a tight black skirt and pumps that had her nearly on tiptoes. Her unhappiness with the situation was apparent to me, though clearly lost on Nitzy and Aidan.

"Isn't she the bee's knees?" said Aidan, before gulping another large mouthful of bourbon. "And you, Nitzy, a vision."

So she was, in a floor-length dress with bunched up fabric growing out of it everywhere, and a narrow neckline that nonetheless plunged about as far as anatomically possible. She struck a pose that had to be restruck after briefly losing her footing.

"We have to stop polishing these floors, Aidan. They're too slippery."

Sober as a judge, I was able to time a strategic withdrawal. Natsumi was alert to the moment, and helped with the transition.

After several rounds of thank you's, two-handed handshakes, cheek kisses and hugs, we were out the door — Natsumi unsteady on the heels, holding a fabric Gucci bag full of the clothing she'd arrived in, as well as a few items more, and me holding her.

"Well," said Natsumi, slumping down in her seat as if to avoid deadly fire from the rear, "that was interesting."

"Love the new threads."

"Women wear these on purpose," she said, kicking off the shoes. "I wouldn't even if my mother hadn't forbidden it. You can get a nosebleed from the altitude."

"I think she likes you."

"As a little Asian doll. I'm ready for anything, Alex, but playing dress-up with Nitzy Bellefonte sort of pushes the creepiness factor."

"It was all a pretext to get me alone with

Aidan so he could pry."

"How did he do?" she asked.

"Fine, for our purposes. Not so sure for his."

"Does money always warp people?"

"I believe money only warps the warpable. But I don't have all the data," I said.

We sat in silence for a while. Then she said, "You're one of the unwarpable. I can tell, even without the data."

I thanked her and we retreated back to our grand mansion, our eager Colombians and a greater appreciation for the deeper pleasures of the placidly mundane, even as fantasy and delusion swept up around us like a swirling, uncontrollable tide.

The weeks before the party sped by with reckless abandon. Mostly because there was so much to do, and so little time to do it. The plan we'd made held firm, meaning each of us had equal amounts of too much to do, but it undoubtedly served its purpose in getting it all done.

Throughout, Natsumi maintained her lively level-headedness and I my dour determination.

Perhaps the only unwise assignment for me was to audition and secure the fire dancers. No amount of online research can prepare one for the sight of attractive, flimsily clad people twirling lit batons and exhaling vast clouds of billowing flame. Nonetheless, I hired one of the candidate troupes, based more on their willingness to reveal the inner workings of their craft than the actual thrill of the performance.

It didn't hurt that they were French Canadian. They pledged the greatest party ever.

"Monsieur Grenouille, nous allons presenter un spectacle le plus stupefiant au monde."

"That's good enough for me."

Distracted as I was, Evelyn was right to be angry over the long delay in hearing from me.

"You didn't answer my last email," she said.

"You're right. I was going to, then forgot."

"That's not like you."

"It's getting harder to tell what is and what isn't like me," I said.

"Is that supposed to be comforting?"

"I have a new accomplice. I stupidly exposed her to a very dangerous person, so I had to bring her along with me."

"Her?"

"Yes, and yes before you ask," I said.

"My, my. Now I know why you aren't

yourself."

"It's more than that, but you're probably right. It changes things."

"I wish you could tell me more."

"I have the name of the person behind the one who pulled the trigger. It's an alias, of course. His modus operandi is to be invisible and unreachable, but I have a plan. It isn't fully formed, but I'm already committed, so we'll have to see."

"But why, Arthur? How could such a person have anything to do with Florencia?"

I hesitated before answering, which made the answer more difficult to frame.

"I think I know. But until I'm sure, I don't want to say. Not over the phone."

"You told me these disposables were secure."

"As long as no one has any reason to listen in," I said. "I can't say that for certain anymore."

"That's disturbing."

"I can't tell you things if you aren't prepared to be disturbed."

"Okay. You're right," she said.

"I just have a question for you. Had you seen any changes in Florencia in recent years? In mood, behavior, anything?"

"No. Never. She had that great Latin, 'The world is crazy, Evelyn, so let's go have some fun' thing about her. All the time. I don't suppose you can tell me why you're asking."

Her imitation of Florencia's Spanish-inflected English was painfully accurate.

"Not yet. By the way, how're the agency's new owners doing? Any word?"

"Haven't heard a thing. Bruce had plenty of time to prepare the transition. Said it went very smoothly. He's now completely retired to his home in the Virgin Islands, God bless him."

I only held her on the line long enough to provide some feeble reassurances and another apology. We hung up with feelings intact on both ends.

That evening I got an alert of a new email connected to the account I'd used to monitor the video camera trained on Shelly Gross.

It said: "Still interested in selling that Mercedes, Alex?"

As the implications sank in, I felt a blast of heat across my torso and a fuzzy roar building in my head. I took deep breaths to calm my mind and short-circuit a blizzard of panic responses that sought to animate reckless action.

In theory, he could know everything that

I'd done under the name Alex Rimes. All the bank accounts, all the credit cards, all the purchases and rental agreements. He could know the identity was purloined from an unfortunate guy in Alaska. He could trace everything back to Gerry's shop at the clock factory. From there, by contacting Gerry in Amsterdam, he could make the link to another dead guy named Arthur Cathcart.

He could learn that Alex had recently bought, and then soon after sold, a food truck business. Linking that to a heist of precious metals from Collingsworth Machine Tool and Metals Company was unlikely, since CMT&M were not yet aware of a potential heist. He also couldn't know that Alex Rimes had now moved uptown and taken on a new identity, since I was meticulous in walling off Alex from Mr. Frog.

On the other hand, my saner self argued, setting up that account required nothing but a bunch of made-up data. No Social Security number, no credit card, just a registration. It was conceivable that the site recorded my computer's MAC address, but unlikely. And even so, I'd paid cash for the computer and given the retail outlet more false information, so it was untraceable to me by itself.

So, also theoretically, all he could have was the name Alex Rimes.

Yet it was bad, especially since I couldn't know for sure what he knew, what had been compromised and so had to be jettisoned, and even that involved further risk.

With nothing left to do, I wrote him back.

"These cars are rare birds, but maybe not for the determined hunter."

His response came in minutes. And the dialog began.

"I want to help," he wrote.

"With what?"

"Your pursuit."

"I don't want the cavalry riding in," I wrote. "It'll blow the whole thing."

"It's only me for now."

"How can I know that?" I wrote.

"You can't. But I no longer work for those guys. I have no legal obligation to communicate what I know."

"So what's in it for you?"

"The offer you already made," he wrote. "To get the big fish on the end of the line."

"How did you get this address?"

"There's another serial number on the lens of the camera. You'd have to break the case to even know it was there. Easy to match it up to the transmitter, and subsequently the wildlife web site. A visit to the web master with my old badge and five minutes later there's your name and email."

There was no reason for me to believe that was all he had, or that was what he wanted me to think. I had to pick my reality.

"Can you tell me any more than you already have?" I wrote.

"No."

"Then, with all due respect, how can you help?"

"There might be a photo," he wrote.

I waited longer to write back than I wanted to.

"Might?"

"It's ten years old, not terribly clear and uncorroborated. Though the guy who took it made a second try. Unsuccessfully. We found him a piece at a time."

"Do you have it?"

"No. I have to get it," he wrote. "Not that easy. Not worth the trouble if you won't play ball."

"Ball? What are the rules?"

"No formalities. Just a little trust."

"Nothing little in this game," I wrote. "Not for me."

"You gave me Frondutti. I didn't appreciate what that really meant before, but now I get it. Proof of trust. Okay, the pic will be in this mailbox in twenty-four hours."

"No. This mailbox is dead. Send it here."

I gave him instructions on posting to wallbox.com, then signed off. A few minutes later I cancelled the mailbox, though I knew it could leave a traitorous little tunnel back to me, if followed by an official digital wizard with all the right secret maps.

I emerged from my computer room a slightly changed man. I found Natsumi on the big metal-framed, glass porch off the dining room that would be the location for the silver and ice phase of the festivities in a few weeks. She and the Costellos were moving tables around. I asked in a lighthearted tone if I could borrow my wife. They said *si, si,* and I led her to the overstocked library where I could at least share the news in comfortable leather chairs in the company of the great works of Western civilization.

She listened intently, showing little reaction.

"You don't know, so what do you feel? Feelings are sometimes smarter than thinking," she said.

"I feel he's far more interested in my quarry than in me. I've given him cause to be wicked curious, but getting to me can't be his prime objective. He's basically rolled up all of the serious organized crime in

357

Connecticut with the exception of Little Boy, Sebbie Frondutti, who I handed to him, and Three Sticks, who I might. Why not play it out?"

"I agree. Sometimes the best place to hide is in the open, and the best way to stay safe is to be exposed."

"Japanese philosophy?"

"Psych 401. The Application of Counter Instinctual Behaviors in Balanced Life Strategies."

"Tell me you made that up," I said.

"I did. But I've taken worse."

She went back to the glass porch and I sat alone in the library trying to let go of my racing thoughts. I was reaching the point where the complexities of the project were oozing out of control. Even with my reduced mathematical capabilities, I knew the science and understood the odds. I'd mapped probabilities and studied chaos theory, where a tiny bit of statistical noise grew over time to overwhelm the dominant equation.

I pictured a graph, with the erosion of my personal security on one axis and time on the other. It indicated that I was running out of time. Rapidly.

I made two decisions. I would trust Shelly Gross, and my feelings, as instructed by

Natsumi Fitzgerald, whose own feelings had thus far proved both judicious and wise.

CHAPTER 21

Even someone as ruthlessly rational as I am harbors a suspicion that mystical beings are out there wielding destructive forces against your better interests. So it was with some relief and gratitude that I welcomed the crystal clear cold, but not unbearably frigid weather that was forecast for the night of the party.

Nitzy and Aidan had come through, if the RSVP's were to be believed, with a head count of Fairfield County's A-list glitterati, numbering just north of fifty. The event had escaped the notice of the *New York Times*, though the local paper had it on the front page of the Sunday lifestyle section, complete with a description of the hosts as "a beautiful and über-wealthy power couple from who-knows-where."

Natsumi and the Costellos looked grey with exhaustion, and I likely looked no better. We'd all put in eighteen-hour days over the last week, and there was still plenty of unfinished business that haunted our fleeting intervals of sleep.

The morning of the event I stole an hour to go online. Shelly was true to his word. In wallbox was a black and white photograph of a man and a note:

"It's already been enhanced as much as possible before distorting the image. You can only work with the pixels you got. Also add ten years."

His skin was on the lighter side of white, his black hair slicked back from a high forehead. Incipient signs of balding were apparent. He wore sunglasses and the collar on his white shirt was pulled up. With the top two buttons unbuttoned, it wasn't a shirt you'd associate with someone named Austin Ott, the Third. He was coming through a door, leaving either a storefront or a restaurant.

Height was difficult to determine. Some fleshiness around the throat suggested a paunch hidden by the door. Age, at this point, mid to late fifties. Shelly was right to lower my expectations.

It wasn't much to go on, but it wasn't nothing.

The guests arrived under a blaze of light from lamps mounted up in the trees trained on the façade of the house and the parking area plowed out of an expanse of lawn. Most accepted the offer of a valet, though a few were insistently self-reliant.

My spot was the front door, where I shook everyone's hand and took their coats, which I passed along to a team of coat managers. Then I directed the guests down a path that led to a succession of bars serving hot toddies and hors d'oeuvres that large men in red and gold outfits were preparing over open-flame grills.

I had just enough time between greetings to jot down the names of men who could possibly fit the Austin Ott criteria. When the last car pulled in, I had fifteen names.

Natsumi worked the house. After running the food and drink gauntlet in the foyer, guests were funneled into the main hall of the house, the walls of which were lined with narrow platforms upon which the French-Canadian fire dancers rendered a variety of performances, from twirling poi and mounting giant stakes to exhaling great gusts of flame.

The live band naturally played songs with a fire theme, though at a volume that permitted conversation, which frankly failed to invoke the proper spirit of Jimi Hendrix.

I found Natsumi engaged with one of my candidates who was accompanied by a woman in a gold bodysuit so tightly fitted I first thought it was paint.

Natsumi explained that the woman had ordered the outfit for a James Bond party where she played the unfortunate victim of Goldfinger's revenge.

"And your name is Auric," she said to me. "So do you find this moment disturbing?"

"I find it brilliant," I said. "Do you agree?" I added to her companion.

"I played Ernst Stavro Blofeld, so of course I find her brilliant," he said. "Pretty cool party, Auric. You know how to make a splash."

"It was all Charlene," I said, putting my arm around her woven silver tank top.

This same conversation, only slightly varied, continued on through the cocktail phase, as we moved around through the crowd. Since most of the partygoers knew each other, the chatter was free and friendly. When I finally banged into Nitzy, she grabbed my arm and guided me around the room, making introductions and subtly taking credit for the event's underlying concept. Her dress was a remarkably soft red velvet held at the middle by a gold chain, which she found a way to tell me was solid fourteen karat.

"I think Aidan must have bought it off a gangbanger in Harlem. Just kidding."

I'd deleted some of the candidates from my list as I learned more about their lives, but not Aidan. He fit too many of the criteria. Not that it meant that much. It was all so highly speculative; though as Natsumi said, sometimes feeling is smarter than thinking.

At one point, Nitzy dragged me over to a server with a tray of edible gold leaf canapés. Picking a sample off the tray was Elliot Brandt, the new owner of Florencia's insurance agency.

"Hello again," I said, reminding him that I'd introduced myself at the door.

"Very nice event, Mr. Grenouille," he said. "Impressive even for this neck of the woods."

"Please call me Auric. We're very flattered at the turnout. What compelled you to come, if you don't mind my asking?"

"A phone call from Nitzy, naturally. She who will not be denied." Nitzy curtsied, a weird gesture even for her. "She was very complimentary of you and your wife. Who I think is divine, if you don't mind my saying."

"I don't."

"I lived in Tokyo for a few years. Stationed there with Goldman. Japanese women, what can I say."

"What's keeping you busy these days?" I asked.

He went on to describe a number of investment and acquisition projects he was working on. All of a faceless industrial nature, all in the hundred million dollar range, and thus well beyond the insignificant purchase of an eight million dollar insurance agency.

"So, do you have kids?" I asked.

Brandt let off the usual parental glow.

"Daughter Elise and son Damien. Elise is studying dance and picking up bit acting parts in the city. Damien's a CFO. For an insurance agency. Can you get any more different?"

"I have no children myself, but I hear that a lot from parents I know."

"Damndest thing."

"Is Damien in the city as well?"

"Stamford. Little town is full of financial services. Probably why you're in these parts, eh?"

"Have to fish where the fish are."

"You're in metals? Definitely not my thing," he said, with a snort, a sneer and a belt of his scotch on the rocks.

"I thought you were interested in the highest profit possible," I said.

"I am."

"What I do is your thing. Squared," I said, shaking his hand again, then walking away. I moved toward a couple standing off to the side, looking around not at the fire performers nor the other partygoers, but at the house itself. I remembered his name, recorded on my list, but not hers.

"So you're Larry," I said, then turned to his wife, "which means you're . . ."

"Jennifer. Easy to forget. Back when I was a kid it was a rare name. Now every broad in the city is named Jennifer."

"I appreciate that you came to the party," I said.

"Not our usual scene," said Larry. "But we made an exception in your case."

"I'm flattered."

"Most of our friends are still in Queens," said Jennifer, by way of explanation. "We moved here for the schools."

"So I'm especially glad you made the effort," I said.

"Maybe it was your name that caught my

eye," he said, with a twitch that involved most of the left side of his face.

"You know other Auric Grenouilles?" I asked.

"None, but that's the point, right?"

"I forgot your last name."

"Antonelli. I was born Anderson, but changed it to Antonelli for business reasons," he said, with another twitch, which I began to understand stood in for a smile.

"So what do you do, Larry?"

"Diversified business interests. A little of this, a little of that. I get bored just doing one thing."

"I'm in metals," I said. "I like the focus."

"So I keep hearing. Which I got to admit, has me a little curious."

"Always ready to talk to any interested party," I said.

"Don't you need to go powder your nose or some crap?" he asked Jennifer.

She got the message and left, with no sign of opprobrium.

Larry cocked his head at the crowd maneuvering their way from food station to food station, or clustered in little groups, juggling glasses and plates of hors d'oeuvres.

"Yeah, we moved here for the schools. The school of bongo bucks," he said with another twitch. "Them people out there?

367

Some of the smartest in the world. More brainpower than the rest of the universe combined. And every megawatt is focused on one thing and one thing only. Making money. None of them could give a rat's ass about the dopey woman's museum. They're here because of you, because Aidan Pico said an opportunity is riding into town, and nobody wants to be the chump sittin' out the game on the sidelines."

"I appreciate your candor," I said, "It's refreshing. I have to attend to the party, but I'd be happy to discuss the possibilities anytime next week."

"Sure thing. But what's the bottom line?" he said, squinting at me.

I squinted back.

"Everybody's dazzled by gold and silver, because that's what they know, what they buy their wives to hang around their necks. What they aren't thinking about is the exotic stuff, like iridium, palladium and rhodium. They don't know that these are essential ingredients in the only things people are actually buying these days — laptops, smartphones, tablets and games. And where does it come from? Places out in the middle of bum-fuck nowhere, in countries where people slice off your hands as easily as look at you. In the next decade we'll be invading Africa just to insure that little Suzy can keep texting her idiot girl-friends."

Then I walked away, offering my hand to the next person I saw, a young toff in gold wide-wale corduroy pants and the most beautiful Italian shoes I'd ever seen. His date wore a red, floor-length, tube-like dress with a meager slit that severely limited her forward mobility. She took it in stride, sacrificing neither dignity nor equilibrium.

The next person I ran into was Natsumi, glittering in her silver, disco-ball outfit. It was sexy to look at, not so much to touch.

"How're we doing?" I asked.

"Only one guest has caught fire, so I guess we're ahead on points."

"Did we call an ambulance?"

"No, but I think we'll be buying a new gold sport jacket. I'm suggesting something noncombustible."

"What's the chatter out there?" I asked, looking out over the crowd.

"You can hear it from here. 'Who are these people? What's their deal? They're not even on Google. Though she's stunningly gorgeous.' Not really. I made that up."

"No you didn't. You are gorgeous," I said.

"The perfect thing to say. For a guy with a hole in his head, you can sure think on your feet."

"Anyone plying you for information?"

"Actually, that guy over there in the green jacket and plaid pants, who obviously didn't read the invitation, offered me a kickback if I got him an exclusive. Ten percent, which I think was overly generous. I'd have done it for five."

In the pulsing light of the flame-filled room, I got a better look at the man in the green jacket, who was also on my list. He was a little old based on the criteria, but his face was the right shape, with a hairline well in retreat. I walked over and reintroduced myself.

"Nathan Charles," he said, shaking my hand. "I was born Chomsky, like the brainy radical, but you can't have a name like that on Wall Street." I wondered if anyone at the party still had their original names. "You got me scratching my head, like everybody else here. And I'm actually a commodity trader. I know by memory the opening and closing price of anything anybody can trade. Oil, wheat, coffee, iron ore, pork bellies. Precious metals? What's the play?"

I gave him a more technical and less colloquial version of what I'd told Antonelli.

"Okay, I can almost buy the concept," he said, "but how're you different from the open market?"

"A nearly limitless supply at prices you haven't seen since they used iridium to make fountain pens," I told him, before executing another departure stage right.

I repeated the story with slight modifications a few more times before the first phase of the event flowed into the second, a banquet in the main dining hall. At my request, Nitzy acted as hostess, delivering a brief speech only slightly slurred by champagne, including mention of my six-figure donation to the museum, a gesture of good faith and encouragement for others to follow.

Most people at the tables followed Nitzy's gaze to where Natsumi and I were standing by the door to the kitchen. I gave a modest little wave when they applauded. As the dinner progressed, Natsumi and I worked the tables, helping the servers pour wine and deliver plates. Nitzy was so charmed by the idea of helping the help that she joined in, failing however, in provoking Aidan to follow suit.

The fire performers had retired, but the walk-in fireplace at the far end of the room compensated nicely. The night's theme was also upheld by the rented, gold-plated flatware and serving dishes. The Costellos had made a careful count when we opened up the boxes from the rental company, a fact they shared pointedly with the servers.

Carvers at strategic locations sliced rare roast beef, dropping the slabs on plates already adorned with golden sautéed potatoes, beets, and in a concession to proper nutrition and visual relief, raw spinach. Once everyone was settled down and eating, I was able to take a break and pay closer attention to individuals. I had spoken to each of the men on my list, and nothing at that point moved me to expand the club. At the same time, nothing told me to make it smaller.

Once the dinner plates were cleared, Nitzy announced the final phase of the event, dessert and aperitifs on the glass porch. Each partygoer had the option of slipping on a fake fur coat and tender kid gloves, since we'd opened all the doors and ceiling vents to hold the temperature below freezing, in part to keep the commissioned ice sculptures looking crisp.

Once everyone had climbed into their furs and helped themselves to silver gelato and icy cordials, the servers lit magnesium sparklers and shot silver ribbons across the room with air guns. With each pop a muted cheer went up from the crowd. A brave keyboard player inflicted upon us jazzed-up versions of "Baby, It's Cold Outside" and the theme from "Ice Age."

Larry Antonelli walked up to me and tried to give me his card. I politely demurred, as I had a dozen times before.

"If you'd like to discuss trading opportunities, just use the email address on your invitation to the party to set up an appointment," I said. "I won't be reaching out to anyone."

He squinted at me again.

"Some people might consider that a little arrogant."

I hoped I looked duly apologetic.

"That would be regrettable. I just don't want to give the impression that I'm wanting for potential investors. A deal will happen. The only question is the size of the offer. And the terms."

"Pretty confident."

"Yes, but never arrogant. I know it's a privilege to engage with people of this caliber," I said, turning and spreading my arms, as if to embrace the room. Then turned back to him. "People like yourself."

He twitched at me.

"Man, I just love the feeling of smoke traveling up my ass."

I patted him on the shoulder, noting that

it felt like molded concrete, and moved back into the hubbub on the porch.

Though entirely incidental to my purposes, I was glad everyone seemed to be having a good time. I'd never held a party before in my life, so I allowed myself to see the irony in a former math geek and social misfit beginning and ending his party-throwing career at the top.

Nitzy intercepted me again and reinforced my self-congratulation.

"This party is just the *best,*" she said, gripping and hanging unsteadily on my right bicep. "You and Charlene are *brilliant.*"

"My only brilliance was asking Charlene to make it all happen."

Nitzy threw both hands around my neck and whispered in my ear.

"She's so precious, you lucky, lucky man."

"Aidan did pretty good himself," I whispered back.

She pulled her head back, trying to get me in focus.

"Are you trying to win amazing man of the year?"

As I sought to form an adequate response I was saved by the appearance of Natsumi, who told me the foyer was ready for the closing ceremony. Nitzy unselfconsciously let go of my neck and asked Natsumi what that meant.

"You'll see," said Natsumi, taking my arm and leading me away.

"Have we secured all the appropriate glassware?" I asked.

"We have."

We went out to the foyer, which had been cleared of all the food stands, decorations and performers. The red and gold garlands along the ceiling were down, and in their place were silver and gold helium balloons trailing lightweight silver and gold chains. Each chain was anchored to a small gift-wrapped box that sat on a shelf above the wainscoting.

I stood with my back to the front door and waited while Natsumi herded our guests off the glass porch and out of the rented furs, and then into the foyer, which was just big enough to comfortably accommodate all fifty of us. There was much animated speculation over the balloons, which some had already tentatively begun to claim.

I rang a little silver bell to capture the group's attention.

"First off, let me thank Nitzy Bellefonte and Aidan Pico for allowing us to support their wonderful museum. We know many of you will follow suit with a generous gift of your own."

Everyone applauded.

"And on behalf of Charlene and myself, our sincerest thank you for giving us such a warm welcome into your lovely community."

More applause. Self-regard filled the air.

"Some of you may have noticed a balloon or two."

Laughter.

"Well, there is one for each of you to take home. You'll want to be sure to bring home the little package attached to your balloon. Inside you will discover a frog, a creature all of you had the good manners not to remind me is my namesake."

More laughter.

"Now, while each frog is identically shaped, they are all composed of different materials. Where Mr. Antonelli's frog may be chrome-plated brass, his wife Jennifer's may be solid gold. Each is unique, some exotically so. Yours may include alloys such as palladium, or osmium. Or it may be pure platinum."

Some of the people who'd already grasped a chain dropped their first choice and took another. Soon every box and balloon had been claimed, with little breach in decorum. Several servers worked their way around the room collecting coat claims and returning with arms full of fur, cashmere and lamb's wool. As I'd greeted by the door, so I bid adieu, shaking hands and kissing cheeks.

The most fervent farewells were the last, as Nitzy and Aidan brought up the rear. While Aidan stood patiently by, Nitzy repeated her effusive declarations of gratitude, and compliments on Natsumi's exquisite taste and compelling appearance. I thanked her so Natsumi could limit herself to a demure and diffident smile.

As soon as the door closed, Natsumi spun on her heel and went back to the big rooms to supervise the breakdown of the party and restoration of the house. Before joining her, I stopped off at my technology array in the room over the garage. Though the room was secured under strong lock and key, I ran several utilities on the computer that would detect, and either destroy or take over, the kind of spyware and keystroke registration software I'd installed at Florencia's agency and CMT&M.

Though no protection was perfect, everything checked out clean and undefiled.

So I went back downstairs to help put the house back together again.

CHAPTER 22

"Alex," said Natsumi, intercepting me in the upstairs hall, "you need to come with me."

I followed her down the long hall to the door that led to the master bedroom suite. We went through a small sitting room, past the walk-in closets and into the bedroom. On the bedspread that covered the king-sized bed was a small bundle of bark-covered sticks, like the kind you pick up from the yard.

"How many?" I asked.

"Three."

"Did you touch it?"

"No."

I stood over the bed and saw how the sticks had been tied together with a piece of silver ribbon, about a mile of which had recently decorated the party rooms. Also tied to the ribbon was a piece of paper. Blank — but there was evidence that something was written on the other side, the side facing down on the bed.

"I'm getting rubber gloves," I said. "Lock the door behind me and wait here."

I also brought back a kitchen garbage bag. I put the gloves on and picked up the bundle by the tip of the largest stick, flipping it over to expose the note.

The note said, in a handwritten, block-lettered scrawl, "Face-to-face with me a non-starter. But if you want volume, we'll give you all the volume you can handle. Conditions: No one gets better terms. Our orders fill first. No shorting. Think about it. We will contact you."

I made sure that Natsumi had a chance to read the whole thing, then I picked up the bundle again, put it in the plastic bag and tied off the open end.

"I guess it worked," she said.

"I guess it did."

"It would have pissed me off if it hadn't. Given all that work."

"Me, too."

"Now what?"

"We go back downstairs and finish up, then go to bed," I said.

"We do?"

My leg hurt, my eyes were losing focus, the wig and makeup felt like it was disintegrating and falling off my face. All I could think of was the king-sized bed and the down comforter.

"I'm exhausted," I said. "That was the hardest thing I've ever had to do."

"Acting like a people person?" she asked.

"Exactly."

"For me, the opposite," she said. "To act shy. I'm anything but."

"I'm sorry to put you through that."

"But at least it worked."

"It's a start. Let's figure out the rest tomorrow."

We didn't actually get to dive into bed until about three-thirty in the morning, and for me this didn't translate into uninterrupted sleep until about an hour later. A busy mind is always the enemy of a good night's sleep, a fact I'd known for most of my life. The only treatment for this that ever worked for me was to force myself to focus on one thing, no matter how obsessive, and put the rest into a holding pen for another day. Or night.

That night I thought about Florencia. I tried to reconcile the Florencia I knew, in such a profoundly intimate way, with a person who would skim money from her own highly successful business and send it off to a numbered account in the Cayman Islands.

It was impossible. I couldn't.

The first thing I did the next morning was email Shelly Gross.

"What are the chances of getting some things examined for DNA?" I wrote. "Also, can you check the criminal records of some of the wealthiest and most socially connected people in Greenwich, Connecticut?"

I had to wait until midday to get a response.

"Doable. But I'll have to know why."

"We need to meet."

"You're not going to follow me around again? Pop out of an alley?"

"The Bulldog Lounge at the Green Club in New Haven. Four-thirty this afternoon?"

"Pretty trusting," he said.

"It makes no sense to take me down now. This is what I trust."

"Fair enough," said Shelly. "I'll see you at four-thirty. Will I know what you look like?"

"You won't have to. I'll know you."

I sat with Natsumi in the cavernous living room and we talked through all the implications. Our exposure had never been greater, on both sides of the legal divide. Our only defense was the self-interest of those who

381

could do us harm. This might have been a reassuring bit of logic, but it did nothing to actually reassure.

"I fear for your safety," I said.

"I fear for yours."

"You could come with me to New Haven. I'll drop you off somewhere, then pick you up when I'm done with Shelly."

"Why is this safer than me staying here?" she asked.

"It isn't. It just makes me feel like it is."

"I have a better idea."

The Bosniaks showed up in a dark purple minivan that looked like an eggplant on wheels. There were four of them, including Little Boy. They were clearly taken aback by the house, but tried to not let it show. Natsumi, the Costellos and I came out to greet them, offering food, drink and earnest expressions of gratitude.

"I hope you got cable," said Little Boy. "The Celtics are acting like they just remembered how to play basketball."

After getting his crew ensconced in the aircraft hangar-sized family room in front of a TV the size of an average billboard — with the Costellos nervously on call to serve refreshments — I took Little Boy aside and elaborated on the situation.

"In about ten minutes, I'm jumping in a car and going to an important meeting. Three Sticks knows we're living here. I can imagine him snatching my wife for leverage. Or for that matter, snatching both of us and simply coercing us out of our product. It would be stupidly shortsighted, but possible. Like I said, I don't know him well enough to know."

"From what I've seen, he's practical," said Little Boy. "But seriously cruel if he thinks you're fucking with him."

"Does that worry you?"

A look of disdain showed on his face.

"You know what we been through? Back there? The frightened ones are the first to die. The crazy ones go next. The lucky ones last as long as their luck. If you're smart and have balls, you live on. After a while, the only ones left are those with no fear."

I shook his hand, instinctively, which was exactly the right thing to do. The gesture seemed to straighten his posture and add another inch to his towering height.

"Post a watch," I said. "You don't want to get massacred in the middle of a free throw."

Before I left for the Green Club, I called Evelyn.

"I need you to do something," I said,

when she answered the phone. "Though you're going to hate it."

"Don't sugarcoat it."

"I want you to contact Bruce Finger and tell him you've learned about an irregularity in the accounting at Florencia's agency that wasn't uncovered during due diligence by the Brandts. It could have a material impact on the deal, post-close, maybe even involving a claw back that will devastate the selling price. You need him to arrange a face-to-face meeting with the buyers to explain the situation."

There was a long pause.

"Okay," she said, stretching out the word. "What irregularities?"

"This is the hard part. You can't tell him. You just say he needs to call the meeting. And to trust you. It will all become clear."

"That's all?" she asked.

"Will he do it?"

"No. Not without more explanation. He likes me, but not that much."

I knew this was true. I was just hoping it wasn't.

"Tell him someone will be in touch to fill in the details. I'll figure something out. The main thing is to impress upon him the importance of this. That you really need him to make that call."

"You sound a little tense. I'm not used to that," she said.

"Sorry. Things are getting complicated. Too many spinning plates, too few hands."

"Okay, Arthur, I'll do my best."

The Green Club was no longer a club in the traditional sense. Anyone could go there and hang around the bar or have a meal looking out at the New Haven Green. Though as with any well-established venue, it featured a distinct clientele — people devoted to Harris tweed, brown leather wing tips and a largely fanciful notion of the dead Ivy League past.

New Haven was about the same distance from Greenwich and Rocky Hill, which I thought only fair, and the club an ideal venue, with its tomb-like quiet and respect for discreet conversation.

I had to stop along the way to rent a motel room where I could switch my look from Auric Grenouille to Alex Rimes, at least the Alex Shelly had met at the restaurant. I brought along my blue blazer, grey slacks and the red and blue diagonally striped official tie of the University of Pennsylvania, where I received my Masters in Applied Mathematics. Natural camouflage.

Shelly, on the other hand, had opted for a

bright yellow, nylon windbreaker over a white polo shirt and an orange baseball cap. If any deer hunters were passing through the Bulldog Lounge, he'd never be mistaken for a grazing stag.

I sat down and put the plastic bag on the table.

"It's a note from Three Sticks," I said. "Attached to three sticks." I told him what the note said. "I provoked him into it," I said, not telling him how. "I'm reasonably certain he picked up the sticks, wrote the note and placed it on the bed. A bit of bravado in response to my provocation, the way I signaled to him. I'm not a handwriting expert, but I'm fairly certain he wrote the note with his left hand. Unless he brought along surgical gloves, the paper should be covered in DNA."

"Should be," said Shelly.

"I also have a list of candidates, wealthy men in Greenwich who could conceivably be modern versions of the man in your photograph. I'm also reasonably sure one of these men left the message. If not, it was a subordinate, which might be good enough."

I handed him a flash drive.

"I have all their names, addresses, business information and email addresses. And the names of their wives or dates. Also, recent photographs of them all, and some at younger ages that I pulled off the web."

"That's pretty good," said Shelly.

"It gets better."

A waiter showed up to launch the standard rituals, which I short-circuited by ordering an iced tea and a cheeseburger. Shelly did the same. When the waiter left, I put a box on the table.

"Cocktail and wine glasses. Fingerprints and DNA. Each identified by name with a piece of tape."

He looked a little perplexed, then he grinned.

"You served them at a restaurant," he said. "Or a party."

"How quickly do you think you could run it through your files?"

He smiled.

"My buddies at the Bureau would find that question amusing. Some of the biggest cases in the country can take months to work their way through the labs."

"I can't afford days. This venture has a shelf life."

"The more I ask of them, the more they'll want to know."

I sat back in my chair and thought through what I was going to say. Calibration was important. For better or worse, he beat me to it.

"As far as I can tell," he said, "you don't exist. That doesn't mean you have no identity. I bet you have several, but none of them are you. They all belong to dead people. Before you get nervous, I don't know this for certain, it's just the result of forty years on the job. But I'm pretty sure if our people ran down the name Alex Rimes, we'd learn some very interesting things."

He tapped his fingers on the box full of glasses, which he held as if asserting fresh rights of ownership.

"You got a dilemma," he went on. "You need me because I can do things you can't, at least not on your timetable. But the closer you get to me, the more I learn, the harder it is to stay invisible."

"You're right," I said. "My risk is trusting you. But if you let others in on it, your biggest risk is losing control over the best, and last, opportunity you'll ever have to snag the big fish that got away."

He tapped some more on the table, and appeared to be chewing on the inside of his mouth. I imagined this as an insight into the state of his mood, a giveaway apparent to his former employees, yet oblivious to Shelly himself.

"Interesting situation," he said.

"Indeed."

"I have no problem keeping things close to the chest," he said. "I'll probably have to use every chit I have left, but we'll do it your way. Up until the moment I learn you're scamming me, and then all bets are off. I'll be after your ass like a starving hound from hell."

"So how quickly can you turn this around?"

He liked that.

"So who the hell are you, anyway?" he asked.

The urge to reveal everything to him, to bare my soul and all my transgressions, was nearly unbearable. It was human nature to confess, to share intimate, sordid information. I'd exploited the tendency many times myself, so I was forewarned. Yet even so, it took willpower to counter the impulse.

"It doesn't matter who I am," I said. "Even if I knew anymore. It only matters what I do."

Our meals came soon after that, and we spent the rest of the time eating and sharing experiences we'd had in and around New Haven. I learned a lot about Shelly's successful campaign to gut local crime syndicates, and he learned something about the historical and contemporary demographic makeup of the city and its environs.

When he asked me how I knew such things, I said, "I absorb a lot of minutiae. It's a bad habit."

An assertion he saw no reason to contend, whether he believed it or not.

I was glad to see nothing had changed when I got back to the house. The Colombians had joined in solidarity with the Bosniaks over the Celtics game, in which the favored team prevailed, and now everyone was swept up in a celebration fully fueled by the voluminous leftovers from the prior night's party.

Little Boy, interpreting the expression on my face, assured me that his best man, cold sober, was outside guarding the periphery, well-armed and in communication with his second best — who was a little drunk, but famous for throwing a knife through the eye of a Serbian infiltrator after an entire night's consumption of tequila shots, wherein he lost the drinking contest, but won the fight.

I found Natsumi in the library, curled up like a cat in an overstuffed chair, reading a copy of *Pride and Prejudice* slipped out of the crammed bookshelves that surrounded her.

"Oh, goody, you're here," she said, looking up from her book. "I'm so glad."

"Me, too. It seems like our guests are settling in."

"I've never met such polite people. We Japanese pride ourselves on social decorum, but I'm often suspicious of the sincerity. These guys seem to mean it."

"You should know I'd only invite the most refined of criminal gangs into our home," I said, then told her about my meeting with Shelly Gross.

"Do you think he'll be true to his word?"

"Probably yes, if only because he's got nothing to lose. I'm sure he has enough to get close to us, if not all the way, if he had the support of the FBI, and wanted to try. But it's not yet in his interest to try. I realize my analysis of his psychological motivation is amateurish, but it's all I have to go on."

"I think your analysis is highly projectable, and this from a recently minted Bachelor of Science in Psychology."

"You don't look like a bachelor."

"Did you use your sense of humor to flirt with your wife?" she asked.

It took a second to adjust to the hairpin turn in the conversation. I tried hard to give an honest answer.

"Yes, I did," I said. "It was probably the foundation of the relationship. Couldn't have been anything else."

"You're probably shortchanging yourself, but it doesn't matter. She's gone, you're back from the dead and trying to reconstitute your life. Whatever existed before is moot. At least it should be."

"We dueled a bit. I liked it, up to a point. As soon as she started to heat up, I'd retreat."

"For fear of conflict," she said.

"Yes."

"So you actively avoided anything that might have put stress on the relationship. You never tested the limits."

"No. Florencia was a breathtakingly beautiful, and successful, woman. I held up my end in the household, but really, I was just a goofy nerd in awe of my good fortune to have the affection of such an amazing woman. No other way to put it. When you find yourself in such an asymmetric situation, you don't question, you simply thank the gods and get on with it."

"Are you questioning now?" she asked.

"Yes. I'm questioning everything."

"How does that make you feel?" she asked.

"Like I love you, but you best not psychoanalyze me. Though I appreciate your good intentions in trying to do so."

"You're not just a goofy nerd," she said.

"Just?"

The next few days would have been unexceptional but for the effort to integrate four Bosniak gangsters into our domestic routine. The burden for this fell mainly on the shoulders of the Costellos and ourselves. For their part, Little Boy and his men had the demeanor of cheerful unsophisticates who'd just won an all-expenses-paid holiday in a fantasy mansion, which essentially they had.

I spent most of my time racing around the Internet, downloading data, stalking Greenwich millionaires and skulking like a ghost in the financial and operating systems at Florencia's agency.

Natsumi was less housebound, though she never ventured outside without Little Boy and at least one other Bosniak in tow.

No word from Shelly Gross. I spent hours on the web trying to keep my mind under load and out of emotional mischief. Though after a while, even I can get tired of staring into a computer screen. I find it can send me into tiresome feedback loops, sapping my intellectual energy. The only remedy was to get out of the house and clear my head with fresh air and a natural landscape.

And so one of those afternoons when Natsumi and three of the Bosniaks were out shopping, I thought driving down to Long Island Sound to look at the water and ruminate was a good idea. I dressed in jeans and a dirty work jacket and took the Subaru as a modest form of disguise.

It was cold, but clear, and though the sun still traveled a low arc across the sky, the light was getting warmer and less harsh to the eye. For some unknown reason, I brought along a beer, thinking I could go whole hog down at the beach, wolf down the beer and perhaps open some hidden doors of perception.

I made it to Greenwich Point and was about to crack open the beer when a crowbar smashed into the side window. The safety glass contained most of the blow, though a blizzard of tiny shards sprayed across the left side of my face. Knowing the next strike would get all the way through, I dropped over the center console and covered my head. I heard the wet, concussive sound of the crowbar penetrating the window, then the sound of the door opening. Cold air and strong hands rushed inside.

They pulled me out of the Subaru and dragged me a few yards across the parking lot. One of them kicked me in the stomach, which caused more shock than pain. I curled up and waited for what was to come.

"We tole you we'd contact you," said a voice I recognized as belonging to Jenkins. "What's with all the Eurotrash? Damn, that's so unnecessary."

"I'm just trying to be careful," I said, without uncurling from the fetal position. "You'd do the same."

"Not careful enough, eh brother?"

"Hurting me serves no purpose," I said.

"Yes, it does. It teaches you to show a little more respect," said Jenkins, before kicking me in the small of my back. Most of the shock was absorbed by the meaty muscles to the right of my spine, but some of it reached the kidney. I grunted, but held my defensive curl.

"Point well taken," I said, picking my face up off the macadam. "From now on I'll hold you in greater esteem. I'm not a physical person. More of this, and you'll have to explain to the boss why his potential business partner died on the way to the deal."

"I've a mind to shoot your ass."

"Go ahead, but you'd only be shooting yourself. If Three Sticks doesn't take you out for insubordination, some Bosniak certainly will."

It was quiet for a moment, then Jenkins said, "You are one strange motherfucker," with a hint of a laugh, which I took as encouraging. Several sets of hands grabbed me by the clothes and pulled me to my feet. I had trouble standing fully upright, my abdomen bruised and clenched like an angry fist. They shoved me back against the Subaru and rummaged around in my pockets, finding one of my disposable phones. Luckily one with no important numbers recorded in recent calls. I also had a wallet, but there was nothing in it but a little cash and a credit card belonging to Auric Grenouille. A minor victory for paranoid precautions.

Jenkins bundled me into the passenger seat of the Subaru and assigned one of his boys, a pockmarked white guy with unnaturally black hair and a fur parka, to drive the car. The only thing the driver said to me was, "Fuck up once and I'll kill you."

Which was a clear enough directive.

We drove in a caravan, following Jenkins' Escalade along the coast into New York. The landscape quickly transitioned from seaside opulence to manufacturing ruin, with train tracks and metal-sided warehouses, forlorn gas stations and brick monuments to the industrial revolution. My driver held his silence and I was just as glad, as it freed up lots of bandwidth for self-recrimination.

We followed the Cadillac south into a suburban neighborhood of early fifties vintage — ranch homes packed close together, carports and curvy streets. We pulled into one of the driveways. It was plain, but better kept than most. Two trash cans were at the curb. The shrubbery, what there was of it, was neatly trimmed. Another SUV, a Range Rover, was parked in the carport.

Jenkins got out of the Escalade and went down the front walk, picking up a newspaper in a blue plastic sleeve along the way. He rang the doorbell and was let in. A few moments later, he came out and waved to us and the guys in the other car. My driver got out, walked around to my side and opened the door. With my driver's encouragement, I led everyone to the door of the house.

The interior reflected the same spare tidiness as the outside of the house. You entered directly into the living room, which featured a long sofa against the far wall and two club chairs. Another pair of wooden chairs, colonial reproductions, completed the seating area, at the center of which was a large coffee table. In the middle of the table was the only object out of place — a futuristic black phone you commonly see in commercial conference rooms.

I sat in one of the wood chairs before they had a chance to direct me. Jenkins took the other one, facing me across the table. The big white guys, including the one who'd opened the door, filled in the upholstered furniture.

"A call's gonna be comin' in," said Jenkins. "We're gonna be discussin' business. I'll give you some inside information. People're gettin' sick of foolin' with you. This is your last chance to make your case. I strongly suggest that you settle down and make the necessary accommodations. Do you understand what I'm saying to you?"

"I do."

That seemed to make him happy.

"That's good," he said, looking around the room. The other guys all nodded, though no one said anything.

He looked at his watch, then at the phone, which buzzed as if on his visual command. He leaned forward and pushed a button.

"We're here," he said.

"With our guest?" the other party asked. It was a male voice run through a distortion device like they use to hide the identities of people during TV interviews, their voices a mechanical drone, their faces in shadow.

"That's right. He's right here."

"Hello," I said.

"I'm interested in coming to an agreement with you, but we need to iron some things out."

"Okay," I said.

"You need to agree to the provisions outlined in the note."

"I agree." It was quiet on the other end of the line. He obviously expected more resistance. So I kept talking. "You get the same terms I gave Little Boy. All product is available at a quarter of the market price set at the opening of the day it is sold. The agreed-upon quantity will be fulfilled. I prefer cash, but a wire transfer is acceptable. You can place your order now, or have Jenkins bring it to my house after you've had a chance to think about it. I'd prefer that he call ahead, in that some of my colleagues may react poorly to an unannounced visitor."

"About that," said the distorted voice. "Aggressive tactics would not be looked upon favorably."

"Good. Then tell your boys to keep their hands off me."

"Don't be too enamored of the Bosnian bravado. It would be a contest they cannot win."

"Conflict is never healthy for business," I

told him. "I'll do my part, you do yours, *everybody* wins."

Jenkins curled his lip at me, a gesture that clearly said, "What a bunch of bullshit."

"You'll hear from us," said the voice, and the line disconnected.

On the way out I looked for the street number of the house, but had to do with the numbers next door and across the street. Likewise, the street name itself, which had been removed from the pole. But I caught the next one we passed, and the one after that.

Though we left by a different route than we used on the way in, it was easy enough to determine, as we crossed into Larchmont, that the house was in New Rochelle. I laid my head on the headrest and closed my eyes, a cheap signal to my driver that I had no interest in our surroundings. And it wasn't that hard an act to fake. I was bitterly exhausted and sore, and now that the adrenalin had drained out of me, my nervous system began to crackle like static electricity.

And all the while, the quiet center of my mind kept asking the question: how, after all these months of vigilance and deliberation, could I be so stupid?

CHAPTER 23

I counted among Natsumi's admirable qualities a consistent failure to overreact, no matter how fair it would be to do otherwise. She held true to that when I told her where I'd been and what I'd been doing.

"And you don't know why you went out on your own?" she asked.

"Actually I do. It used to be a habit of mine, under normal circumstances. Get out of the house and go off on some meaningless chore, just to clear my head and breathe a little fresh air. What I don't know is why my sense of self-preservation didn't tap me on the shoulder and say, ' 'Yo bud, these aren't normal circumstances. You aren't living in Stamford anymore doing market research on feminine hygiene.' "

"You did that?" she asked.

"What?"

"Researched feminine hygiene?"

"Absolutely. Did at least twenty focus

groups in different parts of the country. The product wasn't exactly hygienic. More cosmetic. Essentially perfume for the nether regions. I learned a lot. Once a group gets going, respondents will tell you anything."

After I filled in Natsumi, I went over the story again with Little Boy and the other Bosniaks. I was afraid they'd see it as a flagrant provocation, deserving of ruthless reprisals, which I'd have to struggle to suppress. What I got were grins and some gentle teasing.

"Hey, lucky they not kick you in the nuts," said Little Boy. "That's what we do."

"The nuts, then the head. Not necessarily in that order," said one of his boys.

"I thought they were going to kill me," I replied, I hoped matter-of-factly.

"Kill you? The goose who's laying all these golden eggs?" said Little Boy. "No way. They just working off a little steam. Probably got impatient waiting for you to come out of the house. I been on those stakeouts. It gets damn boring."

Cheered by the outpouring of concern, I slipped away to spend some time with the sort of company that rarely failed to gratify my expectations.

My computer.

I liked to believe aeronautical engineers

never lost their wonder over the proposition that objects heavier than air can fly. By the same token, even a tech hound like me finds it difficult to believe that you can see an image of your house taken from a tin can orbiting the earth so clearly you can make out the Weber grill on the patio. On a clear day, whether you're grilling hot dogs or chicken breasts.

This was the kind of wonder and appreciation that filled my heart as I zeroed in on the house in New Rochelle. Knowing two of the streets in close proximity, it took only a few minutes to identify Newbury Street. Then, with two of the street numbers of nearby houses, it was child's play to pin down number twenty-five.

From there, I used a simple directory service to capture the home's phone number. I could have obtained much more, like the market value of the house, the yearly tax bill, the number of bedrooms and any outstanding mechanic's liens, but all I cared about was ownership. This came up as New Heritage Properties, a real estate management company headquartered in Bermuda. Aside from having an oxymoron for a name, my sense before doing more research was that research would turn up absolutely nothing. Corporate confidentiality in Bermuda wasn't the steel vault of the Cayman Islands, but close enough.

I wouldn't be able to get much further, but somebody else could.

I wrote to Shelly Gross and described the day's events. I included all the information I'd obtained about the meeting house, and ended with another request: "I bet you could dig up the phone number of the guy who called that house today. He might have taken some precautions, on the other hand, maybe not. It could save a lot of lab time."

I also gave him the make and model of both the SUV's and their license plate numbers.

"Surely something will connect," I wrote.

He wrote back soon after.

"So you didn't get high definition images, DNA samples or fingerprints of these guys?"

Evelyn called soon after that.

"I talked to Bruce," she said. "I told him someone from the insurance commissioner's fraud unit had contacted me asking a bunch of questions I couldn't answer. I said the fraud people instructed me not to discuss the call with anyone, but I said screw that and immediately contacted him. He sounded very concerned. He asked me a lot of questions I couldn't answer, mostly because I was making it all up. I told him they wanted to interrogate me, but I was terrified to do it on my own, so could he just do me this one huge favor and come along? I don't do damsel in distress very well, so maybe that's what convinced him."

Evelyn would be the last person on earth, maybe just behind Hillary Clinton or Margaret Thatcher, to make a good damsel in distress. Under any circumstances.

"It probably was," I said. "Brilliant job."

"I hope so. Now it's your turn. Just keep me informed."

I exited the call filled with contrary emotions. Admiration for my sister's courage and imagination, countered by a vague panic over how to play a ploy I hadn't conceived of myself.

Insurance commissioner's fraud unit? Was there such a thing?

I dove onto the web and quickly discovered that there was. Bruce would know that, having spent most of his career in Hartford, the insurance mecca of the nation. Chances were, he knew the commissioner and half the people in his office. Two minutes after Evelyn's call, he probably knew there was no investigation, current or planned. At least I had to assume that.

I couldn't see a way to make this happen

without Bruce Finger. And no way to compel him, least of all without his awareness and willing consent.

I put my head between my hands and tried to force a strategy.

I couldn't do it, because there wasn't any. Nothing elegant, subtle or immune from risk. Which made me recall something I'd heard from a Vietnam veteran I once interviewed. I'd forgotten the original subject, but remembered the discussion taking a radical turn into the limits of human endurance in the face of desperate circumstances.

"Sometimes, man, the only way out is through," he said to me.

I took out my phone and called Bruce Finger.

"Mr. Finger?" I asked in my Clint Eastwood voice.

"Who's calling?" he asked.

I told him I was a private investigator for the insurance carrier who covered the largest number of Florencia's clients. I supplied enough information, gleaned from the agency's files, to prove my intimacy with the company in question, information no one else could possibly have.

"So you're not from the insurance commission," he said.

"I lied to Ms. Cathcart. I didn't think she

406

could handle the truth. You can. In fact, I think you were expecting my call," I said.

"You need to tell me what this is all about," said Bruce.

"You know what it's about."

There was a long period of silence on the other end of the line. I shut my eyes, tightly, adding darkness to the quiet.

"I do not," he said, finally.

"You were the acting president of the agency. The fiduciary responsible for the ethical management of your clients' funds. You don't know that some of them are missing?"

More long periods of silence.

"I had no idea," he said. "I'm retired from all that."

"Do you think retirement conveys immunity?" I said.

"I did the best I could," he said. "My experience was underwriting and product development. I'd never worked in distribution, much less at an agency. Mistakes might have been made. Nothing intentional. Are you in contact with current management?"

"I will be."

"Should I be talking to my attorney?" he asked.

"That's up to you. My clients would prefer a quiet and painless resolution. For

407

all involved."

"What does that mean?" he asked.

"We have a meeting. All the issues are put on the table. We propose a solution, you and your counter-parties discuss, modify and agree. A check gets written, and we move on with our lives. People like the insurance commissioner never have to get involved."

"I still don't know what I'm being accused of," he said.

"Do you think I'd be talking to you if there was nothing to discuss?"

"You're a fixer," he said. "I've heard about you people. I think you're loathsome."

I was surprised on two counts. That I wasn't the only one aware of these mythical characters, and that a man of Bruce Finger's stature believed in the myth.

"More loathsome than a trusted advisor who mismanages what he's been entrusted with?"

"What do you propose?" he asked, in the exhausted voice of a person falling reluctantly into bitter old age.

"A meeting," I said. "Here's who you need to call."

I hardly had a chance to catch my breath when a call came in on the cell number I'd given Jenkins. They were ready to make a transaction.

"Half a mil of merchandise, made up of the following," he said, then read off a shopping list composed of fifty percent gold and the rest an assortment of exotics.

We arranged a meet for that night in the parking lot behind an abandoned warehouse in an old industrial park in the North End of Hartford.

As soon as I got off the phone, I tore Little Boy away from ESPN and had him pick one of his guys to head over to the warehouse, with luck, ahead of the other party. It was four hours before the meet, plenty of time for a capable stakeout man to dig in.

The rest of us bent to the task of loading the goods into Little Boy's minivan. Luckily, I had the quantities to cover the order. I'd have to replenish after the next round. I'd sent a partial payment to CMT&M to stay out of arrears, gaining some breathing space. No reason to start stealing until I had to.

After we loaded the van, Little Boy sent another advance man to relieve the first. There was no way to know for sure, but the first guy was fairly certain no one from the other side was skulking about. The warehouse was in a bland industrial park, but well apart from the other buildings, none of which he thought would make for a decent sniper's nest. That opinion held some authority, given the Bosniaks' painful familiarity with snipers.

We spent the remaining time hanging around the TV room, the Bosniaks smoking cigarettes and me writing myself notes in the little soft notebook I kept in my back pocket. It was a habit I started in the early days of my recovery, when my memory was re-learning how to function and my imagination was running well ahead of my organizational abilities.

At that moment, it really served no greater purpose than keeping my mind calm and my doubts and fears — always looking for opportunities to assert themselves — at bay. Checklists and to-do lists had that effect on me. They ordered the world, and expressed an implied state of optimism. Why bother making a checklist if you didn't think any of the items would ever be checked off?

Finally, the moment came for us to leave. I drove with Little Boy in his minivan and the others followed in the Outback, causing transitory damage with their cigarette smoke, though I was hardly in a position to complain.

When we got to the parking lot, Jenkins was there leaning against a rented box truck with sides advertising cheap moves to Hawaii, embellished by painted images of palm trees and hula skirts. Jenkins, like most of his crew, was smoking a cigarette and looking slightly bored with the whole thing.

He gave a languid wave when we pulled up alongside and dropped his cigarette to the ground, raising a tiny plume of red sparks. I climbed out of the van and Little Boy followed, keeping a few paces behind me. The other Bosniaks parked on the street and walked across the parking lot, keeping at least ten feet between them. Jenkins watched all this with a face that exuded either grudging respect or uncontainable contempt.

Little Boy walked up to Jenkins and offered a fist bump, which Jenkins accepted. Everyone else had their hands in their pockets, exhaling steam and shuffling their feet. The harsh light from the parking lot floods turning us all into backlit cutouts. Soon one or two on either side had cigarettes lit, which did nothing to illuminate the setting, though it did calm a few nerves, some by proxy.

"We got the heavy boxes," said Little Boy to Jenkins. "You got the cash?"

Jenkins swiveled around to show us all a backpack. Then he swiveled back again.

"Even usin' hundreds, a half million's a lot of paper, you know?" he said.

"I need to at least take a peak," said Little Boy, flicking on a small flashlight.

"Dig," said Jenkins, offering up his back again.

Little Boy unzipped the backpack and peered in. A long minute later he looked at me and stuck up a thumb.

"Okay," I said, jerking my head at Little Boy's crew. They proceeded to open up the Outback and off-load the metals into Jenkins' vehicle. Part way through, Little Boy reached over and grabbed a piece of Jenkins' backpack.

"Whoa, dude, not too frisky," said Jenkins.

"We're delivering," said Little Boy. "Your turn."

Jenkins neither gave in, nor moved away. Instead, we all stood and watched the transfer of the little boxes. When the last left the Outback, Little Boy gave the backpack a gentle shake.

That was when Jenkins reached into the inside of his jacket and pulled out a silver revolver.

Little Boy dropped to the ground, and in less time than you can think a thought, had a gigantic, gold-plated automatic in both hands pointed at Jenkins' head. One of

Jenkins' boys thought this was a good time to stick an elbow in the face of one of the Bosniaks, to which the Bosniak responded predictably, swatting away the elbow with his left arm and planting a right jab directly into the middle of the other guy's face.

Things went downhill from there.

Jenkins was yelling, "I'm cool, I'm cool," holding his hands in the air, the only intelligent response to the handheld cannon pointed at his forehead. Though he still held his nasty little gun. His colleagues were not so inclined, even to semi-surrender. At least two all-out fist fights were underway, each evenly paired, the fighters weighing in at around two hundred pounds apiece, experienced and incapable of giving ground, even in the face of sure defeat.

It was a strangely quiet affair. The occasional fist fall yielding barely a wet thud, most of the noise coming from the rustle and frenzy of sloppy physical contact. The grunt and growl of enraged men in mortal conflict.

Little Boy pulled a tiny revolver out of his jacket pocket and tossed it to me. He gestured toward Jenkins.

"If he move, shoot him," he said.

I'd rarely touched a gun, but I'd watched plenty of TV. I knew how to look like I knew

413

what I was doing.

Little Boy waded into the melee, and threw one ferocious punch into the first face that presented itself. When the guy dropped, he planted another on his own guy.

Two down.

The other combatants, instinctively turning toward this new threat, for some reason dropped their hands, allowing Little Boy to slam another fist into Jenkins' boy, and in the recoil, crack the edge of his hand into the face of his own man. Thus in less than ten seconds, all the fighters were safely flat on the ground.

That was when Jenkins shot Little Boy.

A little late on the draw, I shot Jenkins, more or less.

"Fuck, man, tha's just wrong," said Jenkins, slapping a hand on his thigh, where my bullet had winged him, improbably, dropping him on his ass. He flailed his arms trying to get back on his feet, which he finally did, allowing him to level his gun at my face, though before he could pull the trigger Little Boy shot him again, this time in the middle of the body. He fell back in a heap, frantically holding the bullet wound. I soon saw why, as great waves of red blood flowed over his dark fingers.

"Motherfucker," he said, looking down at

his stomach. "I hate gettin' shot."

As last words go, I guess these were as good as any. He twitched a few times, then lay still.

Little Boy was sitting on the ground, gripping his gun in one hand and the fleshy part of his chest near his armpit in the other. Blood covered the front of his jacket, but he was grinning.

"Dope don't know how to shoot, that's for sure," he said.

I walked over to him.

"What the hell just happened?" I asked.

"Just business. Sometimes it get a little rambunctious. Any of our boys dead? Don't want to move too much to look."

I looked around at the carnage.

"Not that I can tell," I said. "Jenkins is done for sure."

"Idiot bastard. Trying to get the drop on me. What he think, I'm a tourist?"

"How bad are you?" I asked.

"Can't be that bad if I'm talking to you, right?" he said. He felt around the wound, pulling away a hand holding a puddle of blood. "Maybe should get this plugged up, though. You think?"

I left Little Boy and stripped the backpack off Jenkins, then walked over to the only one of Jenkins' contingent both still alive and awake. Though not entirely sure he'd stay that way. I stuck the snub nose in his face.

"Consider the transaction complete," I said to him. "Tell Three Sticks we'd appreciate the next engagement be free of gunfire. You could lie and say we started it, but you know we didn't. That you get to keep the product is a matter of good faith. Do you understand me?" I asked.

He nodded, tentatively. "Do you understand me?" I repeated, wiggling the gun.

He nodded more enthusiastically.

"I understand," he said. "Jenkins was being a dumbass."

When we were all back in the minivan I told Little Boy we had to get him to a hospital.

"Not necessary," he said. "Our guy from Hartford already on the way. He get to your house faster than they check me through ER. Better this way. This thing nothing," he added, nodding at his own midriff.

Then he passed out. I was tempted to take advantage of that and just drive him to the nearest hospital, but one of his boys, anticipating the impulse, told me to do what Little Boy said, the threat of noncompliance implied. So I complied.

Their doctor was a half hour away when

we got there, so we kept Little Boy in the van with the engine running and the heat on. His breathing was steady and firm, and as far as we could tell, the bleeding had stopped. One of his men had Little Boy's head cradled in his lap, and occasionally brushed back his unruly hair and said something in their native language. None of them seemed all that concerned.

When I asked about that, one said, "People with bullets in them go to sleep. It protects their strength. Anyway, God is deciding what to do," he said with a shrug. "Why make a big fuss?"

Natsumi brought out blankets to cover Little Boy, and brought water to the men in the van and out on the grounds monitoring the entrance and periphery of the property. She also took over communication with the doctor, who supplied updates every ten minutes on his progress. Each report into the van came with a dose of optimism.

When the doctor finally got there, I was surprised to see a very young Chinese guy in an expensive parka and a duffle bag filled with pharmaceuticals, medical gear and a laptop. The Bosniaks broke away from their defensive positions around Little Boy, and the doc dropped to his knees and began to work. After helping rig brighter lights and providing a tub of warm water and various disinfectants, there wasn't much else I could do, so I got out of the way and went up to my computer room.

Natsumi lingered behind, just in case.

The first thing I did was email everyone who was at our fundraising event, assuming Three Sticks was there somewhere among the guest list:

On behalf of the Bellefonte Gallery, I was truly surprised by your response. So unexpected. However, I hope we can re-engage even more in the not-too-distant future. There is much we can accomplish as trust builds and we get to know each other better.

Then I wrote to Shelly Gross:

Now would be a really good time to get some results from your analyses. Things are warming up around here.

Bruce Finger was next:

Set up that meeting yet? The longer we wait, the worse it gets. For you. All the same to me, I lied.

I went back downstairs and outside to check on Little Boy. An ambulance was in the driveway. Paramedics were in the van working on the Bosniak at the direction of the doctor. I stood there and waited until they had him on the gurney and into the ambulance. Before the doctor could get back in his car, I grabbed him by the shoulder. He turned and looked at me, alarmed.

"Sorry," I said, dropping my hand. "What's the prognosis?"

"Good," he said. "Just a lot of blood loss. He's on IV now. We're fine."

"Where are you taking him?"

The doc shook his head.

"When Mr. Boyanov regains consciousness, we'll talk about it."

"Okay, sure," I said.

Then he drove away, with the ambulance, leaving us with all but one of Little Boy's crew. Natsumi did the intelligent thing and herded everyone back into the house; and subsequently the mammoth kitchen, where she and the Costellos cooked up a small mountain of food — much of it with a hint of the Balkans — which Boyanov's crew washed down with a steady supply of American and imported beer.

Luckily, this diplomatic mission didn't

419

include the two humorless sharpshooters who were still guarding the property. While spirits were still running high, I went out there, and at great risk of life, lured both of them out of their snipers' nests. When I apprised them of the situation, both agreed to stay on until Little Boy was able to clarify their responsibilities.

In the absence of contradictory orders from Little Boy, they would have stayed on duty forever, so we all knew that thanking them was meaningless, though they appreciated it anyway. I shook their hands, and their formal little nods were worth a million words on the subject of valor and forbearance.

I got the call the next day.

"This is not the way I conduct business," said the voice.

"Your man started it," I said. "It wasn't about us. It was about your money."

"I have plenty of other men," he said.

"Good. I see no reason to allow such foolishness to interfere with commerce."

"We need to test out the distribution. We'll be in touch."

"Got it."

Natsumi and I spent the next week buying

guitars. I didn't think it would be possible to soak up all the cash, but we got close. The effort involved a lot of travel, including a few days on the West Coast. Along the way, the two of us ascended to the upper ranks of guitar aficionados, learning more about the resonance of tropical hardwoods, glue chemistry, pickups, frets, machine heads and the hand manufacture of musical instruments than we'd ever hoped to know.

We always had a few Bosniaks along during local forays, one of whom, a fellow named Kresimir, was a pretty good fingerpicker. This came as a welcome relief to Natsumi, who was beginning to tire of my distinctive rendition of "Stairway to Heaven."

I arranged to have everything sent to the storage facility in Danbury. I wrote a beefy check to the guy who ran the place for helping to catalog and organize the inventory. He sent me photos taken with his phone of guitar-filled shelving units, all carefully identified by laminated hangtags.

Since this vastly expanded collection was officially owned by my sister Evelyn, I thought I ought to let her know. And since we were getting accustomed to a lot of travel, I decided the time was right for a personal visit.

"You want me to do what?" she asked.

I gave her the name of the restaurant in Norwalk where I'd met with Henry Eichenbach.

"Park on the street. Go into the restaurant, then out the back door to where a white Toyota will be waiting for you. The key will be under the mat on the driver's side. When you leave the lot, head away from the main road and make your way to Route One. Head over to Westport." I gave her the name and address of another restaurant. "We'll meet you there. Around seven. The food's on me."

"You don't honestly think anyone's following me around," she said.

"No. But the last time I didn't listen to my inner paranoid, I could have been killed."

"Okay."

"Look for the preppy guy with the Asian woman."

I booked two tables, ten feet apart. One for us and the other for Kresimir and one of his buddies, who arrived a half hour ahead. If the person who took the reservations noticed we never spoke to one another, she didn't say.

I was pleased to see that Evelyn looked pretty good, and just the way I remembered her. She couldn't have said the same about me.

"Arthur?" she asked, when she approached our table.

"Better not to use that name," I said.

"That must be his inner paranoid speaking," said Natsumi, standing and offering her hand. "By the same token, call me Charlene."

Evelyn took her hand, but then sat down and stared at me.

"How do you feel?" she asked.

"Mostly okay," I said. "Physically. I've adjusted to the sensory distortions, I've worked my math skills back up to a sixth grade level. I've got a slight limp, but no longer need the cane. I've stayed pretty busy. I think that's the key."

She looked over at Natsumi. I knew she wanted to ask the other half of the question. How was I emotionally, psychologically? I spared her the awkward question.

"I'm me, Evelyn," I said. "Just a different version. We're all born with more potentials than we use. It's up to life's circumstances to make the selection. My circumstances changed."

Natsumi asked her to describe the prior me. After some more awkwardness, Evelyn took a stab at it. And though her perspective differed from mine, there was nothing for me to argue with.

Natsumi listened carefully, then said, "He's right. Same guy, different version. Same with me, I think. I like this version plenty well."

I gave Evelyn a general idea of what I'd been up to, using a lot of euphemism and imprecision when describing the illegalities. I didn't know what made a person an accomplice after the fact, but I'd already made her more of one than I wanted. She didn't press me, on that or anything else, probably so I wouldn't have to say I couldn't tell her.

Thus it wasn't the easiest dinner conversation, but I was glad to see her, and glad she could meet Natsumi, who wasn't the most comfortable person in the restaurant, either, but it barely showed. At the end of the night, before parting company, Evelyn gave us each a hug, which might have been a first for me. I'd never seen her hug anyone.

"I'd prefer driving my own car the next time we go out for dinner," she said, heading for the white Toyota. "Don't disappoint me."

When we got back to the house, Little Boy was down in the family room, watching TV with his crew. He moved a little stiffly when

424

he got up from the sofa, but otherwise looked no worse for having been recently shot.

"It really was just a flesh wound," he said. "Nothing important got hit. Just the rib nicked a little. That's what hurts like the son of a bitch."

I brought him up to the study so I could tell him about the call from Three Sticks. Not to hide it from his boys, but I knew he liked to control important information. A leader's prerogative.

"So he don't want to go to war," said Little Boy.

"I don't know that," I said. "Though probably not for now. That doesn't mean we don't double up on precautions the next time."

"Hard to believe Jenkins acted on his own."

"Impossible, in my opinion. I think it was an intimidation tactic gone wrong."

"Intimidate *us*?" said Little Boy, incredulous.

"He knows now what you guys are made of. Next time, expect the real thing."

Before I went to bed, I checked in on my electronic moles at Florencia's agency and CMT&M. Nothing of any note. I also looked at all my email accounts, and saw nothing of importance there either. Though eager to get some sleep, I felt compelled to visit one other site — one I checked usually every other day — the online reporting for the lockbox at the Blue Hen National Bank in Delaware.

For the first time since Florencia's death, there was a new deposit. Fifty thousand dollars.

I looked away and then looked back at the number, as if it were an hallucination that would disappear. The fifty grand was still there, having been deposited that morning.

I opened the spyware at Florencia's agency and searched all the computers for the password, actually a series of letters and numbers, used to take any action on the Blue Hen account, limiting the search to an hour before the deposit was made.

In seconds it was there. Florencia's.

I searched her computer for any entry or action made from that deposit back to the time of her death. The logs showed where I'd gone in weeks before, when I'd stumbled on the skimming activities. But the computer hadn't been touched again until that morning when someone turned it on, used Florencia's username and password to get on the network, made a ten-second visit to the lockbox account, then logged off.

I switched over to the premium trust account. A distribution had been made the day before to Deer Park Underwriters.

Fifty thousand dollars.

The next morning, a tall, white man with long brown hair tied in a ponytail walked down the driveway with his hands on his head. He wore only a T-shirt and a pair of long underwear in the frigid weather, the cold being less of a concern than the possibility of getting shot.

The Bosniaks on watch got the idea and let him get all the way to the front door. We waited inside until one of them came up behind the man and pressed a pistol into his back. Then we opened the door. Despite the impossibility of concealment, Little Boy frisked him anyway. Then we let him drop his hands.

"What'd you do to get this gig?" Little Boy asked the man.

"What I'm told is what I did. I'm only delivering a message."

"Let's hear it," I said.

"The boss likes your products. He wants to go another round. Only no stupid stuff this time."

He gave a date, time and another venue

427

for making the transaction — a gazebo in the middle of a large open area in Easton, Connecticut. Once one of Fairfield County's last dairy farms, it was now a park committed to summer concerts and readings. That time of year, it was virtually abandoned and as private a location as one could come up with.

The gazebo was accessible from opposite directions. He said they'd come in from the east, we could take the west.

"I have a proposition of my own," I said.

The guy shrugged, as if to say, knock yourself out.

"Just him and me this time. Pretty much eliminates the stupid stuff."

The guy shook his head.

"Not gonna happen," he said. "Nobody sees him. Ever."

"If he shows, I'll drop the price another half."

"He won't care."

"Just ask."

He shrugged again, in the same way as before. I told him I'd be there at the designated time, either way. He put his hands back on his head.

"That's not necessary," I said.

"Oh, yes it is," he called back as he walked

down the driveway, followed by the Bosniak sniper.

"What's their maximum range?" I asked Little Boy.

"The snipers? With our weapons, less than two thousand meters. Give them a better gun, they shoot farther."

"Hm."

Bruce Finger called me that evening. He said the meeting was set for five o'clock the next day. He was going to catch a plane first thing in the morning to be sure he got there in time.

"We'll use the conference room at the agency, as you requested."

"The Brandts?" I asked.

"They'll be there. It took some persuading."

"What did you tell them?"

"The truth, based on what you said to me," he said. "That a private investigator from one of the big carriers had uncovered a serious issue with the books that existed prior to the sale. That it was in everyone's interests to deal with the situation promptly and quietly. But it had to be in person. That's still true, isn't it?"

I told him it was. Then I hung up.

I placed one more call before leaving my

computer room to join up with Natsumi for tea in front of the fire.

I told her about the first call, but not the second.

CHAPTER 24

I had a busy afternoon planned. First exchange my last million dollars' worth of stolen gold and precious metals for $250,000 in cash. Then rush home to change my disguise for a business meeting at Florencia's insurance agency. Further proof that scheduling is often the biggest challenge for the modern multi-tasker.

Natsumi, as with other stay-at-home domestic partners, felt a little left out.

"Couldn't I come along as your administrative assistant? I can take notes."

I told her I needed to know she was safe. Otherwise, I wouldn't be able to concentrate.

"So why is that any different for me? I *know* you're not safe."

"I'm bringing Little Boy along to both meetings. He's worth ten other men, even with a hole in his chest."

"Just come home. Okay?"

When I told her that was guaranteed, 100 percent, I almost convinced myself.

The plan was for the two best Bosniak snipers to set up well in advance, taking advantage of the trees that surrounded the field. That should have put them well outside of range, but we knew better. Three Sticks was a wily American gangster, but he hadn't fought in the Balkans War.

All of us wore Bluetooth earphones connected to our cells, and on the way to the park, we were conferenced in through AT&T.

Once everyone had announced their presence on the line, Little Boy said, "Don't forget I can hear everything you say. No bitchin' about the boss."

Somebody said something in Bosnian which drew a lot of laughs, including from Little Boy. I knew not to ask for a translation.

I had some time in the car with Little Boy, which I tried to fill with small talk. Not being involved day-to-day in larceny, prostitution and illegal drugs, I was at a disadvantage. I knew almost nothing about sports, least of all soccer, which was another impediment. I didn't have children, or even know any. I never watched TV, nor been even close to the Balkans. So I asked him about his home country.

What followed was a rhapsody of description, of the beauty of the countryside, the perfection of the food and warmth of family and friends. He talked about weddings and holy days, some festive, others meant for fasting and prayer. He also spoke of life under Tito when he was a young boy, social tensions that followed the breakup of Yugoslavia, and then the inexorable slide into ethnic war. When we reached this part of the narrative, the joy in the telling died away, and the story dwindled into one simple sentence: "It was very, very bad, leave it at that."

We rode in silence after that, until it was broken by my cell phone. I looked at the screen. It was Shelly Gross.

I put the conference call on hold and took his call.

"I got a match," said Shelly.

I gave him the name before he had a chance to say it. It was quiet for a moment.

"How did you know?" he asked, with a tinge of suspicion.

"Been a working hypothesis for a while. But the confirmation means a lot."

"The office in New Haven is processing warrants. We got a lot of them. I don't suppose you'd be willing to testify," he said.

"The only thing I'm doing is laying low until you got that bastard locked up."

"That's smart. And don't worry. Nobody knows my source, and they never will."

"I know. You're an honorable man," I said.

I hit END and stuck the phone back in its holster. Little Boy looked over at me.

"What was that about?" he asked.

"Change of plans."

I asked Little Boy if it was okay for me to direct the crew. He nodded and said into his phone, "Mr. G. and I got this worked out. He'll be calling the plays. Listen up."

They came back in Bosnian. Little Boy put his thumb up.

I reconnected with the conference call and asked everyone to identify themselves. When all were accounted for, I laid out the setup: There were three of our cars converging on the park. One would cover the west entrance. The other would follow us and cover the east. As soon as the Three Sticks vehicle showed up, we'd drive the Subaru into the park. Little Boy would stay with me slumped down in the front passenger seat, gun ready.

When the Three Stick vehicle reached the gazebo, the snipers would shoot out its tires. We'd take it from there.

"Take it from there?" Little Boy asked, his

phone on mute.

When we got to the park, the east entrance looked clear. I pulled the Subaru just inside the entrance and stopped. Our escort drove past and looked around the area. They called in all clear. The guys at the west entrance confirmed the same.

So we waited.

At the appointed time, a black Ford Expedition with darkly tinted windows drove into the west entrance. It moved slowly, exuding not so much caution as confidence, even arrogance, a lumbering, invincible dreadnaught of a truck.

I shifted the Subaru into drive and drove into the park.

"On my mark, snipers," I said. "You boys at the entrances, kill anything that tries to follow that Ford."

The lay of the land made it difficult to see cars approaching from the opposite direction until you were nearly at the gazebo. So the massive grill of the SUV almost filled the horizon before I was able to give the command.

"Snipers, fire," I said into my Bluetooth.

Little grey puffs appeared around the Ford's wheels. The SUV stopped dead in its tracks and dropped about six inches toward the ground. I slammed the Subaru into reverse and cut the wheel hard to the right. Two men in battle fatigues leaped out from the gazebo and started firing at the Subaru with automatic weapons.

"Snipers — take 'em out!" I yelled into my phone.

The splatter of bullets hitting the car was mostly obscured by the sound of the gunfire itself. But Little Boy was undeterred. He opened his window, then sat up in his seat, looking for targets.

I was busy trying to drive in reverse around the gazebo, hoping none of those incoming rounds would disable us before I could complete what I had in mind. Little Boy threw himself half out the window and began firing away at the guys in the battle gear. With all the noise from the guns and the agonized scream coming from the Subaru's engine, I had no idea where the threat was coming from, so I just concentrated on spinning around the gazebo until the rear end of the Subaru was pointed directly at the driver's side of the Expedition. Then I straightened out the wheel and stuck the accelerator into the floor.

I pulled Little Boy back into the car.

"Put on your seat belt," I yelled.

He did, just in time, as we hit that Ford hard enough to knock it over on its side.

The Subaru was still upright, so I was able to see the two guys from the gazebo being picked off by our snipers, seconds before they had a chance to shoot through our windshield.

I looked over at Little Boy, who was slumped back in his seat holding his chest.

"You okay?" I asked.

"Rib hurt like a fucker. We now go finish off these assholes?"

"We do," I said.

We exited the Outback, and Little Boy climbed up the chassis and looked inside the Expedition. Then he reached down his hand and hoisted me up so I could look in as well. There was only one asshole still conscious, and he was in no shape to do anything but stare in disbelief through a veil of blood pouring from his forehead. The driver was thoroughly integrated with his vehicle, and one other guy in the back, holding a Kalashnikov, looked like someone had removed his skeleton and replaced it with silly putty.

Next to him was a backpack. Little Boy reached through the smashed window and pulled it out. Inside were lots of bundles of cash secured with zip ties.

"Why bring the money if you're only going to steal the merchandise?" I asked Little Boy.

"Good to have options," he said.

He should know, I thought.

After stripping it of the precious metals, the Bosniaks towed the Subaru out to the street. When well clear of the area, they called a wrecker. They left the Expedition, now likely filled with dead people, to be discovered whenever it was discovered.

Little Boy and I went on to Stamford, about a half hour away. On the way, I stopped at a fast food restaurant and used the bathroom to pull off the wig, put on a pair of glasses in place of the contacts, and strip off all the makeup, returning my face to its natural, flawed appearance. This is how Little Boy had originally seen me, when we first met.

"I like this Mr. G. better," he said. "You look less like a rich prick."

I gave him a rundown on what to expect at the meeting. I told him everything I thought I should, in the interest of his safety, and mine, though I might as well have made it all up, since he didn't believe anything I said.

"What you been smoking lately, Mr. G.?"

"Just stay alert and assume I'm right," I

said. "For both our sakes."

We were early, so I parked down the street where we could see cars pulling in and out of the agency's parking lot.

"So who are you really, Mr. G.?" Little Boy asked me, as we sat and watched for incoming cars.

"I used to be a market researcher. Now I don't know."

"I used to be an arborist. I have a degree in Agriculture and Forestry from the University of Sarajevo. Worked all over Europe for a big landscape architect. Got a little distracted by the war."

"Get the hell out of here," I said.

"It's true. You got nice trees here in New England. Someday, I'm going back to the forest. I'm better there."

About five minutes before the scheduled start of the meeting, a new Jaguar drove into the parking lot. I followed. Elliot Brandt got out as we pulled into the slot next to his. I waited for him to enter the building before getting out of the car. He'd already passed through reception when we got there. I asked for Bruce Finger, and the receptionist picked up the phone and announced our arrival.

"Your other guests are here, Mr. Brandt," she said, speaking to Damien, the agency's new president.

A few moments later he came out to greet us. He was a lot shorter than his father, and fleshier around the middle, with darker and curlier hair. Yet the family resemblance showed itself in the shape of his face and the insistent edge in his voice.

"You're the investigators," he said, shaking our hands. "I don't think I have your names."

"You don't," I said, looking up at the ceiling.

"Right," said Damien. "This way."

We followed him down the hall to the agency's formal conference room, the place where Florencia charmed clients and underwriters from the big carriers. The room was unchanged from the last time I'd sat there, eating tuna fish sandwiches with Florencia, and making her laugh over tales of recent one-on-one interviews with earnest, benighted consumers of some dopey packaged good or another.

Damien excused himself with a promise to be back momentarily. He told us to help ourselves to coffee from the machine in the corner. Bruce came in soon after that, carrying a stack of folders under his arm, which he dropped on the table before offering his hand.

As we shook he said, "I've been going through the financials. Everything looks good on this end, unless I'm really missing something."

"You are," I said. "But let's wait for the others."

It wasn't a long wait. Elliot entered with an impatient scowl on his face, his son trailing him, looking more puzzled than affronted. They sat across from us, and with little ceremony, the elder Brandt said, "What is this about?"

Having forced the meeting, it was only fair that everyone looked at me for the answer.

"It's about a beautiful, kind, young woman of Chilean ancestry, whose parents came to the U.S. to escape the political upheaval tearing up their country," I said. "And to give their daughter an American education. She was a bright student, majoring in economics and business administration. Her only weakness was a foolish attraction to this hapless mathematics major."

Brandt's scowl deepened.

"We know to whom you are alluding," said Elliot, jabbing his finger at the conference room table. "The former owner of this company, and her husband, who were murdered by an unknown individual. What the hell does that have to do with us today?"

"Everything," I said.

I reached inside my jacket and took out a piece of paper, folded lengthwise. I unfolded it and slid it in front of the Brandts.

"As you can see," I said, "I have the routing numbers used to transfer funds from the agency's premium trust account to a shell known as Deer Park Underwriters. From there, the money is transferred, automatically, to a lockbox being held at Blue Hen National Bank in Delaware. I also have that account number, along with the username and password that allows me to access monthly statements. But not the funds themselves. These are also automatically transferred out, this time to a numbered account at a bank in Grand Cayman."

As I spoke, Damien stared at the paper. Elliot stared at me.

"I have that number as well," I said, "along with the original code required to access the account. You can see it there at the bottom of the page. It's the phone number at the apartment Florencia lived in when she was going to Wharton. AT&T still has all those old records. Kind of amazing."

"Original code?" said Elliot, in a soft voice.

"I needed a fresh set of numbers when I moved the money to another bank. But don't expect me to tell you any of *that*. I think there's, what, a bit shy of eleven million dollars in that account? Right, Damien?"

Damien looked up from the paper, his face a blank, white wall of misery.

"Who are you?" said Elliot. "You're not from a carrier."

"You're right. I'm not. And you're not Elliot Brandt."

His stare intensified, and he stopped ignoring Little Boy, who had stood up from the table and was now leaning against the wall, arms folded.

"You," he said to Little Boy, "say something."

"Fuck you, Three Sticks," said Little Boy, his Bosniak accent dripping off every word.

A phone at the end of the conference room buzzed, causing Bruce Finger and Damien to jump.

"Mr. Brandt," said a woman's voice out of the speaker, "there's another gentleman here to meet with you. Oh, sir, wait, you can't do that," she said, her voice rising in volume as she held her mouth away from the receiver.

Elliot jumped out of his seat, and leaned across the table.

"It's you, you bastard," he said to me, then

turned toward the conference room door and starting backing away. Bruce stood up as well, nearly stumbling over his chair.

"What the hell is going on?" he said.

The door opened and Bela Chalupnik walked in. In his right hand, pointed toward the ground, was a black automatic fitted with a silencer.

"Oh, God," said Bruce.

Elliot pointed at me, and then at Little Boy, and said, "A million bucks, Pally. You know I'm good for it."

Chalupnik raised the automatic and shot Austin Ott, the Third, through the bridge of his nose. Then he swung the gun toward Damien, who was still sitting at the table, but before it got there, Little Boy put a fifty-caliber round through Pally Buttons' chest, the impact from which lifted the assassin off his feet and into the blood splatter that preceded him to the wall.

CHAPTER 25

It only took about an hour to get all our important belongings, in particular my computers and Natsumi's textbooks, and a single bag of new clothes, into the back of the Mercedes.

Before Little Boy bolted back to Hartford, I gave him the pile of cash taken out of the Expedition that morning, and he made a second distribution to his fellow Bosniaks.

"So no more dreams of golden riches," he said to me.

"Not for now," I said, not knowing what else to say.

The Costellos, to whom I also awarded a stack of cash, said they'd stick around the house until the rental people showed up to take back a few pieces of furniture and all the kitchenware we'd rented. Then they planned to stay with their families in Colombia for a month or two. Or once they figured out how to get their cash out of the country, maybe buy a business there and never come back.

Natsumi and I drove into New York and booked a room at a midtown hotel. Natsumi ordered in room service and I went across the street to another hotel where they had free and untraceable access to the Internet in a room off the lobby.

First I used funds from the Caribbean account to pay my bill at Connecticut Machine Tool and Metals, minus the remaining inventory, which I arranged to have returned. There was no point in giving up the house yet, even if we weren't planning to return. It might come in handy in the remaining months covered by the deposit.

I was able to leave a text message for Evelyn soon after Little Boy and I had walked briskly past terrified agency employees — those who weren't under their desks — and jumped in the car for the trip back to Greenwich.

"I'm okay," I wrote her. "Will explain."

I'd been ignoring calls from Shelly Gross that were coming in every hour or so since news of the shootings hit the media. I waited until I was back in the hotel room to call him back.

"You set me up," he said, his voice ragged with emotion.

446

"I had the guy," I said. "You just confirmed it."

"That's a fine point. You still used me."

"You're right."

"And don't give me any crap about the world being a better place. I told you, no vigilantism."

"You did," I said. "But at least you can check off two big boxes."

"Yeah. And add a new one. Yours."

Then he hung up.

I flushed the phone down the toilet, then dug out the one I used to talk to Evelyn. She'd also called recently. I called her back.

"Oh, Arthur," she said. "What happened?"

"The men killed today were the ones responsible for Florencia's death. Elliot Brandt was also known as Austin Ott, the Third, street name Three Sticks. Also not his real name, but that's irrelevant now. He hired the other guy, Bela Chalupnik, street name Pally Buttons, to kill us both. It was Chalupnik who took care of Three Sticks today. An associate of ours disposed of Chalupnik. That's it in a nutshell."

"Why would this man Chalupnik kill his employer?"

"He had a thing about rats," I said. "I sent a message through his sons that he could pay a call on the biggest rat in town."

447

"Rats?"

"It a long story. I'll explain later," I told her, knowing I probably wouldn't.

"But why would anyone want to kill Florencia?" she asked.

"She'd been running what's called a skimming and lapping embezzlement scheme for years, siphoning off a modest, yet steady stream of premium money and sending it to a shell company, then into a lockbox, and finally a numbered account in the Caymans. She likely could have kept it going indefinitely, except for the bad luck of hiring Damien Brandt as her new comptroller, who unknown to her was the son of the region's most notorious gangster. Somehow Damien stumbled on the scam — probably by discovering the shell, which was on the agency's books as a legitimate insurance carrier. He dug a little deeper, and realized he'd discovered a pot of gold. He shared the news with his father, who hired Pally to get the codes for the numbered account, and then kill Florencia, thus taking control of both the stolen premiums, and ultimately, the agency itself.

"After buying the place, Damien allowed what he thought was a safe amount of time to go by, then re-launched the old scam. I have a feeling he hadn't asked Dad's permission, but that's sort of irrelevant at this point."

"Now what happens to the agency?" she asked.

"I don't know," I said. "The lawyers are going to have a field day. You need to get a good one. We sold a business that had been running a massive fraud. Of course, the buyers were criminals, who knew about the fraud, yet failed to report it, and in fact, kept it going after acquiring the business. I have to think this would destroy their standing as an injured party, but I'm not a lawyer."

"So what are you going to do now?" she asked.

"I'm done with the people who killed Florencia, but not with the reason they killed her. I need to know why she was stealing from her own company."

"So you're not coming home."

"Not yet. There's a chance a retired FBI agent named Shelly Gross has my fingerprints and DNA, which could lead him to Arthur Cathcart. Though I've never been arrested, or tested, or fingerprinted for any reason, so I can't be in their database. Though he's good. And determined. And he's really mad at me right now."

I told her I was shutting down our email

account, and to destroy the cell phone she'd been using to talk to me.

"Stand by," I said. "I'll make new communications links when the time is right."

"I don't know whether to be happy or disappointed," she said.

"Try being cautious, but hopeful. That seems to work for me."

I knew there were plenty of loose ends that needed to be tied off, though nothing that couldn't be handled remotely. There was little reason to stick around New York any longer than it took to steal a new crop of Social Security numbers, from which we acquired driver's licenses — leading to the establishment of a series of new bank accounts and credit cards. And lastly, with a fair amount of tricky work — some involving interaction with less than entirely legal enterprises — two new passports.

Throughout, Natsumi maintained a trusting and thus not terribly inquisitive attitude, though something about holding that fresh, new, dark blue American passport triggered a renewed curiosity.

"So, Alex, or Arthur, or whatever your name is, where the hell are we going?"

"When I finally cracked into Florencia's numbered account in Grand Cayman, I was able to download the account's history. Capturing deposits *and* withdrawals."

"Withdrawals?" she asked,

"Lots of them. I don't know what the money was for, but I know where it went."

"And?"

"Better buy some sunscreen," I said. "The sun can get pretty bright down there in Chile."

ABOUT THE AUTHOR

Chris Knopf lives with his wife Mary Farrell and dog Samuel Beckett in Connecticut and Southampton, NY, where he writes on the front porch until it's too cold to tap the keys.

He's published ten books, including two series set in the Hamptons, one starring Sam Acquillo (*The Last Refuge, Two Time, Head Wounds, Hard Stop,* and *Black Swan*) and a spin-off featuring Sam's lawyer Jackie Swaitkowski (*Short Squeeze, Bad Bird* and *Ice Cap*). The first in a new mystery thriller series, *Dead Anyway,* launched in September 2012, and received starred reviews from *Publishers Weekly, Booklist, Kirkus* and *Library Journal.*